The Rocky Path

By

Hazel Goss

Other Books by Hazel Goss

Forced to Flee
A novel set in war-torn Kosovo in 1992. Follow the journeys of two doctors who make different choices when faced with Serbian hostility and atrocities.

Bookworm24
Reviewed in the United Kingdom on 17 December 2016
Thoroughly enjoyed this book. It really opens your eyes to what refugees have to go through in order to achieve the kind of life most of us take for granted.

The Pathway Back – The first book in the Pathway Series

Mitchell Ward
This story moved very quickly and believably through time. It was thought provoking – the realisation of how much would alter if the past was changed. A really good read. I hope there will be a sequel.

A. J. Wagstaff
Reviewed in the United Kingdom on 20 April 2019
I really enjoyed reading this current day, time travelling ripping yarn. The characters were believable and I could empathise with them, coming as they did from the same world as me. These people drink tea, go for runs in the park, enjoy an occasional cruise and lead perfectly normal lives, apart, that is from the discovery of an old ship's timer and its effect on their family.

The Pathway Forward- The second book in the Pathway Series

C. J. Richardson
Reviewed in the United Kingdom on 15 August 2020
Action packed from start to finish. Couldn't put it down. This is book 2 in this series and it was great to meet some of the characters from book 1 again. There is a definite hint that book 3 will soon be winging its way onto these Amazon shelves. Can't wait for the next adventure.

Sandy Kell
Reviewed in the United Kingdom on 2 September 2020
Despite the complexity of the story already set in the future with several trips backwards and forwards in time this is very easy to follow thanks to the skill of the writer. She made it enjoyable and believable. I loved reading about the lives of all the characters and hope there'll be another story in the series so I can meet them again.

To my sister, Lesley, for reading and critiquing my manuscript and to my husband John for his support, patience and encouragement, with love.

June 1859

'Emily, go and find Major Carstairs and remind him that it's time for Nathaniel's afternoon nap. He said something about going to the lake to feed the ducks.'

Emily bobbed a curtsey as she said, 'Yes ma'am,' and then hurried away. It was not an onerous task; she had been sweet on the Major ever since she'd first been employed as Jane's personal maid in India.

The path took her through the rose garden, a fragrant delight of pink, golden yellow and white blooms. Then she crossed a large lawn, avoiding the croquet course, the metal hoops shining brightly in the sun. From the edge of the lawn the path sloped down to the lake and a wooden jetty with two rowing boats tied to a stanchion. She could see them swaying in the light breeze and wondered what it would be like to be in one and laze on the cushions like a lady.

On the grass in front of the jetty was the Major and his son, Nathaniel, sitting on a picnic rug. They were playing with building bricks and a Noah's Ark with wooden animals. The Major was lying on his side, his head propped up by one hand and Nathaniel was engrossed and laughing when Papa's pile of bricks fell down. It was a happy scene, Nathaniel's auburn hair shining in the sunlight, a contrast to his Papa's brown curls.

When Emily arrived and gave him the message, he stood up with a broad smile, making her heart flutter. He was tall, sturdily built and when he smiled, as he did now, his brown eyes sparkled and crinkled at the edges. She could not resist him.

'Well now, Emily,' he said lazily, 'I suppose I should do as I'm bidden but I think there's no great hurry. Master Nathaniel seems quite happy where he is. I think we've time...' His arm slipped around her waist and he pulled her to him and kissed her. 'Let's move into the long grass; don't want Nathaniel telling mummy we were cuddling.'

They lay in the grass giggling like naughty school children as he released her generous breasts and began to fondle and suck them. His right hand reached down to drag up her skirt knowing she never wore awkward underwear.

1

It was a quick coupling, leaving them both breathless. Emily recovered first, standing, pulling down her skirt, tucking her breasts back into her bodice and combing her fingers through her hair. Cecil – she called him that when they were 'canoodling' – lingered, relaxed and satisfied. He looked up at her, squinting and shaded his eyes with his hand. 'It's so much fun with you, Emily. Jane's so stiff and just does her duty. Anyway,' he sighed, 'I suppose I'd better move and get Nathaniel back for his snooze.'

He stood and adjusted his clothing and then looked towards the picnic rug. There were the toys but no child. A wave of fear coursed through him. 'Nathaniel, Nathaniel. Are you hiding?' He listened for any sound but there was just the long grass rustling, birds singing, bees humming.

Emily ran down to the lake edge and then screamed. Just beyond her reach, floating face down, was Nathaniel's body. Near him bobbed his Noah's Ark. Cecil jumped into the water, and pushed towards the boy, lifting him clear and calling his name. He knew his limp son was dead but still called his name, shaking him gently, willing him to open his eyes and take a breath.

Chapter 1

Daniel looked over the edge of the rock. 'I can see Giraffe caught on a bush, so stop wailing and I'll climb down and get him.' He glanced at five-year-old Ben and saw him nod and heard him sniff. 'Stay there and don't try to watch me. I don't want to be picking you up off a bush too.'

The big rock they were on was dry and not too difficult for Daniel's long limbs to step down carefully beside it. When he was standing safely on a lower rock he was within reach of Giraffe, Ben's much-loved fluffy toy; he grabbed it and stuffed it up his stretchy shirt. He looked at his solafone and swallowed, suddenly anxious. Xen had said he was to get Ben back by nineteen hundred and it was almost that. 'I've got Giraffe and I'm coming up then we've got to hurry, it's eighteen fifty-nine.' As he said that he was grasping both sides of the rock looking up. The rock seemed to vibrate, and it flashed through his mind it might be a mini earthquake. He didn't notice that Giraffe had slipped out and was once again on a bush.

When the vibration ceased Daniel climbed up and Ben was nowhere to be seen. 'Ben? Ben!' he shouted. 'This is not the time to play hide and seek. Come on.' He waited, listening. 'Well, I'm going back without you then.' He didn't set off straight away, he searched around all the closest rocks calling Ben's name and becoming more anxious with every step. His eyes began to prick with tears, while a lump grew in his throat. He followed the path, more overgrown with grass and wildflowers than he remembered.

Brimham Rocks was a local attraction; its rock formations eroded into weird shapes and wonderful for clambering on and around. Daniel's dad, Andy, and his mum, Isabelle, had come with Ben's parents, Xen and Joanna, for an evening picnic. They'd finished eating and Daniel had asked if he and Ben could go and climb on the rocks for a while.

'Just take care of Ben; don't let him try anything too hard but if he does get stuck come and get us,' said Andy.

'Better get back here by 19.00; we'll need to set off home then,' added Xen.

*

Daniel should have come to a broad path by now that ran downhill to the car park or uphill to the café, shop and toilets, but the path barely existed. It was a narrow track. He wondered if he'd gone wrong somewhere but decided downhill must get him to the car park eventually or at least to the road.

There was no car park. The road was not tarmac, just deeply rutted mud; the ruts dry and baked hard. Daniel sat down, squashing the long grass and a myriad of insects flew about in protest. He looked at his solafone. It was dead. Solafones never needed charging; just a dose of light kept them charged, but there was nothing on the screen. It had worked just a short while ago when he'd retrieved Giraffe, so what had happened? The rock had shaken but an earthquake as mild as that wouldn't knock out the service and render it dead. He looked around bleakly and wondered what to do. He couldn't stay here, hoping Mum and Dad would come looking for him. He needed to set off towards Harrogate and home.

The light was beginning to fade when Daniel reached a crossroads. At this point he knew he should be able to see the faded globes of the defunct communication station at Menwith Hill, but there was just a view of fields and dry-stone walls. He resolutely turned left towards Burnt Yates, frightened of being unable to get help before nightfall.

When it was almost too dark to see the road, Daniel saw a dim glimmer of light and stumbled towards it. A farm. He moved towards the light aware of a pungent smell of manure and almost stepped into the midden. He backed away, went around it and then the light went out. He stood still, uncertain, until his eyes became accustomed to the moonlight and he saw the outline of the house. The depth of darkness, the unfamiliar rustling sounds, the stench, made him feel nauseous and his heart raced. He banged on the door hoping their solafones worked and he could ring Dad.

4

Suddenly the door opened. Daniel stepped back as a long-barrelled gun was thrust towards him. 'Wha' do yer want, waking up folks in the middle of the night. Be off wi' yer.'

'Please, Sir. I'm trying to get to Harrogate, but I need somewhere to sleep tonight.'

Perhaps it was the words Harrogate and sir, or the high voice denoting a child, that made the farmer pause.

'That's a long walk, young man. I'm goin' that way tomorrow.' He made a decision. 'You can sleep in't barn and do some chores in the morning to pay for it. I'll get a lantern.'

He shut the door and Daniel sighed with relief. The farmer returned with a lantern, blanket and a jug of water. 'Come on,' he said.

The barn held cattle and stank of manure and urine but with no better option Daniel followed until the farmer indicated a wooden ladder leading to a hay loft. 'Up there. I'll stop while yer get up and then I'm takin' the lantern. Here, tek' these with yer.' He handed Daniel the blanket. Daniel tossed it up and then reached for the jug. He scaled the ladder, carefully so as not to spill the water and when he had settled in the sweet-smelling hay, the farmer left him in the dark.

Daniel sat for a few moments, hoping he would see a glimmer of moonlight. There was none. It was the most complete blackness he had ever experienced. Tears began to run down his face which he tried to sweep away with his hand. He cried quietly at first and then louder for his mum. The tears relieved the tension and he felt for the jug and took a drink. He coughed, caught his breath and tried again. It was not water; some kind of beer, perhaps. He drank again and decided it was drinkable. After several more swigs he began to feel odd. Was he getting tipsy? The ale and exhaustion made him sleepy. He laid down and pulled the blanket round him.

A shout woke him up.

Chapter 2

2048

Joanna and Xen both heard Ben crying and ran towards the sound. He was stumbling, rubbing his eyes, coming down the broad path towards the car park. Xen got to him first and swept him into his arms. 'What's the matter? Where's Daniel?'

'Gone, Daniel's gone.'

'What do you mean, gone? Gone where?' Unable to answer Ben held out his arms to his mother and Joanna took him. She carried him back to where they'd had their picnic and met Isabelle and Andy coming towards her.

'What's happened?' asked Andy. 'Where's Daniel?'

'I don't know. All Ben can tell us is, he's gone,' said Joanna. 'Xen's looking for him now.'

'He could be anywhere. Do you think Ben could show us where they were playing?'

'He might when he's calmed down,' said Joanna.

'I don't think we should wait, let's take a different direction each and do lots of shouting. He might have fallen and be hurt.'

'I'll go straight up the main path,' said Isabelle.

'I'll go to the right and go around the rocks and meet you at the Visitor Centre.'

Daniel's parents were frightened now and moved quickly along their allotted paths, calling repeatedly. Other people joined in and soon there was a dozen shouting for Daniel, but there was no response.

Joanna packed up all the picnic gear and distracted Ben by giving him little jobs to do. When everything was stowed in the car, she hunkered down so her face was on a level with his and said, 'Shall we go for a walk and you can show me where you were playing with Daniel?'

'I dropped Giraffe. Giraffe fell over the edge an' Daniel went down to get him.'

'I see, so perhaps if we find Daniel you can get Giraffe back.' They set off up the main path and after a while Ben pulled her to

6

the left. They threaded their way around huge rock formations and then met Xen. Joanna could see immediately by his haunted expression, that it was serious, but he wouldn't have left Daniel if he'd been injured. He would have called an ambulance.

'Giraffe!' shouted Ben and ran towards his dad who was holding the soft toy. Xen picked up Ben and gave him Giraffe. Ben smiled happily, a contrast to Xen's expression.

'What's happened, Xen. It's bad isn't it.'

'I think Daniel found the portal to the past and has gone back in time.'

'Well can you use it too and go after him?'

'I don't know what he said, and I don't think the rock allows you to come back to your own time. What am I going to say to Isabelle and Andy? It's my fault. I knew about the portal and should never have allowed them to play on their own.'

'You told me, but I didn't know where it was exactly, and I must admit I'd forgotten about it. How long ago did Morgan show it to you?'

'About six years or so. He told me how to do it and I thought it was impossible to do it by accident. Ben, can you remember what Daniel said before he was gone?'

Ben looked up at his dad and said, 'Daniel said it was getting late, eighteen fifty-nine and we'd have to hurry.'

'Good boy. You're certain that's what he said?' Ben nodded several times.

Before they could talk any more the police arrived. There was one car and a large van that spilled out at least fifteen men. Andy ran up to them. Isabelle went towards Joanna, whose face dripped with tears. Xen held Ben as the two women embraced, Joanna's hand rubbing up and down her friend's back as if she could rub away the pain.

It was all too much for Ben who began to cry. The volume increased with high pitched screams and he thrashed his legs until Xen said, 'I'm sorry but we have to take Ben home, but I'll come back and help with the search.'

Isabelle shook her head. 'There's enough people looking now. We'll let you know when we find him.'

'Would you like me to stay?' asked Joanna. 'Xen can manage Ben and Ruby will be home to help him.'

'Yes please.'

Xen wasted no more time and carried Ben to the car, fastening him into his child's seat efficiently. The car drove silently away, and Joanna wished she was in it. She knew, in her heart, they would never find Daniel and would probably never see him again. But, Isabelle needed her support, so she held back her own tears. 'Come on. Let's go up the centre path and help in the search.' The two women held hands, Joanna almost pulling Isabelle into action.

*

The search was called off when it was too dark to see and becoming dangerous. Everyone walked down the wide main path in silence, feeling keenly their failure to find the boy. At the car park the sergeant in charge assured Andy and Isabelle they would return at first light but asked them to stay at home in case Daniel had left the site and was making his way home.

'If he was conscious, he would have called us on his solafone,' said Andy. 'But we'll stay at home tomorrow and wait for you to contact us.' When they got to their car Andy turned to Joanna. 'Thank you for staying and helping. We'll run you home.'

The programmed car drove them home and the only sound was Isabelle trying to stifle her sobs.

When Joanna reached her house, she got out, watched them drive away and then gave a deep sigh of relief and touched the keypad to unlock the door. She walked towards the kitchen and her daughter, Ruby, intercepted her. 'I can't believe Daniel's gone missing. He's so sensible and trustworthy. He would never have left Ben on his own.' She paused, put her arms around her mum and said, 'You look exhausted. Would you like tea, cocoa, drinking chocolate or something stronger? Dad's on his second G and T.'

'Tea and a biscuit would be lovely. Thanks Ruby,' said Joanna as she moved from the embrace and joined Xen in the living room. He looked up at her as she came in and gave her a half smile. 'I assume there's no news.'

'No,' said Joanna, sinking gratefully into an armchair. They sat in silence until Ruby entered with a tray which she set down next to her mum. Ruby was 19 years old, slim, brown haired like her mother, sensible and caring, most of the time.

'I expect Dad told you all about our picnic at Brimham Rocks. How did your day go with Cheryl?'

'It was fine. We played VR games and she's got a great new one but then her mum stopped us and said it was too lovely a day to be indoors. She took us out to the Dales, and we had an evening picnic too, after a long walk. I'm going to bed now; I'm really tired. Night Mum, night Dad.'

When Ruby had gone upstairs Joanna sipped her tea then dunked a biscuit before slurping the soggy end into her mouth. She saw Xen watching her. 'Sorry, I know you think dunking's disgusting, but ginger biscuits just have to be softened.'

'I don't care. You enjoy it. You deserve it. Ben went to bed really well, no arguing, and I finished his book, so we need another.' He saw Joanna nod and then changed the subject.

'Should I tell Andy what I think has happened to Daniel?' The question hung in the air as Joanna struggled to answer.

'I don't know. If you say the portal only works one way, then he can't come back. That's so final; the same as if he was dead. If we say nothing, then they still have hope.'

Xen nodded. 'What if I used the portal and went to find him? He would have my love and support in a strange era, but then I couldn't come back either.'

'No, you can't do that. We need you, not just for the money you earn but...' Tears began to run down her face.

Xen knelt in front of her, gathering her hands in his. 'Please, don't cry. It's late and we're both emotionally drained. Let's go to bed.'

'Not until you promise not to leave us.'

'I promise.'

Chapter 3

1859

'Oi, layabout. Wake up and give us a hand.'

Daniel scrambled to sit up, instantly aware he was still living his nightmare. He gathered up the jug and blanket and stepped down the ladder. The farmer had his hands on his hips and was frowning but his eyes had a twinkle.

'Come on lad. Help me load the cart and then we'll 'ave some breakfast.'

'What shall I do with these, Sir?' asked Daniel, lifting the blanket and jug. The farmer took them off him and placed them on a relatively clean pile of straw, then turned to go out of the barn beckoning Daniel to follow.

They went into a cleaner shed where there were mucky carrots and potatoes piled on the floor. Without a word Daniel was given a sack then they both began to fill them. When they were full the sacks were heaved onto a cart. They repeated the task and then a grunt and a nod indicated they had enough.

'We'll load up the cheese and bread after breakfast. Come on you can wash up 'ere.' Daniel copied the farmer as he washed his hands and then his face and neck at the standpipe, then dried himself with a rag.

'Now, come an' meet the missus.' At the door of the house the farmer took off his boots, so Daniel took off his trainers and they went straight into the kitchen.

Daniel immediately remembered a school visit to Beningbrough Hall. This kitchen had the same deep sink with a water pump, a dresser to hold the crockery and shelves for pans and baking tins. From the ceiling hung a wooden clothes-drying rack and bunches of herbs. In the centre of the room was a huge, solid wood table and beside it, wearing an apron and a mob cap over her unruly blonde curls, was a smiling middle-aged woman.

'So, who've we here?'

'Daniel Mansfield, Mrs …?'

'Mary Smith and you've met Joe already. Well don't just stand there, lad. Sit on't stool and I'll get yer some eggs.'

'You're also gonna taste the best bread and butter in Yorkshire,' said Joe proudly. 'Mary's bin up since dawn bakin', ready for t'market.'

Two fried eggs were dished up on a thick slice of bread, the butter dripping on to the plate. Daniel waited, his mouth watering, for Joe to be served.

'Nay lad don't wait, get it down yer. I'll swaller mine in a blink of an eye, then we must be off,' said Joe.

Daniel didn't need telling twice. He began to eat and said, truthfully, it was the best breakfast he'd ever tasted. Mary smiled happily and she poured him a big mug of milk. It was creamier than milk at home and he felt full and more optimistic after it.

Joe finished his ale as he stood and gestured to Daniel to follow. Just as he was putting his trainers back on, he remembered his manners and shouted a thank you to Mary. He helped Joe hitch the horse to the cart, another new experience, and then sitting side by side they set off to Knaresborough market.

As they approached Joe seemed to know everyone and there were lots of greetings as he pulled on the reins to stop the horse. His trestle table was already erected, and Daniel got down to help unload the cart. The sacks of carrots and potatoes were partially emptied on one side of the table and the cheeses and bread on the other.

'You can go now, Daniel, if yer want. It's still a long walk to Harrogate.'

'I've no money, Joe, so I'm scared of going on in case I don't meet people as nice as you and Mary.'

Joe suddenly had a rush of customers, so Daniel stood and watched, helping by putting more carrots and potatoes out on the table, when necessary.

Joe used scales, putting a one- or two-pound weight on one side and the vegetables into the pan on the other. He noticed Joe always gave them a little extra and realised that was why he had a queue for his stall. There was also a lot of banter. Everyone seemed to like him and usually went away laughing.

11

When there was a lull Joe turned to Daniel. 'I thought you had relatives in Harrogate, a Dad, Mum, Uncle?' Daniel's face turned red and, seeing tears beginning to well, Joe changed the subject. 'If you've no money you'd best get a job. What can you do? It's obvious you've not lived on a farm afore and you speak in an educated way. Can you read, write and reckon?'

'I can read and write but what's reckon mean?'

'It's addin' up the coins an' givin' change.'

'Yes, but I've not really handled money, so I'd have a lot to learn if I wanted to work in a shop or on a stall.'

'There's many a person here, in this market that can't read or write. I wonder if you could be a clerk. Perhaps you could 'ave yer own stall, wiv pen an' paper an' charge per letter.'

'I wouldn't know what to charge but I've got neat handwriting.'

'What about you helping me today. I'll teach you the prices and what the coins are. You come back tonight an' Mary will probably let yer sleep in the kitchen. I'll ask around t'see what we can get you as work.'

'Thank you, Joe.'

The day went by quickly and Daniel soon understood pennies, halfpennies, three-penny bits, silver sixpences and shillings. He knew from history lessons that decimal currency only came to Britain in the twentieth century, but working to the base twelve, instead of ten, was not too hard. He did feel a little daunted when Joe said half a crown was two shillings and sixpence and there were twenty shillings to a pound and twenty-one to a guinea. On the market stall, however, they only dealt with small amounts.

When it was time to go home Joe said he'd bring the cart and Daniel could load up what was left while he went and chatted to a few people who might want Daniel's help. Clearing up did not take long and Daniel stood by the cart for some time.

It felt strange to be in the square in Knaresborough with the ancient chemist shop real and open. The modern chemist shop was not there and everything looked different but also familiar. He kept looking around, hoping to see Joe because he was very tired and hungry. Eventually he saw him, grinning and rubbing his hands. There was a man with him who looked more like a gentleman with a smart coat, stove pipe hat and a tidy beard and moustache.

'Daniel, this is Mister Hancock and he's the steward for most of the farms around here.' He paused and Daniel felt he should shake hands and offered his.

Mister Hancock shook hands and said, 'I understand from Joe here, you can read write and reckon and you need work.'

'Yes Sir, I mean Mr Hancock.'

'Well, most of our tenants can't read or write so you could work for me and visit them with letters and write their answers. They might also need help with their accounts. I'll pay you a fair wage, say nine shillings a week. Joe says you can live with him and Mary until you're older. There are two markets a week, so I'll see you Thursday and set you up with your own stall. You can keep all the proceeds from any personal letters you're asked to write, and I'll tell you how much to charge for a letter.'

'Thank you, Mr Hancock,' said Daniel. 'That's a kind offer and I accept.' He wondered at his ability to speak in a more formal way, but it appeared he had said the right thing. Everyone smiled, made their farewells and Joe drove them home.

That night, feeling warm on a mattress near the fire in the kitchen, Daniel thought about his new life. It seemed weeks ago, not just a day, that he'd been at Brimham Rocks and fetched Giraffe for Ben. He realised now that the shaking rock had transported him into the past, although he had no idea of the year. It was obviously before cars had been invented and he had not seen any bicycles at the market. Could it be Victorian times? Would he be able to go home to his own time? He thought of his Mum and Dad then and tears brimmed over and dripped onto his blanket. He was so tired that even in his misery he slept.

Chapter 4

June 1859

Major Carstairs carried Nathaniel's little body back towards the house. His voice croaked as he said, 'Emily, hurry on ahead and tell Jane there's been an accident. It might help a little if she has a warning before she sees...'

Emily ran, relieved for a moment from the horror that was her fault. As she ran her thoughts were selfish. She was going to get the sack, without a reference. How would she get another job? Then her mood became angry. Major Carstairs would blame her. He had to. Jane would never forgive him otherwise.

When she reached the back door, she could scarcely breathe from the running and anxiety, but she barely paused. Flinging open the door she ran to the parlour, shouting, 'Missus, Missus!'

Jane frowned and stood up at the sight of Emily's obvious distress. When she heard the news, she was the one to start running, back towards the river, until she met Cecil with his arms cradling her darling boy. She held her arms out and he gently handed his burden to her. She stared at her child's perfect face and kissed it. Nathaniel's face was cold. His eyes were shut, but not because he was asleep. She began to scream, 'N-o-o-o-o! Nathaniel! Please God. No.' Jane's legs began to buckle. Cecil tried to support her, comfort her. He put his arms around her, trying to take her weight but she stood upright, rigid and shook him off.

'He's wet; drowned. How did this happen? Where were you?' Then she sobbed; tears unchecked flowed onto Nathaniel's face that was held against her own as if she could warm him back to life.

*

Jane took to her bed, inconsolable. She neither ate nor drank apart from a few sips of water. Cecil had to arrange the funeral. He also fired Emily.

'You realise you can't stay on here, Emily. I have to let you go. You'd have gone already had the mistress not stayed in bed.' He saw her nod and continued. 'There'll be no reference, of course, but I have decided to pay you your wages.' He handed her the cash which she took, head down. She did not curtsey, just turned away as he added, 'Go, pack your things now and leave immediately.'

Emily did as she was told. She had no bag of any kind, so she put her clothes in a bundle, wrapped in an old shawl. Carrying the bundle, she went to the kitchen to say goodbye and hoped to beg some food to take with her. Cook and the scullery maid both turned their backs on her.

'Please, just let me have some bread and cheese. I've got a hard time ahead of me and… I thought we were friends.' She saw the scullery maid look at the cook, wanting to help her but Cook was stony. 'You'll get nowt 'ere. Yer don't deserve nowt. Be off with yer.'

Emily left. She trudged down the dusty lane towards Knaresborough with little hope for the future. She would never get employment in a fine house again, not with her dusky brown skin and no reference. There was only one option and, despite her willingness to couple with Cecil, she was horrified of being a *whore*.

There was another option, begging, but if she was caught it would mean the poorhouse. Emily knew nothing about the poorhouse but understood it was a frightful prospect to be avoided at all costs.

These miserable thoughts were halted when she heard a cart coming down the lane and turned to see a man and a woman, farming folk, sitting side by side. The cart slowed to a walk when it reached her, and the woman asked her if she would like a ride to Knaresborough.

'That's very kind of you, thank you,' she said. The man got down, pulled down the tailgate and helped her get into the back. She saw she was to share it with a pig, lying on a bed of thick straw. Emily only hesitated a minute and sat as far as possible away from her travelling companion. They set off and introductions were made. He was called John Partridge and his wife, Rebecca. They were going to the market to sell their pig.

'When our sow 'ad the last litter we couldn't afford to keep 'em and this is the last one. We call him Henry and he should fetch us a fair price,' said John.

'I would a'thought as 'ow you was going to the market too, but for yer bundle,' said Rebecca. Emily knew she had to say something to these kind folk, but she didn't know what. Finally, she opted for the truth. 'I was lady's maid at Lime Bank Hall. I was accused of something I didn't do and told to leave.'

'Not the death of their child!' John pulled on the reins and the cart came to a stop. They both turned to look at her. Emily nodded, squirmed at their scrutiny, then stood up in the cart. Even the pig shuffled to its feet. In their eyes she was a pariah. She struggled to get over the back of the cart and dropped down to the ground with her bundle.

John flicked the reins and the cart rumbled on; neither of them looked back at her. She watched them go and then sighed and said aloud, 'That's a lesson learnt. I must be a liar and need to go away from here or I might even be lynched.'

It felt unjust. Cecil was in charge of the child, not her, but she was not stupid and understood the way of the world.

*

Emily arrived at Knaresborough market just before it closed. Her feet hurt and she had eaten nothing all day. As she walked through the stalls she glanced furtively around, frightened someone would recognise her and assault her. She was pleased her bonnet shielded most of her face so it would be necessary to look beneath it to see the colour of her skin. She paused at Joe's stall, the smell of the bread and cheese impossible to pass.

'What can I do fer you today? Will it be carrots, cheese or the finest bread in all Yorkshire?'

'A couple of thick slices of bread and one of cheese please,' she said. She held out her thin shawl and he placed the food in it. She paid and it was hard not to stuff it all into her mouth immediately.

On one side of the market was a bench, empty of people because the vendors were closing up for the day. She sat there, eating and wishing she had some water or ale to help it down.

What was she to do? As Emily looked around, she noticed a youth sitting at a table with pen, ink and paper. How much would it cost for him to write her a reference? She saved the second slice of bread for later, put it in her bundle and went to ask.

Daniel looked up at her and smiled. 'Good afternoon. What would you like me to write?'

'I need a reference. I didn't do any wrong, but they've let me go. Please can you write, sayin' I'm a good, honest maid that's not afraid to work hard? I haven't much money. What will it cost?'

'I charge three pence for one page, sixpence for two. She bit her lip and said, 'I'll have just one page please.' Daniel dipped his pen in the ink and asked her name.

'Emily … Miss Emily Green.'

She watched Daniel write carefully and slowly, wiping the nib often to prevent blots.

'To whom it may concern, Miss Emily Green has worked for me as my lady's maid for …?' He paused and asked her, then continued, 'three years. I have found her to be hardworking, honest and respectful.'

He looked up again and asked if she had any special skills. Then wrote, 'She can sew neatly and is able to make clever use of ribbon and lace to trim a frock.

I recommend her to your service and know you will not be disappointed.'

'I will need an address and the name of the person who is giving you this reference.'

She frowned, unsure what to say. Finally, she said, 'What's your name?'

'Daniel Mansfield.'

'Please sign it Amelia Mansfield and the address, erm, Stonely Manor, Norfolk.'

Daniel finished the letter and let it dry before folding it carefully, as he had been shown, and sealing it with wax. He handed it to Emily, and she gave him three pennies.

17

'Thank you, Daniel. I'm grateful.' With that Emily walked out of Knaresborough towards the wealthy town of Harrogate, feeling just a little more optimistic than she had that morning.

Chapter 5

2048

The search for Daniel was called off. There was not an inch of the Brimham Rocks area that had not been examined. It seemed as if the boy had just disappeared. The police labelled the case as unsolved and moved on to investigate crimes.

Andy and Isabelle became reclusive, locked in their misery. 'It's worse than if he'd died. We spend every minute of every day waiting for news. Our lives are on hold and I can see no way forward,' said Andy. 'I think I must go back to work. Perhaps that'll help. The lab has been generous allowing me so many weeks on compassionate leave but ...' He looked at Isabelle. She sat, sunk into depression, her head hanging, and gave no response.

'Please, Izzy. Speak to me. I need your help. Shall I go back to work on Monday?' He'd raised his voice and looked at her, wanting to shake her for a reaction. There was nothing. She sat like a statue. She had lost a lot of weight, barely eating. Her hair, normally beautiful glossy auburn with a natural wave, hung dull and as lifeless as her.

'I'm going to call the doctor. You need help and I'm worried about you. I can't go back to work leaving you all day in this state. I'm phoning now.' Andy picked up the phone, expecting her to object, but she still didn't speak. 'The doctor said he would call within an hour or two.' Andy then phoned Izzy's mother, Catherine.

'Would you and Jason be able to come and stay for a while? Izzy's in a bad way, total depression and I can't leave her, but I need to go back to work.' He listened. 'Yes, the doctor's coming this morning. Thank you, I'm really grateful.' He turned towards Izzy. 'Your Mum and Dad are coming to stay for a few days. They'll be here in time for dinner, about seven. What shall we cook? I'd better get something out of the freezer.'

Izzy raised her head. 'I'm sorry. You decide. I can't. Thank you ... for inviting them.'

19

Andy smiled and hugged her. 'You'll feel better soon, especially if the doctor gives you something to help. I'll go and put the coffee pot on.'

He went into the kitchen feeling happier than he had since Daniel disappeared. He knew it was because Izzy had rallied enough to speak; such a small thing but it meant so much. Before the coffee was ready, he looked in the freezer and found pizza, enough for four, although Izzy would probably not eat much. So, dinner was solved. He carried the coffee into the living room then went back to collect the biscuit tin. He offered Izzy one but she shook her head.

'Your reaction to the state we're in is to starve yourself and I'm comfort eating. I daren't stand on the scales. I don't have to; my trousers are getting tight.' Izzy did not flicker as if she hadn't heard him speak. He sighed and took another biscuit. He was just contemplating a third when the doorbell rang. 'Saved by the bell,' he said and went to the screen. It showed the doctor, so he pressed the entry button. The doctor came into the hallway and Andy met him there. 'Thank you for coming.'

'No problem. Is Isabelle in here?' When Andy nodded, they both went into the living room.

'Hello Isabelle. Andy says you're suffering from depression and that's very understandable under the circumstances.' He was watching her as he spoke, noting her slow reactions. 'There's no need these days to suffer as much as you are. I can give you some pills that will help you to cope. They have almost no side-effects and will just make it easier to do those everyday tasks.'

Izzy looked up at him and whispered. 'Yes, I need help. Please ...'

'Excellent, I'll just key in the script and it will be ready to collect as soon as you can get to the pharmacy. They'll deliver if you'd prefer?'

'No, I'll fetch it,' said Andy.

The doctor left and Andy asked Izzy if she would be all right for the short time it would take him to collect her pills. He was pleased to see her look up at him and then she said. 'I'll be fine. I'll have a shower and get dressed.'

Andy felt lighter as if a burden had now been shared. He used the car and was home again within twenty minutes. He could hear

20

the hairdryer going and when he looked in the bedroom Izzy was dressed, for the first time in weeks. When she had finished drying her hair she came into the kitchen and picked up the packet of pills. 'Better take one straight away, then another tonight.' She took it with water and then moved over to Andy and he put his arms around her. They said nothing, just comforted each other.

*

Xen and Joanna had hardly seen their friends in the last couple of weeks. It was hard to know what to say when they were suffering so badly with grief.

'Do you think we should invite them out for a drink or go for a walk? We can't stop being their friends, can we?' Xen had just come home from work and had obviously been thinking about this.

'I spoke to Andy on the phone, and he said Izzy was deeply depressed and he didn't know what to do. I suggested he phoned the doctor,' said Joanna. 'I'm sorry. I should've told you, but I know you feel guilty, and I didn't want to make you feel worse.'

Ben came bounding in from playing in the garden. 'Is dinner ready, Mum? I'm hungry.'

'Nearly, just waiting for the chips to get a bit browner. Will you go and find Ruby; she's probably in her room and tell her I need a hand to dish up, then wash your hands.' She raised her voice at the end because he was rushing to go upstairs while she was still talking.

During the meal Ben chattered about school and Ruby was quiet, glancing at her solafone until her mum told her to stop. 'Turn it off or at least put it in your pocket. Any message can wait until after we've eaten.' Ruby put it in her back pocket and sighed, loudly.

Joanna remembered how delightful she'd been as a child, but this young adult was very different. She seemed totally self-centred, not interested in any of the family; her friends being *so* much more important. She felt like giving an exaggerated sigh herself. Instead, she began to collect the plates and then asked Ruby to load the dishwasher.

Ruby moved, without moaning, and boiled the kettle too, to make tea. Perhaps she wasn't so bad, thought Joanna.

It was much later in the evening, when Ben and Ruby were in bed, that the conversation turned again to Andy and Izzy.

'Do you think if I wished for the timer hard enough it would come? It's supposed to help the women in Catherine and Izzy's family. It took Jason back in time when Catherine was killed in a car accident. He prevented it and no one noticed the world had gone back in time a few months,' said Xen.

'I know the story. I also know how you saved Izzy from dying. I noticed we'd gone back in time and so did Sonia. Andy, Catherine and Jason were delighted to have her back. So, I think it's possible it could appear again to get someone to help Daniel return to his own time, but it won't necessarily be any of us that finds it.'

'That's some comfort but if it was one of us, we would know exactly what was happening, and could act really quickly.'

'Let's hold hands, shut our eyes and both send a message to the timer. It can do no harm and it might work.' They held hands and both pictured the large ship's sand timer with its brass stand and narrow-waisted glass, the sand drizzling steadily through it.

When they let go of each other, the plea having had no obvious effect, they exchanged sheepish grins and made preparations to go to bed.

Chapter 6

1859

Daniel's moods swung from being pleased he was able to earn his own living and saving a small amount every week, to abject misery when he thought of his family and the life he had before. The misery occurred mostly at night when he went to bed and he often cried himself to sleep.

Once, Mary heard him and came into the kitchen in her long white nightgown with a shawl around her shoulders. She knelt down beside him, gathered him up in her strong arms and held her to him. He cried even more then, but the comfort of being cuddled was wonderful.

'Hush, hush, missing yer Ma, no doubt. It'll all seem better in't mornin'.' She left quietly, when he was asleep, and crept back to her own bed.

When he saw her the next day, he was worried she would say something, but she greeted him as usual with her bright smile and busied herself preparing breakfast. He was grateful to her and Joe for their kindness and wondered if he dared ask a favour.

Brimham Rocks, he knew, was several hours walk away but it would be much quicker if he could go by cart or even ride a horse. Daniel wanted to return to the rock and ask it to take him back to his own time. If he explained his idea to Joe, he would think him crazy, so he was unsure what to do.

Since Daniel first began to live with them Joe had treated him like a son and taught him how to help on the farm, in the vegetable garden, and to hitch the horse, Betsy, to the cart. But he had never been taught how to ride. In fact, he'd never seen Joe ride. When they were picking beans one day, he asked why Joe didn't ride Betsy.

'Nay lad, Betsy's trained to pull a cart or the plough. She's not one to be ridden. I s'pose she could be, but I don't.' So, riding Betsy to Brimham was not going to be possible.

'Joe, do you and Mary ever have a holiday?'

'Yer full o' questions today.' He stood up, took his hat off and scratched his head, put it back, bent down and said, 'Nope, no holidays; that's for rich folks, not the likes of us, apart from Christmas o' course and May Day, oh and Plough Sunday. Now let's get these beans picked, market day tomorrow.' They worked in silence for a while and then Joe began to sing, quietly.

Oats and beans and barley grow
Oats and beans and barley grow
Do you or I or anyone know how oats and beans and barley grow?

First the farmer sows his seeds,
Stands up tall and takes his ease
Stamps his feet and claps his hands
And turns around to view his land.

There were several verses and before long Daniel was joining in with the chorus. His voice was still a boy's treble although, occasionally, it would slip out of control into a lower register. Joe looked up at him and grinned. There was no need for words. They were enjoying the easy activity and the companionship.

Later, when they were putting the sacks of beans in the store shed, Mary came out of the house to meet them waving something. 'Joe, the postman's brought a letter. Hurry and wash up.' They washed quickly and went indoors. Daniel knew this was the first letter they'd received in the six weeks he'd been staying there. He wondered if they could read. It seems they could, if rather slowly.

Joe undid the seal and read aloud,

'Dearest Ma and Pa,

Mrs Hayward and her son have left to have a holiday by the sea for two weeks. We have much less to do while they are away so our housekeeper said I could come home and sleep one night. I can have a ride in the carriage as far as Knaresborough market on Wednesday and then you can take me home.

I hope you are both well,

Your loving daughter,
Ruth'

Joe looked up from the letter, cheered, threw his arms around his wife and twirled her around as Daniel watched, smiling.

'Joe, put me down. She's coming tomorrow. I must make her bed and bake a cake. Oh, I can't believe we're going to see her. This is just the best news ever.'

During dinner Daniel learnt more about Ruth. She was sixteen and had gone away to work in Burton Hall as a housemaid. That was three months ago, and they had not seen her since. She had had days off but was not able to get home to see them, until now. Daniel was pleased for them but worried he would spoil her homecoming.

'Tomorrow night, when we bring Ruth home, could I borrow the cart and go up to Brimham Rocks? I'll not stay to dinner, and if you let me take some food, water and a blanket I'll stay overnight and let you enjoy Ruth's visit, without me.'

'I think that's a great idea, Daniel. If it rains you can sleep under the cart.' The details were discussed, and Daniel felt guilty. If the rock worked, he would not be able to return the cart, unless Betsy found her own way home.

The next morning everyone was excited. Mary had put on her better frock and a clean white apron. She added a bonnet and a light shawl when they were leaving because she was coming to market with them, not wanting to miss even a moment of their time with Ruth.

Daniel sat in the back of the cart with the beans, bread, butter and cheese they were going to sell, and he had his wooden box with the tools of his trade beside him. Mary chatted about what she was going to buy in the market and said she would help Joe until Ruth arrived.

It was warm already and there were no clouds in the sky. If he couldn't get back to his own time it looked as if it would be a fine night for camping.

When they arrived, Daniel jumped down and helped unload the cart then he drove it out of the way, while Joe and Mary arranged the produce on the stall. As he walked back Daniel was

25

proud of how much he had learnt in just a couple of months. He unpacked his writing materials, two wooden pens with steel nibs, spare nibs, a bottle of ink, paper, blotting paper and sealing wax.

When he was ready, with no customers, he began to think about his plan that night. If he couldn't go back to his own time, could he leave a letter to be found? It could be found at any time during the next one hundred and eighty years, but it might be found in his own time. It would be like putting a message in a bottle and throwing it into the sea. He began writing:

Dear Mum and Dad,

I'm fit and well, living in August 1859 at Blackberry Farm near Burnt Yates. The people, Joe and Mary Smith, have been very kind letting me stay with them. I have a job writing letters because many people can't read and write, so all that practice you made me do to improve my handwriting has paid off!

I miss you very much and cried a lot at first, but my life is fine and most of the time I'm happy. I'm going to hide this letter at Brimham Rocks and hope someone in your time finds it, if the stone won't let me come back.

Lots and lots of love,

Daniel xxxxxxx

Daniel put the pen back in its stand and sighed. As he wrote he had pictured them at home and now he wanted to be there more than anything. He fought back the tears, checked the ink was dry and then folded and sealed the letter. Now he needed a container for it, a bottle with a stopper or a tin box?

He opted for a tin box but would need to buy one. He still had no customers, so he asked the man on the next-door stall to keep an eye on his writing equipment and looked around at the other stalls. There was a kitchenware stall with crockery and pans and right at the back he saw a tin box.

'Could I look at that tin box?' he asked.

'This is not a tin box, young sir, 'tis a tea caddy, guaranteed to keep your tea dry and fresh.' He picked it up, holding it as if it was made of gold and held it out for Daniel to take.

'How much is it?' He felt it was going to be more than he could afford.

'Half-a-crown, take it or leave it.'

'I can't afford that, sorry.' Daniel handed the tin back and walked on. From the stalls he moved on to the shops and then found an Aladdin's cave of second-hand things. He browsed and bought a small tin box for just three pence. He hurried back to his stall to find an irate customer, waiting for him.

Daniel apologised and settled down to write. It was another private letter, so he pocketed the money having already covered the cost of his box.

When it was noon and most stallholders were eating, Daniel saw Mary coming along with a pretty, smartly dressed young woman. It was obvious they were mother and daughter. Ruth had the same curly hair escaping from her bonnet but was slimmer and a little taller than her mother. They both had the same welcoming smile.

'Ruth, this is Daniel.' Daniel had stood when he saw them approaching and he held out his hand. She shook it firmly with her gloved hands.

'I'm very pleased to see you, Ruth. Your parents have been so looking forward to today.'

'Oh, me too. It's seemed an age since I was last here. I understand you're letting us have the house to ourselves tonight. That's very kind of you.'

'That's the least I can do when they took me in and let me stay.'

They stood, chatting happily until Mary said, 'We'll be packing up the stall soon as we've sold most of it. I hope you won't mind leaving earlier than usual.'

'No, that's fine.' They turned to leave and Daniel suddenly became busy. It seemed there had been letters sent to several farmers saying their rent would be going up. He had to read the contents to them and then they blustered and got cross with him, as if it was his fault.

It was very unpleasant, and he was relieved when the cart came along to collect him to go home.

Daniel helped unload the cart, left his writing box in a corner of the kitchen and Mary made him a packed meal, enough for breakfast as well, and gave him a bottle of ale to have that night. He remembered to take a blanket and then left the family to enjoy their time together. It had been a long walk from Brimham Rocks but now he was driving the cart and feeling excited and hopeful.

Chapter 7

Emily reached Starbeck and stopped at Violet's bakery to buy some bread. She kept her head down as much as possible but the lady serving, Violet herself, was very friendly, obviously wanting to chat. Eventually Emily looked at her and saw no surprise at the sight of her dusky skin; the smile had not wavered.

'Here's yer cob, nice an' fresh. Is there anything else I can help you with today?'

'I don't know if you can help me with this, but I need work. I was a lady's maid but don't mind doing something else. Do you know of any houses around here who might employ me?'

Violet frowned with concentration and then smiled. 'Burton Hall. I know there was a maid who got in the family way and was sent packing. I don't think they've hired anyone yet. Why not go and see?'

Emily asked directions, thanked Violet and walked along until she found the leafy lane that led to the hall. A carriage and pair was coming towards her so she stepped into the trees and watched it pass. She briefly saw an older lady, in widow's weeds, and a younger gentleman driving. She thought it was almost certainly mother and son so perhaps now was not a good time to visit. The housekeeper would surely have to ask permission before employing anyone.

The grass amongst the trees was dry. Emily sat down, ate some bread while wondering what to do. Should she wait until the carriage returned or go boldly to the back door and ask?

She decided on the latter. She put the rest of the bread in her bundle, picked it up, and walked down the drive. It was a Tudor building with three gables and tall chimneys. Emily thought it would have a large staff and hoped they needed another.

When she went around to the back, she saw the stables held two beautiful chestnut horses. It was tempting to go and stroke their noses but now was not the time. There was nobody outside, so she went to the back door and knocked.

After the third knock the door was opened by a girl of about ten years. 'Cook says what do yer want, hurry up she's busy.'

'I want to talk to someone about a position. Could I see the housekeeper?'

The door was rudely shut on her and Emily wondered if the girl would take her message. She waited for what seemed a very long time and was just thinking of knocking again when the door was opened by an enormous woman. Her face was red, her grey hair escaping her mob cap and the bib of her apron hardly covering her bosom. 'Right, I understand yer looking for work. Can you cook 'cause I'm seriously in need of some help?'

'I can do some very basic cooking but I've not had any experience of anything fancy, Mrs ...?'

'Danby, Mrs Danby. You'd better come in and we'll talk a bit more. What's your name then?'

Emily and Mrs Danby had their little chat over a cup of tea and a large slice of fruit cake. It seemed the family that owned the house was having a wedding the following day. The young man Emily had seen driving out was marrying a girl he had met in India. She had no family in England, so they were organising the wedding breakfast and all the guests were staying there. Mrs Danby needed immediate help in the kitchen and Emily was soon fitted with an apron and cap and set to work.

When the mistress of the house returned Cook asked if she could see her. She entered the airy drawing room and when asked explained about Emily.

'She worked really hard today and has been a great help. I was wondering if we could take her on as assistant cook.'

'Yes, but tell her it's just until the wedding is over. If you're pleased with her after that, we'll consider keeping her on.'

'I'll tell her, thank you, Ma'am.' Mrs Danby bobbed a curtsy and went back to the kitchen to tell Emily.

'Did you tell her I'm from India?'

'No, I didn't mention it. 'Twill make no difference; after all the young master is marrying a lass that looks like you, 'cept she has a black mark, like a beauty spot, just here.' She pointed to her own forehead.

'That's a caste mark and in India it tells everyone that she is high born, like your gentry.'

'Really? Anyway, that's enough chatter; we must get on. Separate a dozen eggs and whip up the whites for meringues.'

When Emily was allowed to go to bed, she was exhausted but looking forward to the following day. She had never seen an English wedding, and everyone seemed so excited. Mrs Danby seemed nice, as long as she was obeyed instantly. Emily felt she had fallen on her feet and hoped Mrs Danby would give her a good report so she could stay.

*

As Emily snuggled down to sleep, Daniel was crying. He was not trying to stifle his tears because there was nobody for miles around. He was sobbing and thought he would never stop. He had hoped, so very much hoped, that the stone would take him back to his own time, but it hadn't.

When he arrived at Brimham Rocks, there had been a smart carriage coming out of the wider space where Daniel had intended to stop. He waited while the carriage drove away and then saw a man standing looking at him. The man walked up to the cart.

'I'm Mr Weatherhead. I live up at Rock House and show visitors around. Guided tours are over now, son, so best be off wi' yersen.'

Daniel nodded, drove the cart round a bend then a little further and pulled off the road. He tied Betsy to a sturdy shrub and walked back to the area where he'd intended to stop. As he approached, he kept a wary eye out for Mr Weatherhead, but he was nowhere to be seen. It occurred to Daniel that Rock House must be where the National Trust had their Visitor Centre in his time.

It took him a few more minutes of clambering between the rocks to find the one where Giraffe had been dropped. He climbed down beside it, faced the rock with his hands in the same place he had before, and said clearly, 'Two thousand and forty-eight', not once but several times. The stone failed to respond, and he was still in 1859. When it was obvious it wasn't going to work Daniel climbed up with his message in the tin box and took

31

it to a tiny cave that Ruby and he used to play in. He had shown it to Ben on the day of the picnic and told him it was a special place.

'Are you old enough to keep a secret?' he had asked. Ben had nodded fervently.

'Then come with me and I'll show you a special place.' Ben had been delighted when he saw the little cave, had sat in it and Daniel had climbed in with him. He wished they had stayed there and not explored further to the big rock.

Daniel left the box in the cave and went back to the cart and Betsy. He lifted his arms and put them around Betsy's neck and put his head against her, feeling comfort in the big horse's warmth. He told her everything and that was when the crying started.

It had been a long, disappointing day and Daniel was exhausted. He unpacked his cloth containing bread and cheese and looked at it. Was he hungry? He didn't know but it was getting dark, so it must be late. He broke off a piece of bread and then realised he was ravenous. He drank some ale, had more bread, and ate nearly all the cheese before he remembered it was also his breakfast.

The simple act of refuelling his body was calming. He knew he would have to accept he had gone back in time and must do the best he could to make a new life but now he had to find a place to sleep. He collected the blanket and decided he would feel safer camping under the cart. Betsy was tethered so she wouldn't move, and it was a flat area with thick grass and wildflowers. He spread the blanket out, crawled onto half of it and pulled the rest over him.

He went to sleep immediately, not hearing the rustling of small night creatures or the call of the hunting owl.

The creak of the cart moving slightly woke him at dawn. Daniel crawled out from under it, dragging the blanket with him. He rolled it up and tossed it into the cart then retrieved his breakfast and finished the bottle of ale.

'Do you know, Betsy, in my time it's illegal to drink and drive. In fact, it's illegal to drink alcohol at my age. Perhaps there's something to be said for living now. No police car's going to pull me up and test me.' He began to smile as he untied Betsy and climbed up onto the hard, wooden seat. He clicked his tongue and pulled gently on the reins so she would turn to head back home. After that he had little to do because the trusty horse knew where she was going and there were no other carts on the road. It was Sunday and everyone would be going to church.

As he neared the farm, he could hear the church bells ringing in Burnt Yates. Joe, Mary and Ruth would walk to church, and had probably left already. Daniel would have plenty of time to unhitch Betsy, rub her down and give her some food and water. He was pleased he could escape the weekly church ritual.

At primary school the assemblies were religious with stories from the Bible, and they had special events in the local church. They had been enjoyable. The pastor at Burnt Yates, however, always talked about sin and how everyone was doomed to go to hell. Each week a new sin would be the subject of his sermon and he would go red in the face; his grey hair would flop about as he banged the pulpit. Sometimes spittle leapt out as he shouted. It was not ideal to sit near the front.

The pastor's wife, though, was very friendly and sometimes came to visit Mary. They had tea and cake and chatted. When she had gone Mary would often say, 'Well, she's done her duty for this month.' Daniel could see how much she had enjoyed the visit and wondered why she would say such a thing. He was discovering that class distinction was much more rigid in Victorian times. The vicar was above a farmer, on a par with the schoolmaster and both of them were below the gentry. Tradespeople like carpenters, or stonemasons seemed to be above farmers but below the pastor and schoolmaster. How complicated it all seemed to be and why did any of this matter?

When Joe, Mary and Ruth returned from church, the roast pork was well done, and Mary and Ruth set about cooking the cabbage, potatoes and Yorkshire pudding. It was served with tasty gravy and everyone seemed very happy.

'How did you like your adventure at Brimham Rocks, Daniel?' Daniel nodded but it seemed more was needed.

'I liked driving the cart and Betsy made me feel safe when I slept under the cart.'

'Why did you go?' asked Ruth.

'I became separated from my family there and decided to leave a message in case they came back. I wrote I was staying here and that everyone was very kind to me.'

'Well, I hope they find it and then find you,' said Ruth.

'I'm not so sure we want that, though of course Daniel would. We've become fond of him and he pays his way with his writing letters. Anyhow, it's time we took you back, young lady. We don't want you to go either, but some things have to be. Daniel, will you hitch Betsy up while we say our goodbyes?'

Daniel did not need telling twice. He jumped up, embarrassed but pleased with what Joe had said. He also didn't want to witness the emotional parting that was bound to happen. If anyone started to cry it might set him off again and he didn't want a repeat of last night.

He waved goodbye to Ruth, Joe and Mary then went back into the house. In the kitchen he boiled the kettle for hot water and then washed the greasy dishes that had been left to soak. It might result in Joe telling him that was women's work, but he knew it would please Mary.

Then there was nothing to do: no solafone, no VR games, not even an old-fashioned novel to read. In the evenings, after a day's work, Joe often went to sleep after dinner while Mary sewed by the light of several candles. Now, without them to talk to he felt lonely. Where were the other boys of his age? He'd even settle for a girl to chat to or go and visit. This living in the Victorian age was boring in the evenings.

Chapter 8

2048

Izzy was feeling a little more positive, having had her mum staying with her for several days and taken several doses of the calming pills the doctor had prescribed. Her dad had gone home after the weekend because he had a town council meeting to attend. He'd been a councillor for two years now and loved being involved in helping to improve things for the community.

Catherine was also going home the next day, so she was determined to make this a productive one. 'When things have been difficult for us in the past, we have found that energetic action helped. You've been in this house ever since Daniel was born and I bet you still haven't cleared out the loft.' She saw Izzy grimace and went on, 'So, let's go armed with a load of refuse sacks and do it now.'

Izzy nodded and stood up. 'You do nag. Do you know that Mum?' She took a roll of sacks and together they went to the loft hatch. 'Loft ladder down, please.' She had no idea why she was so polite to an automated device but couldn't help herself.

The loft lid slid across and the ladder came down gently. Once it was locked Izzy said, 'Loft lights on, please.' She led the way up and together they stood and surveyed the mess. None of it belonged to them. The previous occupants had cleared the house when they moved but the loft was full of their junk. They could see suitcases, packing cases, cardboard boxes and a couple of folded garden chairs and general rubbish.

'Where shall we start?' asked Izzy.

'Let's begin near the hatch and work our way in. You go over to the other side and I'll start here.' Izzy nodded and they began to look in sacks and boxes. Sacks full of soft items like old pillows and bedding were unceremoniously tossed down the hatch. They landed with a *thwump* and several rolled all the way down the stairs.

After they had been working for about an hour Catherine began to sneeze, her eyes felt itchy and she knew she had to stop and get some fresh air. 'I'm going down for a while. I'll dispose of what we've already thrown out and I'll make some coffee.'

'OK. Give me a shout when the coffee's ready. I don't want to stop at the moment. I'm on a roll.'

Once away from the accumulated dust of many, many years, Catherine began to feel better. She emptied the rubbish down the disposal chute where the environmentally friendly furnace would incinerate it. Then she washed her hands and face, made the coffee and called Izzy to come down.

When Izzy arrived, she was carrying a small wooden box under her arm and dragging more sacks behind her to be incinerated. Her face had a black streak across one cheek, there were cobwebs clinging to her auburn hair and she looked happier than Catherine had seen her for weeks. Izzy threw the sacks down the hatch, washed her hands and then sat down at the kitchen table opposite her mum.

Catherine had put a few biscuits on a plate, still trying to encourage Izzy to eat something. Her daughter had lost so much weight since Daniel disappeared. She was rewarded when she picked up a biscuit and Izzy followed suit.

'I suddenly feel really hungry,' said Izzy, taking another biscuit. 'You were right, Mum, energetic action is good for the miseries.' She had another drink of her coffee and then lifted the lid of the box. 'Oh, this is a treasure trove of things.' She tipped the contents onto the table and they both reached for whatever they fancied. Catherine picked up a Spanish fan and flipped it open admiring the glittering picture of flamenco dancers. 'A holiday memento, I think.' She looked up at Izzy when her comment had caused no reaction and was shocked to see her crying, looking at a piece of paper that had once been sealed with wax. 'What's that?'

Izzy couldn't speak. She just handed the letter to her.

Catherine rang Jason who said he would drive over to see it for himself. He arrived about half an hour later having given the situation some thought. After reading it, he sat down. 'Oh, Izzy. I wonder how long this has been in the loft. Whoever got it couldn't have known Daniel and yet they kept it. How wonderful to know he's well and with kind people, but how can we get him back to his own time? We need the sand timer.'

'I want to call Andy, but I'm bound to cry down the phone. Then he'll think something worse has happened and feel he's got to rush home.'

Catherine made a cup of coffee for Jason. After sipping it he said, 'I can't help thinking about the last time we went back in time. It was nothing to do with the sand timer, if I remember. It had something to do with Xen. He had to prevent the destruction of Harrogate, and other towns around the world, by a Chinese laser-beaming satellite turned rogue. That was supposed to happen in 2035 and we know he succeeded because Harrogate's still standing, and we're all alive and well. It seems to me we should show this letter to Xen and Joanna and see what they can make of it.'

'If they know of another way to time travel other than the sand timer, another portal, we might be able to use it to find Daniel,' said Izzy. 'He'll be at work now so we can't ring him 'till this evening. I suppose the letter can wait. It's waited to be read by the right people for one hundred and eighty-nine years so another couple of hours won't matter. I feel all muddled now, excited, confused, hopeful. What do you think about the three of us finishing the loft?'

'We might as well be busy and we need another pair of hands for those heavy boxes of books,' said Catherine. They all worked hard until well after lunch time. Jason agreed to take the heavy but useful stuff, to a charity shop in his big estate car and then said he'd like to stay the night and take Catherine home in the morning.

*

That evening Andy read the letter and reacted by standing up and pacing around the lounge, looking at it again and again, unable to believe he held a letter from Daniel written nearly two hundred years ago.

'It's fantastic. He's well, being looked after by kind people. And all this time I thought he was dead, murdered, or abducted by a paedophile. My mind has tortured me with all these horrors. I'm sure you've been doing the same, Izzy.' She nodded, her eyes filling with tears.

'I was talking about this earlier, and I think Xen might be able to help,' said Jason, his face reddening.

'Well let's get hold of him right away,' said Andy. He seemed calmer and flopped back into a chair, looking at Jason but it was Izzy who replied.

'I did that just before you came home and he's coming over about eight o'clock.'

'Good, so we've time to eat before he comes. I'm famished. I can't smell anything cooking.' Andy looked at Izzy.

'There's nothing cooking my love, Jason's offered to buy us a takeaway, whatever we all fancy.'

'Pizza,' 'Indian,' 'Chinese,' were said simultaneously and everyone laughed.

'I'd rather not order all three or they'll all arrive at different times. Can we compromise?'

They settled on pizza and Jason made the call. It was eaten and cleared away just before Xen arrived.

*

On the phone Izzy had just said they'd had a letter from Daniel. Xen was surprised and delighted. He assumed Daniel had been abducted but had been allowed to send a letter to reassure his parents. The possibility that Daniel had run away from home was not an option. The boy seemed happy and well-adjusted even though he was beginning puberty. So far, he had not shown the teenage traits of becoming monosyllabic and unable to take his eyes off his solafone. That was probably because his parents monitored his solafone and limited his use of all technology, encouraging exercise and healthy living.

These thoughts ran through Xen's mind and, by the time he arrived, he was sure that Daniel had not found the portal to the past at Brimham Rocks. But the atmosphere in Izzy and Andy's house was peculiar. It didn't take Xen long to realise why. He held the letter, read it quickly, his original fear confirmed, and looked up at the expectant faces. Suddenly he realised he was going to be sick. 'Sorry, must go to the toilet.' His reaction to the letter was audible to everyone in the room.

'It seems to me Xen knows something about this, as we suspected,' said Jason. The others nodded, sat still and silent, waiting for him to come back. When he did, his face was white and he sat down, hunched over, his elbows on his knees, hands covering his face.

'When you're feeling up to it,' said Jason, 'we'd like to hear what you know about a portal to the past at Brimham Rocks. Did you tell Daniel about it?'

'God, no! He obviously found it by accident when he went to get Ben's Giraffe.' Izzy stood up, her movements jerky. 'Come on, Xen, please stop avoiding the issue and tell us everything you know about that portal. For a start we obviously want to know if he can come back the same way.'

Xen shook his head, sighed and finally faced everyone. 'Five years ago, Morgan, my boss, told me he was dying of cancer and wanted to show me the portal before he died, in case I ever needed to use it. You must stand facing the rock with both hands holding the sides in small indentations, then say the date you want to go back to. I think Daniel was holding the rock like that and said the time, 18.59. Morgan also told me the rock didn't work in reverse so I've no idea how we can get Daniel back.' He paused when there was a sob from Izzy. She held a tissue to her face and Andy put his arms around her.

'How did you get the letter?' asked Xen.

'Catherine and Izzy were clearing out the loft and found it in a wooden box of mementoes. We don't know why it was kept because whoever lived here then couldn't have known who Daniel was.'

Izzy sat up her face red and turned angrily to Xen, 'Why didn't you tell us that Brimham Rocks was dangerous?'

'I didn't believe anyone could find it by accident, especially not a child, because you have to be tall to touch both handholds. I'm so sorry.'

Chapter 9

1859

Emily had been up before dawn, helping Mrs Danby with the bread baking. While the dough proved they had a cup of tea and Mrs Danby explained they were to make a couple of large loaves, but the rest was going to be made into dainty, fancy bread buns. 'I'll show yer how to do the plaits an' I bet you'll be good at that with those nimble fingers.'

Emily enjoyed the work and the chatting that accompanied it. She discovered that the servants were all going to the church, in their Sunday best, but would have to stand at the back.

'Will I be able to come, or do you need me to be getting something ready for when they come back?' Emily asked.

'Of course you can come! When they all arrive back here, afterwards, they have drinks and those little fancy savouries we made yesterday. That gives us plenty of time to finish off the dinner. Have you got something smart to wear?' She saw Emily look down and it was obvious she didn't have anything.

'At my last job, my uniform was all found, and I didn't need anything else. I lived in and had no social occasions where I needed a smart dress.'

'Didn't you go to church of a Sunday?'

'No. It was a very big house. In the grounds they had their own chapel and members of staff went in their uniforms.'

'Right then. We need to find you something. Let me see. You're slimmer than me by miles, taller than our lady's maid. She would have been a good bet because she gets lots of hand-me-downs. I know, you're about the same size as our Martha what does all the mending. Shall I ask her?'

'Yes please, Mrs Danby. I really want to go to the wedding.'

'You just get on peeling them carrots and I'll go and find her.' A few minutes later she returned with two beautiful dresses.

'Go try these on. Hopefully one of them will fit.' Emily went up to her room and held up each dress in turn, one green with a fitted bodice and the other similar but in blue. She tried them both

40

on and they fitted. She had never worn anything so beautiful and tried hard to see the effect in the very tiny hand mirror she had. Finally, she chose the blue dress with a modest bustle and long skirt that was just possible to walk in without stepping on it. She ran down the stairs, into the kitchen clutching the green dress. 'Mrs Danby they're both lovely but I've chosen the blue. Can I take this one back to Martha and thank her?'

'Go on then but hurry back, no gossiping. I need your help.'

*

The wedding was at eleven o'clock so by half past ten all the servants were lined up on the grass beside the church door, the important ones at the front and lower ones behind. Emily was behind with the scullery maid, under-butler, stable boy, (who was at least fifty with greying hair), and the gardeners. The invited guests went into the church and then the groom and best man, looking smart in grey morning suits with top hats that they took off as they entered. There were some more guests and then Emily felt a shiver of fear as she saw her last employers, Cecil and Jane Carstairs. She looked away and down at her feet, glad that her bonnet hid her face. The excitement of the wedding and wearing the smart dress dwindled as Emily glanced up to see their backs, entering the church.

The arrival of the bride and bridesmaids caused all the servants to cheer. The organ could be heard beginning Wagner's *Bridal Chorus*. The bride was dressed in a sari, draped demurely over her head. The shimmering silk fabric was pale pink, embroidered with silver and gold flowers. She was carrying a bouquet made of pink and white roses and walked proudly with her head held high. As they entered the church, everyone stood and the servants filed in after them quietly to stand at the back.

Emily had been brought up in the Hindu religion. Her name was really Jhoti but Jane Carstairs had thought it easier to call her Emily. Now she wondered about the bride. Was she a Christian, Muslim or Hindu? If she was not Christian, was she going through the ceremony to please her husband? She thought she would never know the truth. As assistant cook, she was unlikely to ever meet her, let alone be able to ask such a personal

41

question. When they got to the vows Emily discovered the name of the young master. He was called Mark Hayward.

When the vicar turned to Mark's bride he said, 'Wilt thou, Amrita Achanya, take …', and Emily knew, by the name, the bride was also a Hindu. She suddenly felt lonely for her own country and the family she had left behind.

When Cecil had been sent back to England after the siege of Lucknow, to rest and recuperate from his wounds, Jane asked if she would come and be her maid in England. Emily had agreed so it was her own decision to be so far from home. She had not expected to be fired from her job, but everything seemed to be working well for her at the moment.

The service seemed to be very long, the vicar enjoying the sound of his own voice and having such a full church. Eventually Mr and Mrs Hayward were formally married, had signed the register and it was time for the servants to file quickly out, ready to throw rose petals over the couple as they left the church.

The rest of the day was hard work for all the staff. They had changed back into day dresses with aprons and caps and the kitchen was busy with cooking and footmen collecting tureens of vegetables, meat platters, gravy boats and then returning with dirty crockery and cutlery, then moving quickly to take out the desserts. They had no time for any formal lunch themselves, just catching a bite of something left over and drinking tea as they worked.

By late afternoon the wedding breakfast was over, the kitchen tidy, and Emily, Mrs Danby, the scullery maid, footmen and maids sat down to a simple meal. They had been allowed to add wine to their dinner, courtesy of the butler who held the keys to the cellar. With this they toasted the happy couple and the butler thanked everyone for their efforts.

The Hayward family still had guests that were staying the night so there would be a cold supper to organise later but for a few hours there was time to rest so Mrs Danby went to lie down. Emily took off her apron and went for a walk. While she was still on the estate there was a danger of meeting Jane and Clive, so she kept looking around and behind her. Once through the gates and on the road, she felt safer and strode up the hill towards

Knaresborough. The market would be closing but there might be a few stalls open to browse around.

The marketplace was busy, as she had expected, with stall holders taking things off their stalls and loading hand carts or horse-drawn carts. She stepped carefully avoiding rubbish and trying not to get in their way. Eventually she reached Daniel's stall. A customer was just leaving, and Daniel had stood to shake hands.

He saw her approach and smiled at her. 'Hello again. Did the letter help you find a position?'

'Yes, so I thought I'd come and thank you for your help.' Daniel asked her where she was working. When she told him he said, 'There was a wedding there today, wasn't there?'

Emily nodded. 'I was allowed to go, and the bride was Indian, like me. She looked beautiful and we all threw rose petals over them when they came out of the church. How did you know about the wedding?'

Daniel laughed. 'Everyone knows about the wedding. This is only a small town and weddings are big news. All the local shops have supplied the food.'

'Yes, I should have thought of that. I must go back now; Mrs Danby will be wanting my help. Thanks again for writing that letter. Bye.' She walked away and Daniel, still smiling, began to pack up his stall. It only took a few moments and then he carried his things to Joe's cart and helped him finish loading. He was looking forward to going home. That thought jolted him and a wave of guilt and homesickness came over him.

Chapter 10

2048

Catherine and Jason arrived home feeling a muddle of emotions. They were relieved and pleased that Daniel was safe and living with kind people. They were also upset because they had no way of contacting him or rescuing him from the past.

'When we all went back in time and found ourselves in the middle of the Indian Mutiny, your ancestor, Jane Carstairs, gave birth to a baby boy. Let's look at your family tree again,' said Jason. Catherine found the file in her computer and opened it. She found Jane and her husband Cecil but their son, Nathaniel, had died in 1859.

'How strange. He was definitely there the last time I looked and he lived until he was sixty something,' said Catherine. 'I wonder where they lived? We know Jane's parents lived in Marshall Hall because you bought the sand timer at an auction there. Perhaps we should do some research. Do you think military records would go back that far?'

'I don't know but you can ask. Whatever we do it won't help Daniel will it? We can't tell him he might have a distant relative living nearby. But I think this is significant although, at the moment, I can't see how. I feel so helpless. If only we had the sand timer. I wouldn't hesitate to use it to find him. He's so young to be coping without his family, earning his own living.' He sighed and added, 'If he did come back, he would be changed, matured, and could find it difficult to have to go back to school. Anyway, I'll go and make us a cup of tea and you see what you can find out.'

'OK, thank you.' A few moments later Catherine followed him into the kitchen. 'You know, I'm surprised Izzy hadn't thought of Jane. She travelled in India with Jane to Lucknow. I think I'll text her.'

When they were both sitting in silence, Jason trying to read and Catherine at her computer, there was a ping on her solafone.

Hi Mum, I can't believe I didn't think of Jane! If something happened to the baby, then it seems Daniel might be in the past for a purpose – to save the boy. Wish we'd told him about our time travel. Wish you'd showed him the family tree so he could meet Jane. Wish this was all over and he was here. X

'Poor girl,' said Catherine wiping away a tear. 'I'm not sure we've done the right thing reminding her about Jane.'

'No, it *was* the right thing to do because now she has some hope. The sand timer brought us back to our own time. I'm just praying that Daniel finds it, or the timer finds him.'

*

1859

Daniel had no knowledge of his family's emotional turmoil. He was back at the farmhouse, had enjoyed a big dinner and was grateful to have been offered the use of Ruth's bed while she was away. He had agreed, happily, to move out whenever she visited. It suited Mary because his personal things could move out of the kitchen, 'out from under her feet', but it had not occurred to her that she had woken Daniel each morning as she pumped water into the sink.

The following morning Joe and Mary had a quiet breakfast together, enjoying the absence of their lodger and amused at Daniel's ability to sleep on and on. Eventually Mary took him a cup of hot milk, knocked and entered the bedroom. It came as a slight shock to see his long auburn hair on the pillow instead of her daughter's, but she moved towards him calling his name, gently. Daniel stirred stretched and she saw he wondered where he was.

'Oh, morning, Mary. Thank you. What time is it?'

Mary's smile widened. 'The church clock just struck nine. Joe's been out in the kitchen garden for an hour and says when you deign to get up would you help him there.'

'Sorry. I think I overslept because Ruth's bed is so comfortable. I'll get up right away.'

'Nay lad, don't hurry. enjoy your milk. I'll go down and fry you a couple of eggs. Joe won't notice the passing of time when he's happy working.' She turned and went out and he listened to her heavy steps on the wooden treads.

There was a jug of cold water and a bowl in the room, so he decided to strip off his night shirt, given to him by Joe, and have an all-over wash. This was a luxury and he felt good after it. He just wished he could use deodorant. His mum had insisted he started to use it last year and now he worried he might not smell good. That thought made him smile because everybody he met ponged.

The pleasanter smell of frying wafted upstairs, and he ran down to see Mary dishing two eggs onto a thick slice of toast. She looked up and smiled as he entered. 'Well, that was good timing. Get this breakfast down yer. Yer goin' to need it 'cause Joe's got a heavy job for yer to do.'

When he arrived to help Joe, he felt embarrassed at being so late, but Joe just handed him a pair of over-shoes. 'I've been clearing this 'ere where we 'ad the broad beans,' and he waved his hand at the compost heaped high with bean stalks. 'Now your job is to dig out a barrow load off the midden and dig it in. In fact, I think two barrow loads would be better.'

Daniel nodded and wondered if the smelly and heavy job had been given to him as a punishment for sleeping late. Immediately the thought crossed his mind he felt guilty. For he knew Joe was not like that. He grabbed a shovel, put it in the wheelbarrow and went to the midden. He filled the barrow until he could hardly lift the handles and then trundled it to the vegetable garden and tried to tip it up. Joe looked up, amused and came over to help him. ''Tis better to not pile it higher than you can manage.'

'I realise that now. Thanks for helping me.'

'Spread and dig that lot into half of it and then fetch some more.' Daniel did as he was told and after nearly two hours, when his back was aching, Joe called a halt for a break.

He fetched a jug of ale that had been standing in the shade with a cloth over it by the barn. He took a huge swig, wiped his mouth on his sleeve and handed it to Daniel. Daniel copied him and they grinned at each other.

'When I first came, Joe, that ale made me feel funny but now I can drink loads of it before it has any effect.' He took another drink and handed it back to Joe who did the same, after he'd stopped laughing.

When it was time for lunch, Joe said he was very pleased with what they'd done. 'You're getting stronger, Daniel. Let's see yer 'ands. Aye calluses. Yer getting men's 'ands.' Daniel smiled, pleased with the praise and proud now of his sore blistered hands.

The afternoon task was lighter, watering the cloches where tender cabbage plants were growing and general weeding. Joe left him to go and check the cows and then bring them in for the evening milking.

While Daniel was stooped, weeding between rows, he heard a horse coming down the lane. He looked up and recognised Mr Hancock, the steward who had employed him to read and write letters. He stood and went over to take his horse's rein, to hold it steady while he dismounted.

'Good afternoon, Daniel.'

'Good afternoon Sir, shall I fetch Joe? He's up with the cows.'

'No, don't bother him. It's you I've come to see.'

'Would you like to come in, Sir?' As he said that he was relieved to see Mary smiling a welcome at the door. She shook hands with Mr Hancock and led him inside shouting back at Daniel, 'Daniel, wash up before you come in.'

Chapter 11

1859

Lime Bank Hall was impressive from the front aspect. Originally it had been a mansion, but previous generations had it enlarged. It now boasted three floors in the central section and two floors in each of the wings. It had two reception rooms, a ballroom, library, billiard room and a well-stocked cellar.

Cecil always felt a sense of pride as he approached it. It was a house that was used to parties, balls and frequent socialising but not lately; not since Nathaniel's death. The guilt and sadness he felt never left him. His wife barely spoke to him. The only way he could forget, for a while, was to immerse himself in the work of running the large estate.

He had spent the morning with George Hancock, his steward, in his study. He stood up now and picked up some papers. George stood too, trying to gauge his master's mood.

'Are you sure these letters are from my tenants? There are three here,' he flapped them in the air, 'that are all penned by the same hand. I suspect some conspiracy.'

'They *are* from your tenants, sir, but three of them can't read or write so they got young Daniel to pen the letters for them.'

'Who is young Daniel?'

George pressed on. 'He's the lad I told you about that has a market stall at Knaresborough. You did approve his employment, sir.'

'Ah, yes. I remember now. He's staying with the Smiths, isn't he?'

'Yes, sir.'

'So, no conspiracy, just the same writer. Well, they all say they can't afford the rise in rent and yet it's been a splendid growing year. Every farm has flourished. Perhaps they could do with some help balancing their books. Do you think that's something this Daniel … What's his surname?'

'Mansfield, sir.'

'Well could young Mansfield help them as part of his duties?'

'I can ask him, but farmers don't readily discuss money with others. They might not trust him, knowing he works for you. They could look upon him as a spy.'

Cecil walked towards the window and looked down at the sweeping lawn. He could just see the drive flanked by lime trees. Without turning round, he said, 'What impression do you have of him? Is he pleasant, hardworking, trustworthy?'

'Yes sir, all of those things. I know when he is not at the market Joe Smith puts him to work on the farm.'

'Right. Bring him here to meet me tomorrow afternoon, say four-thirty. Now I would like you to go and see those three farmers and discuss the matter with them then report back to me in the morning. I'll then know what to say, or not, to Mr Daniel Mansfield.' He indicated that George should go, then looked at his pocket watch, and saw it was lunch time.

When he reached the dining room Jane was there and the smile he had forced himself to wear, dropped. He sat down opposite her, the long mahogany table between them.

'Good afternoon, my dear. I missed seeing you at breakfast. How are you today?'

'I'm not an invalid, Cecil, to be asked how I am.' She looked at him her eyes blazing with anger.

'I didn't mean my greeting to sound like that, Jane. I apologise.'

The first course arrived, and the smell of fish wafted from the platter carried by the butler. Their plates were served, and he was followed by the under-butler with vegetables. Jane sipped her water before picking up her cutlery and eating slowly, without any enjoyment.

That was what was wrong with their lives now, thought Cecil, no joy. How, he wondered, could there ever be any joy having lost their beautiful son. There was also no chance of impregnating his wife again. She could barely cope with being in the same room as him. Emily had been officially blamed for Nathaniel's death, but he knew Jane really blamed him, and she was right. Although he had never admitted his dalliance with Emily, Jane was no fool. He tried to talk to her again. 'It was an unusual wedding wasn't it. I thought Amrita was charming.'

'Cecil I really don't want to talk about the wedding. I found it very stressful trying to behave as if it was a time for celebration.'

'It was for them, my dear.'

'I don't know why you insisted we went. It was hardly seemly during our time of mourning.'

'But everyone was very kind to us, and we can't be reclusive for ever.' She stood up, waving away the dessert just being offered. 'I'm going for a walk.'

He stood too. 'Shall I keep you company?'

'I think not.' Her parting shot was final, so he sank back into his chair and accepted his dessert. As he ate, he thought again about Amrita, so exotic, and hoped the couple would have a happy life and that she would be accepted by the local society. He would have liked to invite them here when they returned from their honeymoon, but Jane would never allow it. He sighed and stood up to go back to his office.

*

George Hancock began his round of illiterate farmers at the most distant farm; the tenant being a Mr David Fairhead. He had much ribbing about his name because his hair was a rich blonde much envied by his wife, Eve, who had mousy brown hair. They were a couple in their forties and had not been blessed with children, but they were always cheerful, and he had been looking forward to the refreshments Eve normally offered him.

As he approached, George curled his lip in distaste. The farm was a chaotic mess with broken fences, a gate hanging on one hinge, tools thrown down on the ground, rusting and it was very quiet. Why were there no animal sounds? Chickens normally ran freely around and Fairhead kept one cow for their own use and some pigs. He wondered if Fairhead was ill. If not, why was it in such a state?

There was no sign of life when he dismounted and tied his horse to a metal ring. He went to the door of the house and knocked. There was no answer, so he knocked louder, feeling anxious now. He heard a shuffling step coming to the door and stood back. The sight and smell of Eve made him recoil. Her hair was matted and her skin erupting with unsightly pus-filled spots. Smallpox!

'Mrs Fairhead, I can see you're ill. I'm sorry to intrude, but is your husband similarly infected?' He saw her confusion as she shook her head, then nodded. Finally, she managed to whisper, 'Dead, my David's dead. This morning. I couldn't wake 'im.'

'I'll fetch some men to remove his body. I'll organise his funeral and you need a doctor.'

'No, sir. No doctor. I'm dying an' all.' She shuffled away from him and through the door George saw her collapse to the floor. His instinct was to rush in and help her to her bed, but smallpox was a killer. He left the poor woman and mounted his horse. He rode to the doctor's house to report what he had found and to ask if there were any more cases.

'Yes, several more in the village,' said Doctor Scott. 'I've isolated them and forbidden the family to go out until the patient recovers. The children should be immune, having been vaccinated but older people ...' He shrugged. 'The modern thinking is the illness is a germ and people pass it on in the air or by touching. If you value your men, get them to cover their faces and wear gloves when they deal with your tenant's body. They must burn all bedding, towels and clothing.'

'Thank you, Doctor. I'll visit the other tenants to see if they're ill. If not, I'll warn them to be careful.'

*

George visited the other two illiterate tenants who were in good health. He was welcomed and given refreshments. He told them both about the smallpox outbreak and the plight of the Fairheads.

Then he broached the difficult subject of having help with their cash books. There was a lot of squirming and humming and ha-ing. It was obvious they were not keen on the idea, as he had predicted, but did not want to offend George or their master.

He asked what they thought of the young man that had written their letters. They nodded and agreed he was pleasant. He told them about Daniel's circumstances and they both felt less anxious when they heard he helped Joe Smith about his farm

51

when he wasn't writing letters. Eventually, reluctantly they agreed.

Now he had to visit Daniel at the Smith's farm.

Chapter 12

2048

'Catherine, I've had an idea, but I'm not sure if it's a stupid one.'

'Then you'd better tell me and I'll let you know.' Catherine was smiling at him, but Jason's next words removed it.

'What do you think of us both using the rock to go back to 1859? We could find and support Daniel and then visit Jane and Clive and see if we can get hold of the sand timer.' He watched her face crease into a frown and waited a long time for her answer.

'Phew, that's quite an idea. No wonder you were reluctant to share it. We might not be able to come back. There's no saying that we'd find the timer. It could still be on board a ship. What about money? Clothes? We'd have nowhere to live. Oh, I don't know.'

'Well at least you didn't say a definite no. This doesn't have to be done today. We can work towards it. I've no idea about money. They used pounds, shillings and pence and they'd all have to be minted before 1859. As for the clothes, we could hire them from a theatrical costume shop.' He could see she was warming to the idea as she nodded and was obviously thinking.

'Perhaps we could take something for Daniel, say a letter from Izzy and Andy. We'd have to tell her. We must also take a present for the people who are looking after him. What would be useful to farmers of that time? How can we carry everything? I don't think they had rucksacks in those days. We'll have to have good shoes because we'll have to walk all the way to Burnt Yates, carrying our bags.'

'Stop, Catherine! Your mind has gone into overdrive. I think the first thing we must do is to see if Izzy agrees with the idea. She might be upset at losing both her parents as well as her son. If she says no, then that's the end of it.'

'I think she would think it worth the risk because we might be able to bring Daniel back. Let's go and see her. I'll check she's in.'

It took only moments for her to text Izzy and receive a reply. They wasted no time in getting into the car and driving to her house.

When they arrived, Izzy let them in, and the rich smell of coffee was in the air. Izzy was smiling and seemed to have recovered from her depression. 'I didn't expect to see you today. What a lovely surprise. Coffee?'

'Yes please,' said Catherine. Jason nodded.

When they were sitting down in the living room, sipping their drinks, Jason told Izzy their idea. Different emotions crossed her face; hope, fear and confusion.

'I can hardly believe it. You'd be willing to do that, possibly never to come back, for Daniel.'

'We do love him, but we're also doing it for you and Andy. We're retired, getting older and quite like the idea of one last adventure,' said Catherine, handing Izzy a tissue. 'Talk it over with Andy before making a decision.'

Izzy nodded, too full to speak and blew her nose. When she felt calmer, she drank the rest of her coffee and said, 'Andy's come to look upon you as his parents since he lost both of his. Yes, I must ask him first.' She stood up. 'I think you're wonderful, but would you mind going home now so I can think? I'll ring you tomorrow.'

*

'It's all a question of balancing the good that could come out of it with the possible bad consequences,' said Andy. 'Being a scientist, leaving the emotion out of the equation, let's look at the facts.' He raised one finger. 'One, Jason and Catherine might be able to rescue Daniel.' He raised another finger. 'Two, they might not find the timer, in which case they cannot come back either. Then we've lost three people we love.'

'Huh, you don't have to be a scientist to figure that out. Look, *we* have to make the decision, Mum and Dad were quite clear about that. I just don't know what to do.'

Izzy stood up from her chair and sat next to Andy, resting her head on his shoulder. He shifted so he could put his arm around her. Holding her close he rested his cheek against her head and whispered, 'If I make the decision for them to go and they don't come back, you'll blame me.'

'So, I have to decide. That's not fair, Andy.' She sat up and looked at him with a frown.

'Alright. This is what I think. I'd do anything, risk anything to get Daniel back, including losing your parents.'

'That was brave. Thank you. I feel the same, so the decision is made.' She leaned towards him and they kissed.

Andy resisted the desire that surged through him and said, 'Give them a ring.' Izzy moved to pick up her solafone and within five minutes she was saying goodbye.

'Sorry I should have put it on speaker. You heard me offering to help in any way we can, and Dad said would we find them some old money. He said half-crowns, shillings and I can't remember the rest.'

'There must be coin collectors, so I'll look online. Was there anything else?'

'Yes, Mum asked me to write a letter to Daniel and to think of anything small he might like. She'd also like ideas for a gift for the people who have given him a home.'

'OK. Did they say when they might be going?'

'No, I think they want to be properly organised. Dad even said he was going to see their solicitor to update their wills. It will be a week at least.' Andy nodded. He had been researching coins before 1859 and had found some. 'This sounds good, a mixture of silver coins and copper. Ideal it says for the beginner. I suppose that means they are not rare or special, but you have to bid. Shall I do it?'

'Yes. If it's successful, but not really enough, we can always try again.'

'OK, but it's going to be expensive. There have already been bids of £850. I'll need to bid about £900.'

'Spend whatever you have to, Andy. Nothing is important except helping them bring Daniel back.' She sat silent for a while, waiting for Andy to finish. When he had, he looked up at her, smiled and said, 'Shall we go out to dinner tonight? I feel we have something to celebrate.'

*

55

Three days later, Izzy and Andy went to see Catherine and Jason to take the old money they had bought. Izzy had found some black velvet and made a draw string bag, hoping that would look authentic. They had also written a letter between them for Daniel. They had both shed tears. It had been difficult to write.

Catherine hugged them when they arrived. She and Jason were smiling and seemed to be alive with excitement. Usually, on arrival, they would offer coffee or tea, but Catherine said, 'Come and look at all the things we've got.' They followed her upstairs to the spare bedroom. Two long dresses were hanging up, one was cream and decorated with bark brown embroidery. The bodice had an inset panel shaped from the shoulders to a point at the waist. It had long sleeves and the skirt was very full. There was also a brown bonnet trimmed with cream ribbon around the brim and cream ribbon ties.

'That's a very pretty dress, Mum. I can just see you curtseying as you arrive at a ball in that.'

'Yes, so that's why I've also got what's called a day dress. A more serviceable colour and slightly less full skirt. I can't imagine how I'm going to clamber around Brimham Rocks hampered with all that around my legs.'

Izzy giggled, 'You'll have to tuck them into your knickers, or have you got bloomers?' Catherine went over to the bed and held up a corset, then long underpants. She waved the underpants around and said, 'Apparently, these are not authentic because in those days gussets were considered unhealthy but who's going to look at my underwear?'

Izzy picked up two underskirts. 'These are heavy. I suppose they had to wear layers because there was no central heating.'

'Look at it all! I've also got a thick cloak and a wool shawl. I don't know how I'm going to cram it all into this bag.' Standing on the floor were two large Gladstone bags and Izzy also had her doubts that it would all fit in.

'It's my turn now,' said Jason. He held up a long coat, waistcoat, shirt, close fitting trousers, boots and then put on a top hat.' They all laughed, and he feigned indignation but then went on, 'I also have a warm overcoat, an extra waistcoat, and trousers, plus long johns.' Now everyone exploded with laughter and Catherine led the way downstairs saying, 'I'll make some coffee now.'

Once they were all together in the living room Andy gave the money and the letter to Jason. He opened the bag and tipped the coins onto the coffee table. Then he sorted the coins and added it all up, slowly. 'There's twelve pennies to a shilling and twenty shillings to a pound. I make it one pound, twelve shillings, threepence and a halfpenny. I have no idea how far that will go but it doesn't sound very much does it?'

'I looked it up and a loaf of bread cost about three pence so if all you did was eat bread you could last quite a while on that,' said Jason.

'I can get you some more, if you're worried, but you might have to help with the cost.'

'What did you pay for this?'

'Nine hundred pounds.'

Jason spluttered his mouthful of coffee. 'I'll transfer double that into your account and please get us a little more. It worries me, not to have enough, because if we become destitute, we could end up in the workhouse. How long do you think it will take? We're so keyed up and ready, we don't want to wait much longer.'

'Well, I bid for that.' Andy pointed to the piles of coins, 'so I had to wait for the bidding to finish which was a couple of days. I could probably get it sooner than that.'

'See what you can do, Andy, and thanks for getting this. I know, if I hadn't asked, you wouldn't have told me how much you spent.' Andy shrugged with a smile.

Catherine stood up, went into the kitchen and came back a few minutes later. 'I've just been checking; there's enough in the fridge to offer you lunch. Will you stay?'

Izzy looked at Andy who nodded. 'That would be lovely. It all felt so exciting when we arrived this morning but now, I'm feeling like I want to see lots of you before you go,' she paused, 'just in case.'

'That's how I'm feeling too. So, no maudlin thoughts. I've got some soup and you can help me make sandwiches.'

Chapter 13

1859

Mary ushered George in, bobbing a curtsey as he passed her and went into the main room. 'Please sit down, Sir. Would you like a cup of tea, blackberry wine or ale?'

'I had the blackberry wine last time I came here, and it was delicious. Perhaps a glass of that? Thank you.' While the pleasantries were going on Daniel stood, feeling uncomfortable and unsure what to do.

'Now, while Mary's getting the refreshments, perhaps we can have a talk, Daniel.' He gestured for Daniel to sit and continued. 'I engaged you to work for me, but in fact you're working for Major Carstairs at Lime Bank Hall. He is Joe and Mary's landlord too. The estate is large and there are five farms as well as the house and grounds. I've been visiting all the farms today and this is my last. I can share with you that I have had so much tea and cake I'm almost bursting.'

This last comment helped Daniel relax and they were both still smiling when Mary came in with three glasses of deep red wine. She placed them on the table and then went back into the kitchen to retrieve a plate of cheese scones, split and thickly buttered. The butter was beginning to melt, the scones still warm from the oven. 'Eat 'em while they're hot,' she said and Daniel looked at George, saw his lips twitch with humour as he stretched his hand out and took half a scone.

'Sit with us, Mary,' said George, sipping the wine. 'I've things to say to Daniel and other things to tell you.'

While he was speaking Daniel took two scone halves, ate them very quickly and then took a gulp of wine. It made him cough, and his eyes water. The others looked at him, amused.

'Mary makes excellent wine, but you need to sip it, not glug it like ale.'

Daniel nodded and took a sip. It was fruity, mellow and the alcohol made him relax until he heard George's next sentence.

'Major Carstairs would like to see you this afternoon to increase your work to keeping cash books for two of the farmers.'

'But I don't know how to keep cash books, Sir, and … and I don't think they'd want me to know how much money they had.'

'You can learn, and they've both agreed. You'll be paid a little extra and be given a horse to use for your visits.'

Daniel squirmed with anxiety and embarrassment. He spoke quietly, his head lowered. 'I can't ride either.'

'You mayn't 'ave ridden a horse, but you know how to tek care of 'em and how to hitch one to a cart.'

Daniel looked up at Mary and smiled. He knew she was trying to give him confidence.

'Well, perhaps you could have the use of Joe's horse and cart to start with and we'll charge them a bit less rent.'

'We mostly use it on market days, sir, so that could work,' said Mary.

'Ah, that reminds me. The market will be shut down as from today because there's smallpox around. I'm really sorry to tell you but David and Eve Fairhead have both died of it.'

'No! I saw them just a few weeks ago and they were fine. Poor things. How they must've suffered.' Mary pulled up the bottom of her apron and wiped away tears. 'Are there many more cases?'

'I saw Dr Scott this morning and he said there are a few in the village; not too bad at the moment. There's still a lot of anxiety about the safety of vaccinations, so not all the children are protected and none of the adults, unless they've already had it. What about you, Daniel? I don't want to send you into farmhouses if you've not had a vaccination.'

'I was vaccinated as a baby.'

'Good, well go and get changed, lad, and you can ride behind me to see Major Carstairs.'

While he was upstairs changing from his working smock into trousers and a shirt, Daniel heard Joe arrive home and could hear his exclamation, probably at the news of smallpox.

*

59

Jane and Cecil were having tea in the parlour when George and Daniel arrived. The butler hesitated, not sure whether to take them in there or to leave them in the hallway until he had announced them. He decided on the latter and was told, 'I'll see them in the study, Joseph. Please offer them tea and say I'll be along directly.'

'You could've brought them in here. It would not bother me. George often joins us for tea. Are you hiding something from me?'

'No, my dear. There is a young man called Daniel Mansfield with him. I employ him as a clerk to the farmers. I thought you might find his presence intrusive, that's all.'

'Oh, well, I'd like to meet this young man of yours. Get Joseph to bring them in and I can hear the discussions.'

Cecil stood and rang the bell to summon Joseph, the irritation he was feeling manifested in his brisk movements and scowl. He never knew how to please his wife.

A few minutes later George and Daniel entered, and bowed respectfully. They stood for what seemed a very long time in silence, while Jane rudely stared at Daniel until he began to go red.

'Good afternoon, George and Mr Mansfield. Please sit down and have some tea with us,' Jane said, eventually.

'Not for me, thank you,' said George and Daniel might have laughed in different circumstances.

'And you?'

'No thank you. We've just had tea at my house,' said Daniel. He was relieved when she finally stopped staring at him. Major Carstairs and George began to talk about the smallpox outbreak and the dire state of Mr and Mrs Fairhead. It seemed shockingly callous to Daniel when he heard the Major say, 'As soon as the house is cleaned see about some new tenants. We can't afford to have the place empty.'

Suddenly Jane interrupted them, her cold voice cutting above the men. 'Mr Mansfield, come and sit next to me. I'm interested in your background.' Daniel obediently moved and sat as far away as possible on the two-person sofa.

'There's something about your face and hair colouring that seems familiar. Do you have relatives in India?'

60

'No Ma'am. Not as far as I know.'

'Hmm. When we were travelling to Lucknow there was a young woman we rescued along the road. She travelled with us and was a great help in my … when I was unwell. She had the same bright auburn hair, freckles, pale skin as I have. Her mother had similar features.' She shrugged. 'It doesn't matter. Nothing matters.' She abruptly stood up and all the men did the same, Daniel a little after the others. She walked to the door, turned and said, 'Mr Mansfield, George.' She inclined her head and they bowed. Then she was gone, and the atmosphere lightened.

'George tells me you're willing to learn bookkeeping and to help our illiterate farmers. There's no time like the present so go with George into the study and he'll get you started.'

Daniel nodded, hoped it would do as a bow and followed George. The study was obviously a man's room. The furniture was heavy dark leather, bookshelves lined the walls and there was a huge oak desk covered in papers, ledgers, pens and ink. The fire was laid but not lit and the room felt chill. George sat at the desk, brought a ledger towards him and opened it. 'I want to show you how a cash ledger is set out with expenditure on one page and income on the other. Each entry on either side has the date, a description of the goods bought and the cost. Does that make sense to you?'

'Yes sir, but how am I to know what has been sold or bought when I'm not there all the time?'

'That's a valid thought and I can only say you must take the farmer's word for it. He may have receipts for some things and that will help. Now I'll give you some new ledgers. You can set out the headings as I've shown you then I'll take you home.'

George left Daniel to do the task and when he returned Daniel was standing by the bookshelves reading a book. He replaced it, guiltily but George just said, 'What were you reading?'

'Waverly, sir.'

'Would you like to borrow it? I'm sure Major Carstairs won't mind. He's not one for reading and these books were his father's.'

He was rewarded by a wide smile as Daniel nodded. 'Joe and Mary don't have any books and I've missed reading. Thank you, Sir.'

'Take a couple of books and don't forget your ledgers. We must get you home. I'll meet you tomorrow morning, early and we'll use your horse and cart to visit the tenants who need your help.'

Chapter 14

2048

Xen led the way up the main path at Brimham Rocks. It was just dawn, no other people around, misty and drizzling with rain. The huge, rounded shapes loomed almost threatening, as they walked in silence. Catherine was frightened and imagined she would feel almost as bad as this if she was going to her execution.

When they reached the portal they stopped, and Xen helped them strap their bags to their backs so they could have their hands free to climb down and hold onto the rock.

'We've decided to try and go together if there's room for me to stand behind Catherine. We tried to toss for who should go first but then agreed it must be together or not at all.'

Catherine was looking over the edge, taking in the drop to the valley below and useful hand and foot holds. 'I would find this easy if I wasn't encumbered with this heavy bag and long skirt, not to mention this bonnet that makes me feel I'm a horse with blinkers.' Her effort at levity helped her own anxiety and Jason smiled at her.

'I'll go first and then I can help you down.' He turned to Xen and shook his hand. Xen then drew him into a hug. While Jason was climbing down Catherine hugged Xen and then climbed down herself needing no assistance.

'Good luck,' shouted Xen, peering down as they shuffled on the narrow ledge. Catherine reached up to the hand holds and Jason covered her hands and was touching the rock as he said, 'Eighteen fifty-nine.' The rock vibrated. When it stopped Jason climbed up and helped Catherine. They both stood, bleakly looking around. It was hard to believe Xen had disappeared when the rock formations looked just the same.

1859

'It's not raining and it's colder,' said Catherine. She looked at Jason. 'I'm scared. Have we done the right thing?'

'Yes, and, if you think about it, we've done something drastic like this before. We sold our house and everything to buy a yacht so we could explore the world. That felt scary but exciting like this. Come on,' he said, taking her hand. 'Let's find Daniel.'

They walked along the rough road remarking on the differences they noticed. After an hour Catherine said, 'I could do this much more comfortably if I was wearing my hiking boots, but I must say all these layers of clothing are keeping me warm. How are you?'

'My boots are fine, and this overcoat is really too warm. I think I'll take it off and carry it for a while. I'm getting hungry and thirsty, though.'

'Me too but we couldn't fit any more into our bags. It's odd not knowing the time. I'm missing my solafone already.' She smiled up at him and added, 'We'll just have to get used to a simpler way of life. Up with the dawn and sleep when it gets dark. No television, no electronic games, no electricity so no washing machine, dishwasher, automatic vacuum cleaner. It sounds like hell!' She laughed and Jason joined in. They were both nervous and trying to keep their spirits up.

It was mid-afternoon when they arrived at Blackberry Farm. They skirted the midden, Catherine covering her nose and mouth with her hand and Jason knocked on the door. Mary opened the door and Catherine felt she was at some kind of enactment as Mary bobbed a curtsey and smiled. 'Can I help you, Sir, Madam? Are you lost?'

Jason smiled back and said, 'Thank you, we're not lost but we have lost our grandson, Daniel. I understand he's living here.'

Mary's eyes opened wide. 'Oh my,' She stood back, waving them to come in saying, 'Please come in. Daniel's not here at the moment but I'm expecting him back soon.' Mary indicated the only chairs with arms and Catherine sat down gratefully. Jason continued to stand. 'Please, Sir, sit down and I will get you some refreshment.' She bustled into the kitchen and returned quickly with two pewter tankards of ale. Then went back and returned with cake. The ale was refreshing but Catherine had been hoping for a cup of tea. It occurred to her that tea might be a luxury in Victorian times and only the wealthy could afford it. She wished she'd done more research. 'Thank you, the cake's delicious and the drink really welcome. We've walked a long way.'

Mary took a breath as if to speak when there was a clatter of horse's hooves. 'That'll be him with Mr Hancock.'

They all stood and went to the door in time to see Daniel climb off the back of a horse onto the stone steps attached to the farmhouse wall. George waved at everyone and said, 'See you tomorrow, Daniel. Have the cart ready.'

'Yes sir,' shouted Daniel as George rode away and then he turned to look at Mary's visitors. He was about to bow when he realised who they were and ran into Catherine's arms. 'I can't believe you're here. Did Mum get my letter? Why didn't she come?' Tears were running down his face as he pulled away from Catherine and hugged Jason. In that moment of reunion, they all forgot Mary who was watching, her own eyes moist.

'We came the same way you did, and Xen told us there was no way back. Your Mum and Dad wanted to come but we said it should be us because we're old and retired.'

'I tried to come back. I borrowed the horse and cart and went to Brimham Rocks. I shouted two thousand and forty-eight, but nothing happened. That was when I left the letter.'

'Your Mum found it in a box in the attic. Someone who lived in the house before must have kept it and that's how we knew where to come.'

'He's a good letter writer, Mr …?'

Jason turned to Mary. 'I'm so sorry. We never introduced ourselves properly. I'm Jason Brownlow and this is my wife, Catherine.'

'Grandpa, Grandma, this is Mary Smith. She and Joe have been really kind, looking after me.' There was a moment of curtseying and bowing then Mary ushered them all inside.

When they were all seated, Daniel on a stool, she said, 'I know you have a lot to talk about but before that, have you a place to spend the night?'

Catherine shook her head, 'We came straight here. Finding Daniel was our priority.' At that moment Joe came in and introductions were made again.

'I was just asking Mr and Mrs Brownlow if they had anywhere to stay and they haven't so what do you think of The New Inn, Joe?'

'Yes, it's clean and the food's good. It's just ten minutes' walk, or Daniel could hitch Betsy to the cart.'

'That's a kind offer Mr Smith, but we can walk. Could you spare Daniel to show us the way?'

'Of course, of course. Mary'll keep yer dinner hot, Daniel.'

Joe and Mary watched the three of them walk away and then Mary said, 'I think we're going to lose Daniel, now he's found some family and I've really grown to love him. He seems like the son we always wanted.'

'I feel the same. He's been a great help, learns quickly and the money he's brought in's been a bonus. We'll just have to bide our time and see what happens. When he first came Daniel said he had relations in Harrogate. Perhaps he was referring to his grandparents. Anyway, I'm parched and starved so let's eat.'

*

When they had walked to the edge of the village, Catherine stopped. 'Just a minute, I've got to give you this, Daniel.' She took the letter out of her bag and handed it to him. 'I didn't want to give it to you before in case it made you feel too homesick.'

Daniel opened it immediately and, as she had anticipated, tears began to run down his cheeks unheeded until he'd finished reading. Catherine gave him a hug and he cried noisily for what seemed like a long time. Finally, he pulled away, wiped his face with his sleeve and sniffed several times. 'I miss tissues.' He tried to smile and then took a deep breath. 'Dad says we may be able to return if we find the sand timer and you would explain what he means. Is there really a chance I could go home?'

'Yes, but it's not any sand timer. It's a specific one that was made for a ship called the *Daphne* and stands about this big.' Jason held one hand above the other to show the size. 'We'll tell you all about it, but not now. Your dinner was ready and will be spoiling and we really need to get a room and something to eat ourselves. I can see The New Inn from here, so why don't you go back now, and we'll see you tomorrow.'

'I have to work tomorrow, and I don't know what time I'll be back. Will you stay here and let me come to you? It'll be easier to talk without Mary.'

This was agreed and they separated.

At the inn they were shown a room and told it would cost two shillings and sixpence for a week. They agreed and asked if they could also have an evening meal. Once alone, Catherine sank wearily onto the bed and removed her boots and bonnet. Jason hung up his overcoat and looked around. 'I'm not sure where we go to the toilet, but this seems to be our means of washing.' He poured cold water from a large jug into a bowl, found his simple washing kit and freshened up. 'There's enough water left for you, but I don't know where to throw mine out.'

Catherine giggled. 'Out of the window? Don't worry I'll use your water for now.' She rose wearily and washed her face and hands.

'Daniel's changed hasn't he in those few months. He seems taller, grown up, yet vulnerable and young. If we manage to get him home, I've no idea if he'll be able to fit into the regime of school.'

'Don't think about that at the moment. Let's just get used to life here in Victorian times. I'm really hungry so I hope dinner will be something stodgy like steak and kidney pie or Yorkshire pud with thick sausages. I'm ready; let's go and find out.'

One hour later they were both bursting with food and feeling much more optimistic.

*

Daniel arrived at the farmhouse feeling in an emotional turmoil but that did not hinder his appetite. Mary and Joe had finished eating and Joe was sitting, staring into the fire, while Mary was peering at some needlework in the poor candlelight.

When he had finished eating Daniel cleared away his plate and washed up. He was waiting for Joe to joke about women's work, but he was unusually quiet. When he sat down with them, Joe turned and said, 'I don't feel very well, really tired and my throat's rasping. I'm going to bed.'

67

'I'll bring you some honey in hot water, my dear. It's not like you to be taken ill.' She put her sewing down and said to Daniel, 'You've had quite a day meeting Major Carstairs and then coming home and finding your grandparents.'

'Yes, I met Mrs Carstairs too and she seemed very odd. She kept talking about my hair colour saying hers was the same and did I have relatives in India.'

'She's grieving, you know. Her little boy, nowt but a babe really, fell into the lake just a few months ago and drowned. That's really hard. I feel sad for her. Anyways did your grandparents get settled in?'

'I think so. They made me come back here once they could see the inn sign. I think Grandma was very tired.'

'Talking about tired, I'd better get that honey and hot water and then I think I'll be off to bed too.' Daniel stood up when she did and said goodnight.

Chapter 15

2048

The detective stood wearily, 'I'm really sorry, Mr and Mrs Mansfield, but your son will remain on the missing list and his case will be reopened from time to time. There is really nothing more we can do at the moment.'

Andy stood up to see him to the door. 'Thank you for all the efforts you have made, Inspector.' When he returned to the living room he smiled at Izzy. 'I feel almost guilty, now we know where he is, but I don't think such a stolid man as that would believe us if we'd said, 'Oh he's gone back to Victorian times, Inspector.'

'No, it does take some believing.' She sighed, 'I wonder if Mum and Dad have found Daniel yet.'

'I suppose it all depends if he's still living at Blackberry Farm. We'll just have to wait and hope.'

*

1859

The following morning Joe felt too ill to do more than get himself dressed. Mary fussed over him giving him honey in milk to sooth his throat and help him keep his strength up because he refused any breakfast.

'Now I've banked the fire up. You stay here and I'll see to the milking. The poor things will be bursting by now.' She pulled a heavy cloak on and put on some over-shoes. 'I won't be long, and Daniel should be down soon if you need anything.'

Joe nodded and closed his eyes. When Daniel arrived for his breakfast, he was surprised to find Mary out and Joe asleep. He quietly skirted into the kitchen and cut himself a wedge of bread and poured some milk. He was feeling nervous and excited. He was anxious about meeting the two farmers and helping them with their accounts but could hardly wait for all that to be done so he could see Grandma and Granddad again. He put his dirty

69

dishes by the sink and dressed warmly then went to hitch Betsy to the cart.

Outside it was so cold his breath wafted white as he hurried to the stable. He finished just in time as Mr Hancock reined in his horse and nodded to him. 'Good morning, Daniel. I'm glad to see you're ready because I've got a busy day today and hope to get this done before lunch.' He led his horse into the stable, still warm from Betsy's body, and then joined Daniel on the cart. Daniel drove out of the farm and followed Mr Hancock's directions until they reached the farm of Mr and Mrs Elliot.

They were given a friendly but guarded welcome and offered refreshments which George Hancock refused. Daniel opened the new ledger and work began. When they'd finished Mr Elliot said, with a touch of pride, 'Well now, before you gentlemen came, I counted what we had and there it is now, written down, the exact amount.'

'That's good,' said George Hancock. 'Now you can work out what you can afford to spend on planting for the spring and what you can spend on essentials. We must be going now but Mr Mansfield will come back in one month and update your books, so please keep any receipts and lay them in the ledger then you don't have to try and remember everything.'

When they were back on the cart Daniel said, 'He was amazing. He knew exactly what he'd spent this year down to the last halfpenny.'

'Well, that's what happens if you can't read or write, you have to have a good memory. You'll find Mr Carter a great contrast. Turn left here.'

George was right. Mr and Mrs Carter made them really welcome and insisted on mulled ale, now the weather was cold and slices of cake before they began the work. Daniel could see Mr Hancock was restless to move on, so he hurried his cake and let the ale cool as he stood and placed the ledger on the table and got out his pen and ink. Mr Carter went to him and stood beside him.

'Please sit down, Mr Carter. Can you tell me what you spent on seeds this year?'

Mr Carter shrugged and scratched his head. 'Dunno. Mabel, she'll remember.' Mrs Carter went to the dresser and picked up a wooden box that rattled with coins.

'When we buy summat, and are given a bit of paper I keeps it in 'ere, along wi' the cash.' She opened the box and gave Daniel all the receipts. He sorted them into date order and then began to record them in the ledger. When he had finished, he asked her if she knew what money they had got for the things they sold. This took longer and there was a lot of time spent thinking and discussing but eventually he had sufficient written down to calculate what she should have in her box. It was quite close, there was five shillings extra in the box. When he said that Mabel smiled. 'I completely forgot the sewing, Mr Mansfield. I'm really good at making clothes and altering. That five shillings is, let me see, five alterations, and three shirts.'

Everybody was smiling then and George Hancock stood, saying Daniel would be back in one month and they should keep any receipts and he would enter them in the book. They went out into the sunshine and the air was less chill as they returned to Blackberry Farm.

'So, Daniel, will you be happy to go and see both tenants in a month, without me?'

'Yes sir, as long as they are just as helpful without you being there.'

'Don't worry about that. They'll be too scared to be rude to you, knowing you'd report back to me.' He mounted his horse and waved goodbye as Daniel set about unhitching Betsy and rewarding her with an apple as he led her back to the stable.'

He went into the farmhouse and was shocked to see Joe still sitting in the chair by the fire. He was not asleep, but his eyes were bloodshot, and he said nothing, just watched Daniel walk in and go to the kitchen where Mary was preparing lunch.

'What's the matter with Joe? I've never seen him like this before.'

'I don't know but I'm worried it's the pox. He says he can't eat with his sore throat, so I keep giving him drinks. I made some soup for us and it's ready now if you'd like to sit down.'

Daniel sat down and ate the thick soup and several chunks of bread and butter. When he had finished, he took a drink of ale and said, 'I want to go and see my grandparents this afternoon, but I will do any tasks you want me to do before I go.'

'Thank you. I'd really like you to churn the butter for me. I've had to milk the cows and set on the cheese. I'd like to see if I could get Joe to go to his bed.'

'I've seen you make butter lots of times, Mary, so I know how to do it.'

'The cream is in the can next to the churn.' She stood up and went to wash the dishes.

'I'll do that. You see to Joe.' She nodded and went into the living room. He used water from the kettle to wash up, and then went straight into the dairy and began the laborious job of turning the churn. While he was doing it, he thought about his previous life where butter came in packets from the supermarket, milk and cream in recyclable cartons. He fervently hoped Joe had not got smallpox. He had not really heard of it before, but George's description made it sound very frightening and dangerous.

'How's it going?'

Mary's voice made him jump. He smiled and said, 'I think it's nearly there.' They both listened and heard the steady slosh of liquid change to sloshing and thumping as the butter turned into lumps.

'That's grand, Daniel. You go off to see your family now and I'll finish it.'

He wasted no time and was soon walking briskly along the lane, swinging his arms and humming a pop tune. Granddad was going to explain how they could return to their own time and he felt excited.

Jason and Catherine were sitting outside in the sunshine, drinking tankards of ale. They both waved when they saw Daniel coming and he broke into a run, a broad smile on his face. He sat with them and Jason asked him if he wanted to have a soft drink although he had no idea what was on offer in the pub. Daniel said, 'I really don't need anything at the moment, but I do like ale and drink it at mealtimes, otherwise Mary gives me milk or water.'

'So, you drink alcohol; what would your mum say?'

'She'd be shocked, but I think everyone here thinks I'm about sixteen because I'm so tall, so I get treated like a young man. I'm doing a man's job, now. I'm not just writing letters for those that can't write, I'm also helping two farmers do their accounts. I'm really good at adding up pounds, shillings and pence, now.'

'You're certainly coping well with this life, Daniel. We're really proud of you.' Catherine pulled him into a hug, and he had difficulty in holding back the tears.

'I struggled a lot at first with feeling homesick and although I wanted to help Joe, I was pretty useless because I didn't know how to do anything on the farm. It's good that I'm more capable now because Joe's ill. Mary's worried it's smallpox. George asked if I'd been vaccinated as a younger child and I said yes.'

'That's worrying news, Daniel, because people in our time don't vaccinate against smallpox anymore because the disease no longer exists. I'm afraid you're not safe living there if he has it. I wish I had the internet. I'd like to find out the symptoms.'

'Well at the moment he's just complaining about a sore throat and can't eat anything, but he's got no energy and after lunch Mary persuaded him to go to bed.'

Catherine swept her hair back from her face that was frowning with worry. 'I can remember in 2020, before you were born, there was an outbreak of a virus called Covid-19. It swept all over the world frighteningly quickly and millions of people died. They didn't have spots. It was a disease that affected the lungs and there's still no cure. We are all now vaccinated against that but in some poorer countries it still breaks out occasionally. The only way to keep safe was to isolate yourself from other people.'

'Our doctor has already closed the markets, but we haven't had any other advice. What should I do if Joe gets spots?'

'I think you should come here and stay with us at The New Inn.'

'I can't leave Mary to cope with everything. It's been hard for her today having to bring in the cows to be milked. How could she nurse Joe as well as feeding the chickens, collecting the eggs, making bread, cheese, butter and all the other jobs. She needs me, Grandma.'

'No Daniel. She needs someone but it doesn't have to be you.'

'Well, who else is going to help her?'

'Doesn't she have any children?'

'There's Ruth but she has a job where she lives away from home. I could write her a letter, but Mary would have to agree, and I don't think she would want to put Ruth in danger, unless of course Ruth's been vaccinated.'

'When you go back, I think you should suggest that.'

Daniel nodded. 'I thought you were going to tell me today about a way we might return to 2048.'

'Yes,' said Jason. 'It's a complicated story.' He related how Daniel's mother touched a ship's sand timer that took her back in time to India during the mutiny. She met a lady called Jane Carstairs. Her husband had sent her to Calcutta to get a boat home to England because she was pregnant. Jane, her maid Emily and Izzy survived an ambush and eventually made their way to Lucknow where Jane's husband, Captain Carstairs was fighting.'

He paused to take a drink and Daniel, unable to contain himself any longer, said, 'I've met Major Carstairs, his wife, and Emily too. Mrs Carstairs made me feel very uncomfortable, sitting there dressed all in black. She kept staring at me and asked if I had relations in India. She's got the same colour hair as me and seemed to think we might be related. Granddad, I work for Major Carstairs.'

Jason looked at Catherine, his eyebrows raised. 'Well, that's amazing. We believe Jane, or her father, will know where the sand timer is. It may even have guided you into finding the portal at Brimham Rocks. Over the years we, your mum and Xen have all found our lives disrupted and confused by this sand timer.'

'Uncle Xen knows about all this too?'

'Yes. He was the one who showed us the portal you found by accident. When you get back you must ask him to tell you all about it.'

There was a brief silence while Daniel seemed deep in thought and then he said, 'Do you think I could have a drink of ale now?'

Jason laughed and got out his bag of coins. 'I don't think there are any licencing laws so you can get it yourself,' and he handed him sixpence.

While Daniel was inside Catherine said, 'I think we should call on Major Carstairs, but do you think we should send a letter first? I'm not sure of the etiquette.'

'I think a letter's a good idea. It will come as a surprise to them that we're here and we need to have a plan before we do anything. They're bound to ask us why we left Lucknow so quickly. From their point of view, we were rude not to come and say goodbye. We can hardly say the sand timer brought us back to our own time and we had no control over it.'

'No, we can't, but I've thought of something else. When they saw us, Izzy was not even married and now she has a son of 13 and the siege of Lucknow was only a couple of years ago. We've aged fourteen, no fifteen years.'

Jason breathed in quickly, 'Carstairs was badly wounded, and Jane was having a baby, so they probably can't remember exactly how old we looked then. Let's face it, in that field hospital everyone looked pretty grim.'

'You're probably right. I think having a grandson of nearly fourteen years is the hardest to explain.' Catherine smiled. 'I always wanted more children, so I think we'll have to invent another son or daughter, older than Izzy. Daniel can still be our grandson but not Izzy's. That's another thing. When we talk about her, we must call her Isabelle. It sounds more Victorian. I really hate lying and we still haven't got a good reason why we disappeared so quickly after the baby was born.'

Jason frowned, thinking. 'I suppose I could say I was sent back to fight because my wounds were healed but that doesn't explain your and Izzy's disappearance. They thought you were both nurses so could you have been moved to another field hospital?'

'My God,' said Catherine, holding her head in her hands. 'Listen to us making up a load of old flannel. We'll have to explain this to Daniel too, so he doesn't say the wrong thing.'

At that moment Daniel returned with his ale, so the subject was dropped. They watched him as he took a deep glug, wiped his mouth on his sleeve and looked at Catherine with a grin. 'I know what you're thinking but there are no tissues, and I don't have a handkerchief. Anyway, everyone does it, unless they're gentry. You look like gentry. Where did you get your clothes?'

'We hired them from a theatrical shop for a month so I really hope we can get back before that. We also had to buy old money at great expense, and we don't have that much. Another reason why we'd like to get you home soon, before it runs out.'

Daniel nodded. 'I'd like that too. It's getting dark so I think I should get back to Mary.' He stood up. 'I've no work of my own tomorrow so I'll come over in the morning, once my chores are done.' He hugged them both and then set off, running, back to the farm.

Chapter 16

'A masked ball, whatever next? We've only just got o'er the wedding.' Mrs Danby paced around the large kitchen table. 'I s'ppose people'll stay overnight, so it'll be breakfast for a dozen or more. Then they'll go shootin' and those'll want a picnic lunch, not forgetting a lunch for the ladies what don't like shootin'.'

'Don't worry, Mrs Danby. I'll help. I've learnt such a lot about cooking now, since the wedding, so I can take much more off your shoulders. I think it's exciting and young Mrs Hayward won't be able to socialise once the baby shows,' said Emily. 'At my last position I helped my mistress deliver her baby.'

'Hush,' said Mrs Danby. 'We don't talk about 'delivering babies' in this country. We say, brought to bed with child or even, when she was unwell.'

'I'm sorry. In India we are more ... erm forthright.'

'Humph, you're not in India now so let's get back to the problem in hand. How are we goin' to cope with all the extra work?'

'Could you ask if we can hire a temporary assistant, to help with the rough jobs like vegetable preparation. Someone who wouldn't mind helping Ann wash dishes.'

Mrs Danby sat down onto a chair that creaked a protest. 'Make us a cup of tea, Emily, while I think about that. It's a good idea, mind, but how do I explain to Mrs Hayward senior we can't manage, without it sounding like, well like we're not capable?'

Emily had no answer to that, so she made tea and sat down opposite Mrs Danby. She looked at the big clock on the wall and said, 'It'll soon be time for afternoon tea. Perhaps, if there are no visitors, you could ask then.' Mrs Danby nodded.

*

'Ring the bell for tea will you, Amrita,' asked Mrs Hayward. Amrita did as she was asked, her hips swaying gracefully in her sari, as she walked. She did not like her stiff mother-in-law but

77

tried hard to please her. The older woman had expected her to dress in English clothes, but she found them so cumbersome and thought the enormous skirts ridiculous. Perhaps when the weather grew colder, as Mark had said it would, she would have to comply. She had already resorted to a thick shawl indoors and often gravitated towards the fire in the evenings. She hoped Mark would be back in time for tea. As she thought that he strode into the drawing room and both women awoke from their reveries and smiled at him. They did have one thing in common; they both loved him.

'So how are my two favourite ladies? I've been riding around the estate organising the shoot after the ball. Have all the invitations gone out now?'

'Yes,' said his mother. 'We have not had all the replies, but I think there will be twelve staying overnight so you'll have at least six for your shoot, maybe more if some of the women wish to be included.' She gave a little sniff of disapproval.

Mark rubbed his hands together and sat next to Amrita. The tea tray was brought in by the butler. Mrs Danby followed him in with a tray of dainty sandwiches and cake.

'Mrs Danby?' said Mrs Hayward, 'You don't usually appear at teatime.'

'No Ma'am,' she bobbed a curtsey, 'No Ma'am, but I need to ask something about the masked ball.'

'But we've gone over all the menus so what's the problem?'

Mrs Danby straightened her back and said, 'I want to do you proud with the food, Ma'am, but we really will need some extra help in the kitchen. Someone who can do the unskilled work, while Emily and I do the actual cooking.'

'Hm. Is this any more complicated than the wedding?'

Now Mrs Danby went very red and was silent, screwing the bottom of her apron with her hands.

'Are you thinking of someone to come just temporarily,' asked Mark, 'say a few days before and leaving as the last guest goes?'

Mrs Danby nodded and then she looked up, curtsied and said, 'Yes Sir, thank you Sir.'

78

'We can run to that can't we, mother. We want a smooth efficient staff with no one collapsing under the weight of too much work.'

'Hm, I suppose we can but no more than five days in all and we'll pay her the same as the scullery maid.'

'I'll see to it, thank you Ma'am, Sir.' Mrs Danby escaped from the drawing room and let out an audible whoosh of breath. By the time she reached the kitchen her face was its normal colour and she walked in with a smile.

'I think your smile says we can have some help. Can we?' asked Emily.

'Yes, and I was thinking of Ann's sister. She must be sixteen and in the few days before the ball we can teach her how we like the veg prepared. If she's anything like Ann, she'll be a good solid worker.'

*

The butler bowed, handing a silver salver towards Cecil who took the letter offered. The butler withdrew then Cecil broke the seal and opened it. As he read, he was aware that Jane was watching him with curiosity. 'It seems Mr and Mrs Hayward would like us to attend a masked ball on Saturday November 5th. We can stay the night and the next day there will be a shoot. That's two invitations we've had from them so we really will have to invite them here. What do you think, dear?'

Jane frowned and he waited for her to explode with anger, remind him they were in mourning and storm out of the room. Instead, she said, 'I think I could go to the masked ball. With a mask on I wouldn't feel everyone was looking at me and pitying me, or even being critical because a year hasn't passed since … but I'm not sure about staying overnight. Would you mind terribly missing the shoot? You could even go back in the morning and join in. It's not that far.'

Clive walked over to her and kissed her cheek. 'That's wonderful. I can miss the shoot. I'm just so pleased you're happy to go to the ball. Will you reply, or shall I?'

Jane stood and took the invitation from him. 'I'll do it.'

Clive watched her move to the escritoire and suddenly desired her. She looked so beautiful, the black dress highlighting her auburn hair, piled on her head with little ringlets at the side of her face. He could see her profile, the sweet nose tipping up at the end and the full lips, smiling slightly as she wrote.

The atmosphere in the house and between them was improving, slowly. He made no move towards her; just grateful she was thawing. He didn't want to spoil the moment. 'Shall I ring for some tea?' She nodded and he moved to the bell and pulled it.

The tea arrived at the same time as George who was invited to join them. He told them about Daniel's reception at the tenants and Jane sat up straight, listening with interest.

'The young lad has such a pleasant way with him and in no time, they were bringing him receipts and cash for him to record. I have no concern about leaving him to go on his own next month.'

'That's good news, George,' said Cecil. 'Perhaps now they can see their way to paying me what they owe. Did you mention this to them?'

'No, Sir, not on that occasion, but I will visit in a week or so and give them an ultimatum. They cannot argue when all the figures are in front of them.'

'Hm. You should have demanded it there and then. You're giving them time to drink away the profits. Go back sooner, at the end of this week. Don't forget we still have a farm with no tenant so we need all the money we can get.'

George, always in control even when being reprimanded, said, 'Yes, I'll do that, and I'll make enquiries to see if there's anyone looking for a farm to run.' He picked up his teacup and drained the last drops. 'I think I'll make a start on that now.' He stood and Cecil rose too to ring the bell for the butler.

'Don't ring, I can see myself out.'

*

Daniel arrived at Blackberry Farm to find the cows protesting because they had not been milked and Mary asleep in the armchair. This was so unusual he stood, unsure what to do. He

80

had never milked a cow although he had helped with herding them into the milking shed and washing their udders. It looked like he might have to teach himself. He went back outside and brought the cows into the shed, washed them all and took a bucket to the first one, sat on the stool and squeezed a teat. Nothing happened. He tried again and again but no milk came out. He stood up, frustrated and went back to the house.

Mary stirred and opened her eyes. 'Oh, my goodness I fell asleep. The cows ...'

'I've got them into the shed and cleaned them, but I don't know how to milk them. You must show me so I can do it if you're ill.'

'I'm not ill, Daniel, just tired. I'll get my shawl and show you.' They went out together and after a few poor efforts Daniel's pail began to fill.

'Joe's got spots now. I'm sure it's the pox. I'm that worried I can't think. How will I manage without him? If anything happens Mr Hancock will evict me. He'll know I can't run the farm on me own.'

Daniel moved onto the last cow and sat down, then said, 'People do recover from smallpox, don't they?'

'Yes, often horribly scarred but knowin' he *might* get better doesn't stop me worryin'.'

'I'll do what I can to help, Mary. I can certainly do the milking tomorrow, although I see you've done two cows to my one.'

Mary managed a snort of laughter. 'You'll get quicker, lad with practice. Now let's get this milk into the dairy.'

When they were both back in the house Mary sighed and dragged herself into the kitchen. 'I'm not sure what to cook.' She banged her forehead with the heel of her hand, 'Just can't think.'

'Why don't we just have bread and cheese and finish with an apple. I'll go and get some from the store shed.'

Mary had no time to argue and was relieved to have no dinner to cook. She went slowly around the kitchen fetching the bread board, bread, butter and cheese then two plates. Daniel returned with the apples and told her to sit while he cut the bread. 'The slices might be bigger than you cut but I love it as thick as doorsteps.'

They ate the simple meal and Daniel told her about his grandparents having met Major and Mrs Carstairs in India. 'I think they're going to call on them soon. They didn't know they lived so close and were amazed when I said I worked for them.'

'That sounds good. From what I've heard of the uprising in India it was a cruel affair. Servants that were trusted, even loved, turned on their masters and killed all the family. Many a gruesome story was shared at the market when someone got hold of a newspaper. Major Carstairs was wounded and had a really bad limp for ages.' She stood up and began to clear the dishes.

'I'll do that, Mary.'

She nodded her thanks and looked directly at him. 'Did I hear you say you've been vaccinated against the pox?'

'I thought I had, but then my grandma told me I haven't.'

'Then it's not safe for you to stay here. You should go to the inn and stay with your gran'parents.'

'But I've learnt how to milk the cows. I want to stay and help you. What if you get it too?'

'I've been thinkin' about asking our Ruth to come home. She's been vaccinated and wouldn't be in any danger. Would you write a letter to her an' I'll sign it in the morning? I'm too tired now and I'm going up to bed.'

'Yes, of course, then I could take it to the post office.'

'No, I think you need to take the cart and go to Burton Hall. Then you can bring her back. We'll sort it out in the morning. Goodnight.'

Chapter 17

2048

'Can I stay here? I really don't want to meet Izzy and Andy tonight and listen to all their grief.'

'That's a very selfish attitude, Ruby. I can understand that being with them is hard but it's important we support our friends.'

'You can support them without me. You can say I'd already agreed to go out. They won't miss me. I tell you what, I'll babysit Ben so you can go without either of us. There'll be no children then to remind them of Daniel.'

'Look, Ruby,' said Xen. 'We can't physically drag you there, but I'm disappointed in you. I thought you were kinder than that. Still, if you're adamant, then we'll put Ben to bed before we go. I'll text them and let them know. If Ben doesn't go, then they might want to make the meal later.'

*

Izzy and Andy had invited the Baxter family to a meal. The weekends were always hard for them. The house was too quiet. Daniel's music was not playing. The game console had a blank screen. There were no outings to plan with his entertainment in mind. That was when they missed him the most. During the week they both went to work so it was a little easier. They wanted to see people to fill the silence, hence the invitation.

Izzy had prepared a warming casserole now the weather was colder, and Andy had created his speciality – a chocolate roulade. They were both in the kitchen, sipping red wine when Xen and Joanna arrived. There were greeting hugs and more wine was poured, then they all sat in the living room to relax and chat.

'How are Ruby and Ben? Did it take a lot of persuading to get them to stay at home so we could have adult time?' asked Izzy.

'No, it was really easy, just a little bribe,' said Joanna. They all smiled and she continued. 'Ruby has her exams coming up soon and having to stay in will give her time to do some revision.'

'Well, that's the plan but who knows what she'll actually be doing. It was easier when she was younger and was so lovely, helpful and obedient. We hardly know this Ruby,' said Xen.

'Just remember, when she annoys you, how lucky you are to have her. I think about Daniel all the time and miss him so much. I also miss Mum and Dad. Anyway, you both know that, so I think it's time we ate. Let's move into the dining room.'

They carried their glasses and Xen and Joanna hovered until Andy indicated their seats. He then busied himself topping up their glasses. 'I'll leave you for a moment and help Izzy bring everything in.' He went into the kitchen and Xen looked at Joanna with a sympathetic smile. They both understood why Ruby had refused to come because being with Andy and Izzy was not easy. They were as bereaved as if Daniel had died and there seemed to be nothing they could do or say, to make it better.

'I often think of Jason and Catherine; wondering how they're coping with blending in as Victorians,' said Xen.

Joanna grinned. 'Well rather them than me. I'm definitely not an actress. They'd see through me in no time.'

Andy came in carrying the steaming casserole followed by Izzy balancing a tureen of vegetables on top of four plates. The business of sharing a meal meant there was no need to make conversation and when it was time to clear the plates before the sweet course, Joanna stood and helped Izzy, leaving the men sitting.

'Izzy seems more positive now. Is she really coping better or putting on an act for us?' asked Xen.

Andy wagged his head from side to side before saying, 'A bit of both. Grief catches you out unawares. One minute you're feeling fine and the next you're suddenly crying and bereft. During the week, when we're both at work, things are almost normal. We share a taxi so we both arrive home at the same time, then together we enter the house, so silent and empty.'

Izzy came in at that moment, smiling and carrying the cake followed by Joanna holding a jug of cream. 'Andy's made his famous pud for the occasion, so we can be indulgent and to hell

84

with the calories.' Xen made positive noises, and everyone refrained from saying that Izzy could do with eating more calories.

When everyone had finished and refused second helpings, Izzy said, 'I've been thinking of taking up sailing again. Uncle Phil wants to sell his Enterprise. He's having to give up sailing because of gammy knees.'

Andy looked at her with eyebrows raised. 'You didn't tell me.'

She dismissed his protest with, 'I got a text today. He's given me the chance to buy it and if I don't want it, he'll advertise it at the club. I didn't tell you because I was thinking about it. I know you've no enthusiasm for sailing, but I used to love it when I was a teenager.'

'I think it's a brilliant idea. I can come to the club with you, make the tea and help out, as long as you don't ask me to go in a boat.'

Everyone laughed and then Xen said, 'I've never tried sailing as a sport. Perhaps Ruby would like to learn. She needs an outdoor interest, other than boys.'

'If you're serious that would be great because I'll need a crew. You need two people to sail an Enterprise and I'd be happy to teach her the basics or she could go on a course. The club used to run them, and I expect they still do.'

The whole atmosphere of the evening had lifted. Izzy's face was alight with enthusiasm and Andy persuaded her to ring Phil and agree to buy it. She did that and came back glowing. 'I'm to meet him tomorrow to take ownership and to join the club. I'll have to pay to keep the boat at the club and a joining fee.' She looked at Andy with eyebrows raised.

'That's fine. The money's not a problem. I'll come with you tomorrow.'

When Xen and Joanna left to go home, they agreed the evening had been much better than they had anticipated and were looking forward to suggesting the idea of sailing to Ruby.

*

1859

Daniel got up early, brought the cows in and began milking. He expected Mary to join him at any minute, but she didn't appear. He finished all the milking, placed the milk in churns in the dairy and went indoors. The fire in the range was nearly out so he put some wood on, filled the kettle and waited for it to boil. He felt very anxious. If Mary was still in bed, then she could not be well.

He took two cups of tea upstairs and gently opened the door to their bedroom. He wrinkled his nose at the putrid smell and walked to Mary's side.

'Mary, I brought you some tea.' There was no answer and he realised he had whispered so he said it again, much louder. They both stirred and Mary sat half up, peering at him.

'Daniel, thank you. I've had a bad night, but I'll be down shortly. Leave both drinks here. Don't go round to Joe. He's very poorly. Not sure he can take hot drinks now.'

Daniel looked across at Joe and saw his face was so swollen with spots he was almost unrecognisable. He left their bedroom with tears running down his face. He drank his own tea and cut some bread for them both. He then set about frying eggs. Mary came down dressed and looking exhausted. 'What about the milking?'

'I've done it. Sit down and eat this then I'll take your letter to Ruth.'

'Thank you, I'm not ill you know, just tired.'

They sat eating in silence until Daniel finished and stood up.

'Daniel, take all your things with you, clothes, writing box. You mustn't come back here until the pox has gone.'

His head drooped and he went upstairs to clear the bedroom of his things, tying the clothes into a bundle for want of a bag. When he came down, put on his coat and was ready, he said, 'I don't know what I would have done without you and Joe. Take care of yourself, Mary.' He opened the door to a damp, chill, autumn day and made his way to the stable.

The stable was warm. Betsy looked up as he entered, dipped her head towards him and he went to her putting his arms around

86

her neck, pressing his face against her head. 'Mary thinks Joe's dying.' His voice cracked as tears fell. 'I want to stay and help but fetching Ruth is all I can do.' He stroked the soft nose, sighed, and got her ready to pull the cart.

When she was hitched, he climbed up onto the cart and flicked the reins. Betsy moved away from the farm and he felt so sad tears were threatening again. Would he ever see Joe again? Would Mary catch the pox? He had not really understood that he had grown to love them so much. He flicked the reins again and said, 'Faster Betsy. We must hurry and fetch Ruth home.'

Daniel stopped the cart at the back of Burton Hall and an ostler came out and offered to give Betsy a drink. He nodded his thanks, handed him the reins and knocked on the door. As he waited, he rehearsed what he was going to say, hoping whoever opened the door would be pleasant. When the door did open there stood Emily.

'Daniel, what are you doing here?'

He was so surprised he dismissed his spiel and stammered, 'Emily, I didn't realise … erm.' After a deep breath he started again. 'I have an urgent letter for Ruth Smith from her mother.'

Emily smiled, stepped back and gestured to him to enter. 'Sit down and I'll go and find her.'

He sat at a huge wooden table looking around with interest. It felt like a film set or a museum. His reverie was broken by Mrs Danby.

'Well now, young sir. Are you being attended to?'

Daniel had stood when she came in, his chair scraping over the flag stones. 'Emily let me in and has gone to find, Ruth Smith to give her a letter from her mother.'

'I see. Well, sit down while you're waiting. Would you like a cup of tea?'

Daniel shook his head and said no thank you. He was anxious for Ruth to come and to get her back to the farm.

When Ruth did arrive, she was tearful. Daniel stood again, hoping she was ready to leave.

'Daniel, I'll have to ask permission to leave from Mrs Jarvis, our housekeeper and she may have to ask Mrs Hayward. If I get permission, I'll have to pack some things.'

'In that case,' said Mrs Danby, 'I'll put the kettle on. I'm sure a cup of tea and a piece of cake will go down well if you've got a while to wait.'

'Do you think there'll be a problem with Ruth leaving?' he asked, watching Emily baking something with flour flying out of the bowl.

Mrs Danby replied. 'It depends on the reason she wants to go. Emily, take more care, no need to waste all that flour.'

'Her father is dying of smallpox and her mother can't cope looking after him and the farm.'

'Oh, deary me. That's awful,' said Mrs Danby, turning to Daniel with a plate of fruit cake in her hand. 'Poor, poor Ruth. She loves it here you know, and that Mrs Hayward might sack her. She won't want her back in case she brings the pox with her.'

Daniel didn't know what to say so he concentrated on sipping his tea and trying to eat the delicious cake daintily.

'Then there's the masked ball coming up,' Mrs Danby continued. 'We'll need all the help we can get. Mrs Hayward won't want to let Ruth go, she's such a good, hard worker.'

'Her parents really need her. I hope Mrs Hayward allows her to have leave rather than sacking her.'

'A lot depends on her mood. There's not a lot of human kindness in that woman.' She sniffed. 'I know I'm not supposed to speak ill of my betters, but she's really not a nice woman.'

Ruth came in, red eyed, the letter screwed up in her hand and spoke to Mrs Danby. 'Has he told you?'

'Yes love, and I'm really sorry.' She moved towards her and hugged her. 'What happened when you asked?'

'She sacked me; told me to pack my things and go. Mr Hayward said he would write me a reference and send it to me. So, this is goodbye. Thank you for all you've done for me.'

Mrs Danby pushed her gently away. 'Now you must make haste. Have you got everything?'

Ruth lugged a heavy bag towards the door and Daniel took it off her. He opened the door and waited for her to go through, then they both said goodbye and he closed it behind them.

That had been too emotional for Daniel and he breathed in deeply, welcoming the chill air and oblivious to the smell of horse dung. Soggy leaves squashed under their feet as he heaved the bag onto the cart and helped Ruth get up on it. He sat beside her, flicked the reins and they moved forward, away from Burton Hall.

They travelled for a while without talking, Ruth crying quietly. Then she said, 'Have you seen my pa? Is he really that bad?'

Daniel kept his eyes on the road as he replied. 'I'm really sorry Ruth. His face is covered in pox and Mary thinks he doesn't have long.'

'But my ma's well, isn't she?'

'Yes, but she's been trying to do everything so she's exhausted. She didn't wake up this morning until after I'd milked the cows and taken her a cup of tea.'

'You've been milking? Thank you, Daniel.'

There seemed nothing more to say and they drove in silence, each with their own thoughts, until it began to rain.

'I didn't expect this,' said Ruth lifting the hood of her cloak over her head then pulling the folds over her knees.

'It's colder too,' said Daniel. He had no hat, so the rain poured over his head and ran down his neck. With both hands holding the reins there was nothing he could do to prevent it. He sat there getting soaked until they entered the village, and he drew up at The New Inn.

'Mary told me not to come back but to let you drive the cart home. My grandparents are staying here so I'm staying with them.' He handed her the reins and climbed off the cart. While Ruth slid across to the driving position, he collected his soggy bundle of clothes and his box of writing materials from the back. Ruth set off and he ran into the inn.

It was lunch time. There were meaty smells filling the warm air as Daniel made his way towards the blazing fire, nodding to several people he recognised. He stood close to the flames enjoying the warmth and watching his clothes steaming. When he began to feel hot, he turned to dry his back and saw Jason and Catherine coming down the stairs. They saw him waving and Catherine rushed to give him a hug. 'No, don't hug me grandma, I'm really soggy.'

'Well come up to our room and change.'

He looked down at his bundle. 'Not sure I've anything dry to change into. This morning I collected Mary and Joe's daughter, Ruth, to look after them both. I think Mary was worried I would catch the pox and said I was not to come back to the farm. So, I've nowhere to stay. Do you think I could sleep on the floor in your room?'

Chapter 18

Ruth jumped off the cart and ran into the farmhouse. 'Mama, Mama?'

'Ruth! Thank God. Stay there I'm coming down.' Ruth watched her descending slowly as if she had suddenly grown heavier, but she looked thin, wasted. Ruth moved to give her a kiss and Mary put up her hands. 'No, pet, no hugs. I've been seeing to your father and may have the pox on me.'

'I'm safe, immune, so don't worry. You look like you could do with a hug.' Mary's hands dropped and Ruth cuddled her, scared to hold her too tight in case she broke. They both cried and stayed holding each other for several minutes. Then Ruth said, 'It's good to cry and let out all that misery but better still is a cup of tea. You sit down and I'll make it.' Mary sat, too tired to argue, and when Ruth brought the tea, her head was on her hands and she was fast asleep.

Ruth went quietly around the kitchen, looking to see what there was to eat and the cupboard was empty. She began to bake some bread and hoped the cold store still had some butter and cheese. While the bread was proving she went outside and unhitched Betsy, taking her into the stable and giving her some food and water. The stable needed mucking out but she needed to be dressed differently to do such a dirty job. Before returning to the house, she looked in the dairy and saw there was still plenty of cheese, but butter needed to be made. Finally, she visited the chicken house, filled a bowl with eggs and tossed some grain around for them.

Mary woke when Ruth went back in and drank the tepid tea. 'I'm so glad you're here. Daniel was doing well but I needed you. Were they kind when you asked to leave?'

Ruth grimaced, 'Not really. Mrs Hayward gave me the sack.'

'No! That's so mean and cruel.'

'She needs a housemaid more than usual because she's going to have a big, masked ball for what seems like all the gentry in the county. So, you've got me for a while until I can find another position.'

'Did she give you a reference?'

'No, but Mr Hayward said he would send me one in the post.'

'That's something I suppose. Is that bread proving? I must have been asleep longer than I thought.' She stood up, levering herself on the table. 'I'll just go up and see Joe. Perhaps you'd put the loaves in the oven.'

Ruth nodded and stood too. 'Shall I come up and say hello to Pa?'

'No! Sorry love, I said that a bit sharp. I want you to remember him as he was, not the horror he's become.' Mary went out of the kitchen and Ruth wanted to cry again but fought back the tears. She knew that work was the only way to combat the tears and kneaded the dough viciously as if punishing it for her father's illness.

By the time her mother returned the bread was baking in the oven and Ruth was in the dairy churning butter. Mary went out to talk to her. It was cold and she had not thought to put on a cloak or shawl. She shivered and then offered to take a turn if Ruth would fetch her thickest shawl.

Ruth ran indoors but the shawl was not downstairs. It had to be in the bedroom. She went up, trying to be quiet so as not to wake her father. She pushed open the door to the bedroom and the stench of faeces was overpowering. Her instinct was to grab the shawl and run back to the dairy, but she covered her nose with her hand and went to the bed. She could not believe the disfigured wreck in the bed was her father. She looked down at him and saw his eyes were open a slit. 'Papa, Papa?' She looked at his chest. It was not moving. There was no sound of beathing. She shivered with shock as she realised he was dead.

Ruth ran down the stairs and out into the dairy. 'Mama, Papa's dead.' Mary nodded and kept turning the churn.

'Did you know?'

'Yes. I came out here to tell you, then I couldn't.'

'So, you let me fetch the shawl and find out for myself.'

Mary nodded and hung her head. 'I'm sorry.' Ruth moved closer and held her tightly, feeling her bony frame shake with the tears she had held back for so long. Ruth managed not to cry. She needed to be her mama's rock and was resolved to do everything in her power to help her.

When they let each other go, Mary said, 'I'm going up to clean him and lay him out. Will you finish this?'

'Of course I will, but then we'll have to tell Mr Hancock. I'll do that and then he'll make the arrangements. I'm not sure what happens with a death from smallpox. We might not be able to have a proper funeral. It might be a massed grave.'

'It doesn't matter. It's not my Joe anymore; just his wrecked body.'

They both went about their tasks and Ruth even managed to remember to take the loaves out of the oven before they burnt. The bread smelled delicious, and she realised they had missed lunch. Despite the emotional turmoil, she felt hungry. When Mary came down, carrying armfuls of bedding, there was food ready for her.

'I'll just take this outside. It will have to be burnt along with the mattress, later.' When she returned, she washed her hands and sat down, her face grey with exhaustion.

'I don't expect you feel like eating, but it will help to give you some energy.' Mary nodded and drank some tea. Ruth was pleased when she then took a slice of warm bread and buttered it.

That night mother and daughter shared a bed and the warmth of their bodies comforted them in their grief.

*

The following morning Mary insisted she could milk the cows on her own and begged Ruth to go and see Mr Hancock. 'We need him to organise the collecting of Joe's body and he needs to know we're now alone, managing the farm. I'm frightened he'll evict us because we've got no man to run things.'

'Mr Hancock is a fair man. If we are evicted it will be his master that makes him, that Major Carstairs. But let's not anticipate disaster. Just take one step at a time.'

Mary nodded and together they hitched Betsy to the cart. Ruth set off, pushing Betsy to go faster but then let the old mare slow and go at her own pace. It really didn't matter if the journey took twenty minutes or half an hour.

She arrived at George's cottage, climbed down from the cart and rang the bell. A maid opened the door with a feather duster in her hand. She looked at Ruth with eyebrows raised.

'I'm looking for Mr Hancock. Is he in?'

'Yes, but he's just getting ready to go out. If you would like to come in, I'll go and tell him. Who shall I say is here?'

'Ruth, Ruth Smith from Blackberry Farm.' The maid stepped back and led Ruth into a pleasant parlour. There was a fire lit and Ruth walked to it and stood warming herself. She turned from contemplating the flickering flames when George came in. She bobbed a curtsey and waited for him to speak.

'Good morning Ruth. What can I do for you?'

'I'm afraid it's bad news, Sir. My pa passed away this morning of the pox. My ma needs some men to collect him, and we don't know what to do about a funeral.'

'Oh, dear that is bad news indeed. Please sit down, Ruth. Would you like some refreshment, tea?'

'No, thank you, Sir. I need to get back to the farm soon to help my ma.'

'I was about to do my rounds of the estate, visiting all the farms but before I do, I'll go to the undertakers. There are many people now, dying of the pox so I'm afraid it may well be a massed grave with a shroud rather than a coffin. I will find out and come and visit you and Mary towards the end of the afternoon. Have you still got Daniel with you?'

'My ma asked him to stay with his grandparents at The New Inn. She was afeared he'd catch it too.'

'I didn't know he had relatives here. I was just thinking Daniel could be a man about the farm for you. We can think about that later. Meanwhile, you must get home and I must go about my business.'

They both stood and George helped her climb back onto the cart. As she drove off, he stood for a moment, watching her, before collecting his coat and hat and going to the stable. While he saddled his horse, he kept thinking about her. Ruth was a lovely young woman and he was attracted to her.

*

94

Ruth arrived home to find her ma tending a fire, burning the contaminated bed linen. It reminded her of November 5th celebrations. Autumn had turned to winter and a chill wind was blowing, fanning the flames. Everywhere in the yard was covered in soft wet leaves. The bright fire contrasted with the grey sky and the grim expression on Ma's face.

Ruth unhitched Betsy and gave her some water and feed. Then she went up to Ma. 'Shall I make some tea? It's too cold to linger out here. Please come in.'

Ma nodded and threw the stick she had been using to poke the fabric into the flames. Once inside, Ruth told her what George Hancock had said and that he would be visiting later that day.

'In that case I'm glad I cleaned the house while you were gone. What can we give him for refreshment?'

'I'll make a fruit loaf, but I suspect he may not even come in, just in case the pox lingers in the house.'

'Yes, I hadn't thought of that. Did he say anything about our being asked to leave?'

'No but he seemed to be hinting if Daniel came back to live here then he could be considered a man and we may be able to stay. He might say more on the subject when he visits. I think he's a kind man and wouldn't evict us while Pa's not even buried.'

The two women worked for the rest of the afternoon until it was too dark to work outside. Then they went indoors and put on the kettle and buttered the fruit loaf, ready for Mr Hancock's visit.

He arrived at five o'clock and, as Ruth had suspected, refused to come in.

'I've arranged for Mr Smith's body to be collected and I'm afraid he will be interred with others, in a massed grave. But his name will be added to the headstone that will be erected once the pit is full. I regret it cannot be a more personal affair with a church service, but it's too dangerous to have people congregating. Are you both well?'

'Yes Sir, thank you Sir,' said Ruth. 'My ma is very tired, but she's not ill. We wanted to offer you some refreshment but understand that you may feel the pox is still in the house. My mother has burnt all the bedding and cleaned everywhere. We can do no more.'

'I will call on you next week and if you're still well, I would be glad to come in and take some refreshment. But now I must go.' He bowed and they curtseyed. They watched as he mounted his horse and only closed the door when he was out of sight.

'He's a good man,' said Mary. 'He didn't mention eviction as many others would have done.'

'Let's not worry about that now. I'll make some tea and we can eat the buttered cake. I'm really hungry.'

Chapter 19

George ducked his head as he entered the inn. He was exceptionally tall, slender but did not stoop as many tall people did. He had an upright, military bearing. His hair was brown, eyes blue with crinkles around them showing he laughed more than he frowned. He could stand upright inside the inn and stood for a moment, absently rubbing his hand over his beard. His eyes adjusted to the gloom and he looked for Daniel. He could not see him but there were several men he knew who called out greetings or nodded. George went to the bar.

'How are things, Sam?' he asked.

'I allus likes this time o' the day, when the meat's roasting and folk are comin' in for a bite and a drink. What can I get you, Mr Hancock?'

'I will have some ale and supper later, but now I'm looking for Daniel Mansfield and his grandparents.'

'Ah, they're in their room, number six if you'd like to go up, Sir.' George nodded his thanks and went upstairs. He knocked at number six and the door was opened quickly by Daniel.

'Oh, Mr Hancock. Please, come in, although there's little space. May I introduce my grandparents, Mr Jason Brownlow and Mrs Catherine Brownlow.' They had both stood and Catherine curtseyed while Jason bowed.

'This is Mr Hancock who employed me to be a scribe,' Daniel said, looking at his grandparents. Then he turned to George. 'Would you like to sit, Sir?' and pointed to the only chair in the room. George did so and everyone else perched on the edge of beds looking at him.

'I'm afraid I'm the bearer of very sad news. Joe Smith has died of the pox.' Daniel looked away, trying to hide his tears. 'There will not be a funeral because there are many bodies needing burial so I'm afraid it will be a massed grave.'

'How are his wife and daughter?' asked Catherine.

'Well, that's what I came to talk to Daniel about. Major Carstairs has already lost one tenant to the pox and if the Smith's cottage has no man, I'll have to evict them.'

He heard a sharp intake of breath from Daniel who wiped away his tears angrily. 'That's awful. Mary has been managing to keep everything going as well as nursing Joe. She could run that farm as good as any man, especially with her daughter to help.'

'You're letting your emotions get the better of you, young man. You know full well that women are not able to be tenants. My proposal is that you go back to live with them and then you can be the man, the tenant. The Smith ladies can stay but the farm would be in your name. What do you say?'

There was silence for a moment as Daniel thought about the offer. 'Thank you, Sir, for the offer but I must tell you I don't intend to stay here indefinitely. I would be happy to do it for a while, especially if that will help Mary and Ruth.'

'Excellent. You've solved my problem. Now I can go back to Major Carstairs and let him know.' He stood, so everyone else did the same. He had turned to leave the room when Jason spoke. 'Before you go, Mr Hancock, I wonder if you would give this letter to Major Carstairs. We would like to visit him and his wife. We met them both in Lucknow and would like to renew our acquaintance.' He held the letter out and George took it.

'I'm sure they'll be pleased to see you, Mr Brownlow, Mrs Brownlow.' He bowed and left the room. When he got downstairs the inn seemed full. He went to the bar.

'It looks like I've left it late to get a table, Sam. I'll just have a mug of ale and then be on my way.'

'Per'aps one'll become vacant ere you go, Sir.' George nodded, downing half the tankard in one glug and then turned his back on Sam, surveying the room. He was not only thirsty but hungry too. The smell of roasting meat and the sight of everyone eating was making him salivate. Just as he emptied his tankard a couple of men stood to go. George turned back to Sam. 'It looks like my luck's in, Sam. Another of these and the roast beef please.'

'Coming up right away, Mr Hancock.'

He sat down and thought about the Smith family. Ruth was such a comely lass. If she were to wed a farmer, they could still keep the farm even if Daniel left.

His thoughts turned to Daniel. He had come from nowhere, claiming he had become separated from his family. Now his grandparents had found him. So why was he still here? The answer was probably something to do with this letter. Should he take it this evening or would tomorrow do? The arrival of a steaming dinner with a chunk of bread on the side interrupted his musing. He picked up the bread, dunked it in the gravy and ate it with enjoyment. It was truly delicious.

When his meal was finished, he sat back and surveyed the room. Everyone was conversing, many with animation, hands waving. He caught the gist from one particularly loud man. They were talking about the lack of work for spinners and weavers. The machines in the big mills were producing so fast and so much cheaper than an individual could do at home.

'It's that Castle Mill in Knaresborough, producing linen for the Queen! How can anyone compete wi' that?'

He sympathised with them but no amount of wrecking of machines could stop progress.

George sighed and stood up, reluctant to leave the warmth but his horse had been standing a long time and needed to return to the stable. He paid the inn keeper and went out into the clear cold night. The beauty of the moon and myriad of stars was ignored. He felt weary and decided the letter could wait until the morning. The ride back to his own cottage was short and soon his horse was stabled and he could get to bed.

*

'I understand you wanting to go back to the farm, Daniel, but I really think it's too soon to go tomorrow,' said Catherine. 'These viruses can stay virulent on fabrics and other materials for quite a few days. Then, of course, Mrs Smith or Ruth may contract it. That will also take a few days to be sure. Stay with us until the beginning of next week. What you should do is write to them. Say how sorry you are about Mr Smith and explain the plan to help them keep the farm. They must be worrying as well as grieving.'

'I'll do that now and take it to the post office tomorrow morning.'

'While you're doing that I'll go and order us some dinner. The smells are wafting up and they don't serve all night.' Jason left the room and when he got to the bar the room was quieter than George had seen it. George had gone and so had most of the other people.

'Am I too late to order food, Sam?'

'No, Mr Brownlow there's some meat left on the bone. For three, is it?'

'Yes, please. We'll be down in five minutes.' He went back upstairs, and Daniel was just sealing his letter.

'Daniel's very good at his job. I read the letter he wrote to Mrs Smith and it had just the right tone.' Catherine turned to Daniel. 'Perhaps you'll be an author when you leave school.'

'I can't believe I'll have to go back to school, like a kid. Everyone here treats me like a young man. I'm even trusted to be a tenant farmer.'

'Don't let that go to your head. Come on both of you, our dinner's ready.' Jason led the way down to the bar area, and, like George, they made the most of the succulent meat.

When they were replete Jason grimaced and said, 'We do have a problem that I've been reluctant to share but now I have to. We've very little money left. It doesn't look as if we'll be going back to our own time for a while. Have you any ideas?'

'I still have some,' said Daniel. He took a little drawstring purse out of his pocket.

'Don't open it here, in public. Wait until we get upstairs. I have enough to pay for the meal, so I'll do that and see you back in the room.'

When Daniel tipped out his cash on the bed, he found he had four shillings and sixpence halfpenny. 'Granddad, you can have this but I'm not earning while the market's shut so there won't be any more.'

'Thank you, Daniel. I hope that will see us through our time here.'

*

The following morning, while Daniel was taking his letter to the post office, George gave Jason's letter to Major Carstairs.

'So, have you added postman to your duties now?' He undid the seal and read. 'Do you know who this is from, George?'

'Yes, Mr and Mrs Brownlow, Daniel Mansfield's grandparents. I met them yesterday evening at The New Inn where they're currently staying.'

'It's intriguing. They say they met us in Lucknow, but I have no recollection of the name. He also calls himself mister, no rank so what was he doing there?'

'I don't know, but I'll be happy to take them a reply if you or Mrs Carstairs would like to pen one.'

'I'll take it to Jane and then you can update me on the estate.' He left the room, leaving George alone in the study. The bookcase was laden, and he perused the titles. He had a volume in his hand when Cecil returned. He placed it back on the shelf and they sat and discussed Blackberry Farm and what to do with the other empty farm.

'So, you think young Daniel Mansfield can run a farm? Unlikely I'd have thought. He is but what thirteen, fourteen years? You're getting soft, George. I think the daughter Ruth has caught your eye. Perhaps you should wed her yourself. Then she'd have a proper man to take over the lease.' He was grinning as he said this, but George's face turned red. 'Ah, I think I've touched a nerve. Admit it; you're fond of the lass.'

'There is another possibility, said George, stiffly. 'Daniel's grandfather is fit, and he might be persuaded to take the lease temporarily.'

Cecil laughed. 'I see you've evaded the question but that is an idea. I will put it to him when they visit.' A maid entered to announce that coffee was being served in the drawing room so, business concluded, they joined Jane. When they were sat, drinking their coffee, the biscuits having been handed round, Cecil spoke to Jane.

'What do you think of the letter from the Brownlows? Do you remember them?'

'I certainly do and so should you. Mr Brownlow saved your life and Mrs Brownlow, who I remember as Catherine, helped me during my, erm … confinement. I would like to reply and invite them tomorrow afternoon, for tea if you agree.'

101

'I agree, of course, but I don't think I was properly introduced to my saviour and he and his wife and daughter seemed to disappear when we were both well enough to thank them. Now we can do just that.'

'You know, Cecil, when that Daniel Mansfield came, I felt he was familiar. Now I know why. His mother had the same auburn … No, it can't have been his mother because Daniel's too old. Now I feel confused.'

'It's possible that the Brownlows have more children than the daughter we met a couple of years ago. That would explain it, but you can ask her tomorrow.'

Jane fumbled to find her handkerchief and both men realised she was weeping. 'It's going to be a difficult meeting. They're bound to ask after Nathaniel. I don't know if I can bear it. Perhaps the invitation should not be issued.'

Cecil moved to sit next to her and took her hand. She allowed this and he was grateful. 'I think we must invite them my dearest. If they ask about him, I will be the one to explain. Perhaps it's not a great help but it's the best I can offer.'

*

During breakfast the following day, Sam told Daniel that there were several people who had asked if he could write letters for them. 'So, I took the liberty of suggestin' they came 'ere this mornin'. I hope that would be convenient for you.'

'That's kind of you, Sam, and I'm happy to work here.'

'Well, I've no doubt but they'll need some ale, or a bite to eat, while you're writin'. So, we'll both benefit.'

When Sam had gone back into the kitchen, Jason said, 'I feel embarrassed but really pleased you're going to earn some money today, Daniel. It should be me working but I really don't have any skills to offer.'

'You could do what I do but the local people have got used to me, and anyway, I don't want any competition.' This made them laugh and at that moment George arrived with a reply to their letter. They all stood up, Daniel and Jason bowed, and Catherine curtsied.

'Please, there's no need to move from your breakfast. I just wanted to give you this and then I must be on my way.'

Jason opened the letter and then read it aloud. 'Do I need to reply by letter, or would it be acceptable to give you our reply verbally?'

'I'm going to Lime Bank Hall this morning, Sir, so you may trust me with a message.'

Jason nodded. 'Please would you convey to Major Carstairs that my wife and I will be delighted to accept their kind invitation to take tea.'

'I will do that, Mr Brownlow, and now I must take my leave and let you finish your breakfast.' They watched him duck through the door and then sat back at the table.

'This is not going to be an easy meeting,' said Jason. 'The Major might ask about my rank and why I call myself mister. Then there's the difficulty explaining how we disappeared without saying goodbye. We'll have to invent another child because Daniel's too old to be Izzy's son. Do you want a son or another daughter?'

Before Catherine could reply Daniel spoke. 'You know, Granddad, you've always insisted on telling the truth and here you are listing a load of lies. Why don't you tell them the truth?'

There was silence as his grandparents stared at Daniel and then looked at each other.

'He has a point,' said Catherine. 'They might find it difficult to believe but it would enable us to explain our need to find the sand timer.' She paused and looked towards the door. 'I think the man that's just come in will be wanting Daniel. Let's go back to our room.' They all stood up and Daniel smiled at the stranger who hurried up to him. He explained, as his grandparents went upstairs, that he needed to collect his writing box and asked the man to sit at a clean table.

Sam left his place behind the bar, greeted the man, and as he cleared the breakfast things, offered him some refreshment. Daniel ran up the stairs reaching the bedroom door just as his grandparents did. They let him enter first and barely got inside themselves when he was out again, clutching his box. He ran along the short corridor to the stairs and then slowed and walked steadily down. His client was drinking a mug of ale and another man came in and nodded to Daniel. It seemed he was going to earn some much-needed cash this morning.

*

George went from The New Inn to Blackberry Farm. He wanted to tell them what Major Carstairs had said. He also wanted to see Ruth again. Her gentle smile, general demeanour and her love for her family were pleasing. She was no longer a child, but a young woman and he was deeply attracted to her.

George was a man of principle, unlike his master, and would not consider a dalliance even had she been willing. He realised his life was empty and a wife would offer him companionship as well as sexual gratification. There was just one problem: her lowly status. She would bring no dowry to a marriage and he, if he married her, would be considered to have married beneath him. How much would that matter to him? He was often invited to events at Lime Bank Hall but never to social events at other large houses.

George dressed and behaved as a gentleman. He had no fortune of his own, had to be employed so was not considered a gentleman in the local society. People respected him but he was not eligible to marry their daughters.

All these musings led him to the realisation that he would offend very few people if he took a wife who was socially beneath him. Cecil had joked about it, but would his job be in danger if he was to embark on courting Ruth? He decided to risk it and arrived at Blackberry Farm with a smile on his face. He knocked on the door and stood back a little, changing his broad smile to a sympathetic lesser one as the door opened. His heart flipped when he saw Ruth, neat and tidy with just a few of her lovely rich brown curls escaping from her cap.

'Mr Hancock, how kind of you to come. We were not expecting you for several more days. Please come in and I will fetch Ma from the dairy.' He ducked through the door and sat in the one comfortable chair Ruth indicated. She then went out to call her mother from the dairy. Mary came in and greeted him, offering to make some tea which he accepted. She put the kettle on to boil and noticed his eyes straying expectantly to the door.

'Ruth will be in presently, Sir, she is just finishing the churning for me.'

George nodded. 'May I ask if the undertakers have been?'

'Yes, Sir, and they said there will be a service held outside for close relatives on Wednesday morning at eleven. I would like to go but I'm not sure if it would be safe.'

'If you could bear to stay at home you would be guaranteed to be safe. I know you have cleaned this house and burnt all bedding, and clothing but not everyone will be so vigilant.'

Before Mary could reply Ruth entered, her face pink with cold. George thought she looked beautiful. He stood up and motioned to his seat. 'You look as though you could do with warming yourself by the fire. Please take my seat, Ruth.'

She smiled and looked fully at him, then lowered her eyes, curtsied and said, 'No, thank you, Mr Hancock. I see Ma has made tea and that will warm me just as well as the fire. I made a seed cake this morning. Would you like a piece?'

George would have said yes even if he abhorred seed cake. A small, low table was carried close to where George was sat and Ruth pulled up two wooden chairs as Mary carried a tray with teapot, milk jug, cups, saucers and little plates for the cake. She sat down to begin the ceremony of pouring the tea and Ruth collected the cake, already cut into slices.

'Thank you,' said George. He bit into a piece and said, 'The cake's delicious.'

There was silence as he ate, the women anxious to hear what he had to say.

'Now I need to ask if you received my letter about Daniel taking on the lease of the farm?' He saw them both nod and then told them of Major Carstairs' reservations. 'I'm sorry but there are some other ideas. Daniel's grandfather might be persuaded to take on the lease and work here temporarily. Daniel led me to understand that now he's reunited with his family he may not stay in the area for much longer.'

'So eventually we'll still have to leave,' said Mary. 'This is frightening, Mr Hancock, because without the farm we have no home or means of earning our living. It would be the ... the workhouse. Ruth lost her job, you know, to come home and help me. She's young and may get another position but no one would employ me.'

George turned to Ruth. 'I can see Mrs Smith is upset and I fully understand. Would you be kind and allow me to talk to her alone?' Ruth stood and stepped carefully away from the table. George had stood too but sat back down when she had taken herself and her sewing basket upstairs.

Although George would normally consider himself a brave man, he was daunted by the step he was about to take. He wished he had a whisky instead of a teacup. Mary was quiet, picked up the tea pot and looked questioningly at him.

'Yes please,' he said and handed her his cup. The silence was broken only by a thank you once the full cup was received. George took a deep breath and said, 'The other alternative is that I should court and wed Ruth. Once we're married, you would be welcome to live at my cottage, which is bigger than this one, having three bedrooms.' He looked anxiously at her watching her face redden and tears glisten in her eyes.

'You've flabbergasted me. I don't know what to say. Surely, Sir, you'd be marrying beneath you.'

'This is not something that has only just occurred to me, Mrs Smith. I have found myself attracted to Ruth for some time and know I love her. I needed to ask what you thought of the idea, and, naturally, if Ruth didn't want me to court her the matter will be dropped. I'll take my leave now and ask if I may call again, soon, and hope you'll have an answer to my proposal.'

He watched her nod, then he stood, bowed slightly and as Mary stood, he turned, collected his hat and cloak and left. She curtsied to his back and then slumped into the chair he'd just vacated. 'Ruth,' she called, 'Come down. There's something we need to discuss.'

106

Chapter 20

After lunch, having completed his letters for the day with a purse now jingling with coins, Daniel offered to show his grandparents a short-cut across the fields to Lime Bank Hall. 'You can save at least a mile this way so it will only take about half an hour to get there.'

'That would be lovely, thank you. I'm not sure how comfortable my best boots are so the shorter the better. I'm going to our room to get changed so give me ten minutes then come up. I really haven't mastered buttons all down the back, so I'll need some help.' She saw Daniel's eyebrows raise and laughed. 'I was talking to your Granddad about the buttons. I'm sure you can eke out that rather large mug of ale you've got there.'

Daniel grinned and raised his tankard in salute. This was something else he would have to relinquish if he managed to get home. His mother would be horrified to see how much ale he could drink without getting tipsy. He remembered his first night in the hay loft, taking a huge swig thinking it was water, and how he'd felt the effect of alcohol immediately. He realised he had stopped longing for electronic games and even his need for his parents had faded now his grandparents were here.

When they descended the stairs, Daniel stood and bowed. As they approached, he said, 'You both look fantastic, real gentry.'

'So, you think we'll meet with Mrs Carstairs' approval? Now all we have to do is play the part as well as we can,' said Catherine.

'You might not be the only people taking tea. Sometimes there are several others so be prepared.'

'Don't worry about us,' said Jason. 'We'll be careful and we'll wait before we do anything, like starting to eat before the hostess, or whatever the protocol is. Now lead on and show us the way.'

The short-cut, shown to Daniel by George, brought them to a side gate near the house so there was no need to walk or ride the length of the drive. Daniel left them at the gate and decided to go and see Mary and Ruth. He was going to give them some of his morning's wage, as he had done when he was living there. He hoped he could give them a hand with any jobs they needed doing too.

A butler took Jason's hat and coat, then Catherine's coat. She was not sure if she had to remove her hat, but the butler did not make any move to relieve her of it, so she assumed it was etiquette to keep it on.

They were shown into a most beautiful room with soft, upholstered armchairs, and a welcoming log fire with a huge white marble surround. The walls were hung with portraits and landscapes. The large window was sumptuously draped with curtains touching the floor and there were rich mahogany cabinets and occasional tables. There was even a piano with candlesticks to light the music.

Catherine did not take her surroundings in immediately because she was welcomed by Jane, who seemed thinner than she remembered, and Major Carstairs whose features she could scarcely recall.

They were ushered to seats and, contrary to Daniel's expectations, there were no other visitors. For a moment there was silence, Catherine and Jason having no idea how to proceed, but Cecil, still standing, spoke. 'We were surprised, but delighted, to receive your letter. I would like to thank you both, formally, for your services to us in Lucknow. It seems so long ago, but if you had not tackled that murderer my wife would be a widow now. So,' he said, bowing low, 'please accept our deepest thanks.'

Jason stood up and bowed back. 'We accept, of course, and are pleased to see how well you both look and to see your lovely home. A world away from that awful hospital and all the misery it held.' He sat down after that little speech and stole a, how-am-I-doing? glance at Catherine. She smiled back and gave a tiny nod. He relaxed back in his chair and tried to slow his breathing.

No more was said for a few minutes while Jane proceeded with making the tea. When it was ready, she served it herself to them and then offered tiny sandwiches. When Jason took one that seemed to contain ham, she said, 'Please Mr Brownlow, take one of each flavour to save me offering more. We really are informal at teatime.'

Jason obliged her and Catherine did the same, but she noticed her hostess only took one. Now she wondered if she would be considered greedy. During the eating and drinking there was general talk about the weather, the smallpox outbreak and Jane asked if they were comfortable in their lodgings.

'The innkeeper is pleasant, and the accommodation is … adequate. It is a little crowded in our room because we have our grandson staying with us. He had to move from Blackberry Farm when Mr Smith contracted smallpox,' said Catherine.

'We have many unoccupied rooms here. I wonder if you would consider staying with us. It seems the least we could do, for saving my husband's life.'

Cecil was amazed at these words coming from his, recently unsociable, wife but smiled and added, 'You would be very welcome indeed, and our staff would see to your every comfort.'

'Thank you, that's very kind.' Catherine looked at Jason, saw him nod and smile so she added,' We accept your gracious offer.'

'That's settled then. When you go back to the inn, pack your things and I will have them collected. You must not spend another night in merely *adequate* lodgings.'

'If Daniel wishes to be with you, we can give him a room of his own, unless he is going to return to the farm,' said Jane.

'He was busy writing letters for people this morning and may even want to stay at the inn so he can keep earning. We'll acquaint him of your generous offer and let him decide,' said Jason.

For a few moments there was silence as teacups were refreshed and sweet cake and biscuits offered. Jane sat back, sipping her tea and then said, 'You know the first time I saw Daniel, he reminded me of someone. I now think he looks very like your daughter Isabelle. I spent a long time in her company and the likeness was striking. Daniel cannot be her child, so do you have other children?'

Catherine slowly placed her cup back onto the little table and took a deep breath. 'We only had one child, Isabelle, who, since you met her, has spent three years at university and then married a lovely man called Andy. A year later Daniel was born, and he is thirteen years old, nearly fourteen.' She noticed the incredulous faces looking at her and pressed on. 'When Isabelle met you on the road in India she was confused because she had touched a ship's sand timer that transported her back in time. The sand timer sent her to help you.'

'I've never heard anything so, so preposterous. A magic sand timer that can transport you to different times. No, I cannot accept that.' Cecil stood after that outburst and looked at Jason, hoping another man would agree with him.

Jason stood up too and said, 'Please Major Carstairs, listen and try to understand, difficult as this story is. The sand timer was especially made to help women in your wife's and my wife's family. They are related. I believe it was originally used on a merchant ship your father-in-law owned called, the *Daphne*.'

Jane gasped. She stood up and went to her husband. 'Cecil, that's the ship I was supposed to go home on to be safe from the fighting. Instead, I found you, in the hospital at Lucknow.' She turned to look at Catherine and her eyes swivelled to Jason. 'You all disappeared before we could properly thank you for all your help. Where did you go?'

'The sand timer's task was complete, so it transported us back to our own time,' said Jason. 'We normally live in the year 2048.'

Cecil's arm was around his wife who was leaning heavily against him. 'Has the sand timer brought you here to help my wife then?'

'No,' said Jason, shaking his head. 'Not directly but we believe it is somehow involved. Please would you both sit down so we can tell you how we came to be here and what we believe we have to do.' He paused until they had obediently sat and then he continued to explain how Daniel had found the portal to the past at Brimham Rocks.

He had just finished when the butler entered to announce some more visitors, Major Mark Hayward and his wife, Amrita, from Burton Hall.

'I'm so sorry to be late, Cecil, Jane, but one of the horses cast a shoe so I had to drive back and change horses. I do hope we haven't completely missed tea. I'm dying for a cup,' said Mark.

Jane rang for some fresh tea and a further supply of food as Cecil introduced everyone to each other. Amrita was shown to a chair next to Catherine who smiled a welcome.

'Cecil hasn't mentioned you before, Mr Brownlow. Do you live locally?'

'Yes, we live in Harrogate, but Cecil and Jane have kindly offered us to stay for a few days with them.'

'That's excellent. You'll be around for our masked ball on Saturday. Do join us. There's a shoot on Sunday morning. Can you shoot? Would you like to stay overnight? Cecil and Jane have decided to return home after the ball but Cecil's coming back for the shoot.'

Jason found this enthusiasm overwhelming and was unsure which question to answer first. He looked towards Catherine for help, but she was engrossed, talking very quietly with Amrita. Cecil came to his rescue, grinning. 'Slow down, Mark. Mr Brownlow is not used to your battery of questions.' He turned to Jason. 'If you would like to go to the ball then you may come in our carriage and we will bring you home. Then, if you like the idea, you may return on horseback in the morning, with me, to join the shoot.'

'We have never been to a masked ball,' said Jason. 'Are the masks elaborate affairs because we have very little time to organise them?'

'No, no they can be simply attached to a stick to hold in front of one's face. Some people will, I'm sure, produce more elaborate ones but you do not have to. Please say you'll come.'

Both men were looking at him and Jason nodded. 'Thank you, we'll be happy to accept your invitation.' Jason stood up and said, 'Thank you for the tea and delightful company but my wife and I must leave now. We will see you later,' he said to Cecil and Jane. Catherine stood and everyone else did too. Jane rang for the butler and soon they had their coats on and were walking back to the inn.

'That was quite an ordeal. I'm not really looking forward to staying with them. Everything is so formal. I'm scared of making a faux pas all the time.'

'Me too,' said Jason 'but it would solve our financial problem. Oh,' he grimaced, 'you haven't heard the worst of it yet.'

'What do you mean?'

'Major Hayward has invited us to a masked ball on Saturday and I said yes.' Catherine stopped walking and looked at him with horror. 'I can't go to a ball, with or without a mask. I've nothing to wear. This is my best outfit, and I can't wear it to a ball when I've just worn it for afternoon tea. What were you thinking?'

'I suppose I wasn't thinking really but they were very persuasive. I have also been invited to go back the next morning to join a shoot. Perhaps Jane can lend you an outfit. She will understand, knowing you come from the future.'

Catherine started to walk again. 'They seemed to take that information remarkably calmly. I think they would have said a lot more had we not been interrupted by Mark and Amrita.'

'I saw you chatting to her. She looks a very exotic Indian beauty. How's her English?'

'She speaks it very well. We were chatting about her pregnancy. She told me she was worried about having the baby because it seemed no polite person discusses such things. Isn't that awful. I felt she was lonely and needed a friend. Apparently, Mark's mother lives with them and Amrita finds her very stiff and disapproving. She can't confide in her and misses her own family very much.'

*

Daniel sat alone in the room at the inn. He had been writing a diary when he had first begun writing letters for people. It was all on separate pieces of paper, but he hoped to bind them together at some point to make a book. He had written about all his experiences since arriving in 1859 and now dipped his pen in the ink and began to add to it.

> *I've just had dinner, roast pork, one of my favourites, and have to say this has been a day of surprises. This morning I wrote letters to people and after lunch showed*

112

*Granddad and Grandma the way to Lime Bank Hall,
then went to see Mary and Ruth.*

*I hadn't seen them since I collected Ruth to come
home. Since then, Joe's died and I was nervous in case
they were crying, and not sure how to comfort them. I
planned to offer to do any jobs that might need doing but
when I got there, they treated me like a visitor. I was not
sure if I liked it. They served me tea and cake and then
told me that George had asked if he could court Ruth!*

*This was a great surprise to me, and it seemed they
were still reeling. Ruth said she'd agreed to accept him
because he was a good, kind man. I asked when the
wedding was to be and Ruth shrugged, laughed and said,
'I haven't even told him the answer is yes, yet.' After they
were married, they would move into George's house and
there was space for Mary too. So, the whole problem of
tenancy of the farm will have gone away!*

*As if that wasn't enough, I went back to the inn to find
Grandma packing and Granddad explaining to Sam that
they were leaving. He put me on the spot by asking me if
I wanted to go with them to stay at Lime Bank Hall or to
stay at the inn. I didn't know what to say, but Sam said
I'd be welcome to stay at the inn and keep using the bar
as a workplace. He even said if my trade increased, he
would waive my rent!! I said I'd stay.*

Now I'm feeling lonely.

The next morning Daniel went down to breakfast and was
greeted by a cheerful Sam. 'I've got news for you', he said as he
wiped a dripping tankard. 'There've been no new cases of the
pox so the market's opening this week. Now you have to decide
if you want your stall back or would prefer to write here in the
warmth and cheer of my inn.'

Daniel laughed. 'I expect you know my answer after our chat
last night, but I'm pleased the market's opening. It'll give
everyone a chance to sell their wares and make some money
again.'

Sam smiled and nodded then turned to serve a customer.

Chapter 21

Daniel was not the only person feeling lonely. Mark was out somewhere in the estate grounds, organising the shoot and his mother had gone for a drive. Amrita felt restless and useless. Her mother-in-law was in charge of the house. Amrita was expected to be pleasant to visitors and amuse herself with sewing. She enjoyed sewing and her baby was going to be well dressed but today she felt wretched. The need for activity and company drove her to the kitchen. She would ask how the preparations for the ball were going.

Amrita had never visited the kitchen before but had been introduced to the staff when she first arrived. She had also seen Mrs Danby when her mother-in-law had called her for a discussion about meals. Sometimes Amrita dreamt of Mrs Hayward's demise and being in control of all the household staff. In the dream she was firm but pleasant and the atmosphere in the house was much lighter than it was now.

Emily opened the kitchen door when she knocked, curtsied and said, 'Mrs Hayward. How can we help?'

Mrs Danby, and everyone else in the kitchen, stopped what they were doing and curtsied. Amrita nodded and managed a smile although she was feeling awkward. 'I have come to see how the preparations are coming along for the ball and to see how our latest recruit is settling in.' She was looking at a very young girl, no more than thirteen whose hands and forearms were red from the hot water. Strands of her black hair had escaped from her cap and were stuck with sweat to her forehead. Her face coloured to the same hue as her arms, knowing Mrs Hayward was addressing her. She curtsied again and whispered, 'I really like working here, Ma-am, thank you.'

'That's good to hear.' Turning to Mrs Danby, she asked, 'Will you be able to cope now?'

'Yes Ma-am, thank you, Ma-am. We're still waiting on a delivery of two turkeys but everything else has arrived. Emily,' and she indicated the Indian girl who had admitted her, 'has been working on those puddings that can be made in advance. She's a dab 'and at decorating 'em. I'm sure we can impress your guests.'

'Well, thank you. I feel our catering is in good hands and I'll look forward to seeing your creations, Emily. Tell me; were you born in India?'

'Yes Ma-am,' she said as she curtsied again.

Amrita then spoke a few words of her own language, wondering if the girl spoke the same one. Emily replied in the same dialect and smiled broadly. They spoke for a few more minutes and then Amrita turned to everyone.

'I apologise for excluding you all by speaking with Emily in our own language. I simply asked her if she missed her family and friends she left behind in India. I'll leave you now to continue your work.' She turned and left the room smiling to herself, knowing she would be a source of conversation for the next few minutes.

Amrita went back to her room and her maid helped her dress for the extreme cold of an English winter. When she was ready, she set off down the drive and then turned away to use a small path that took her by a stream and through woods. It was her favourite walk, in leafy summer, but now the trees were naked and her breath streamed from her mouth in a white cloud. She walked quickly and found herself warming with the exercise. She thought about Emily and wished she was her maid. It would be so relaxing to chat to her instead of the formal, deferent girl she had now.

She had also enjoyed talking to Catherine Brownlow and she was determined to ask her mother-in-law if the Brownlows could be invited to tea one afternoon after the ball. Perhaps she could find out more details about giving birth. That, however, would be difficult during tea with everyone sitting close together. She would prefer to talk to her alone. Perhaps they could take a walk together, after the tea. No, it would be dark then. It would have to be a morning walk. They would be meeting again at the ball on Saturday so she could ask her then.

*

When Jason and Catherine had arrived at Lime Bank Hall the previous evening, they had been greeted by the butler. He showed them to their room and said, 'Dinner will be served at eight and Major Carstairs has asked if you would join him for drinks at half past seven in the drawing room.' He then turned to Catherine and said, 'Mrs Carstairs' maid will attend to your needs at seven. Please make yourselves comfortable until then.' He bowed and left them. They stood looking around and smiling at each other.

There was a high, four-poster bed and a wealth of heavy, dark oak furniture. The curtains, closed against the dark, were rich brocade draping from the ceiling to the floor. A log fire crackling in the grate made it seem cosy.

'I've never slept in a four-poster bed,' said Catherine She went to it and found it was so high she struggled to get on it. Then she sank back against the pillows and sighed with pleasure. 'If I have to get up in the night, I'll not climb back in without waking you.'

'Ah, madam, you must use this,' and Jason knelt down and pulled a step from under the bed. 'Mind you I'm not sure how madam will have a pee because there's no chamber pot.' He stood up and looked around, then saw a door by the window. He opened it and said, 'Wow you're going to love this. It's a proper bathroom. There's a flush toilet, with a chain to pull, a bath and a wash basin.'

Catherine slid off the bed, ignoring the step and went to see for herself. She put the plug in the bath and turned on the hot tap. It ran cold but warmed up to very hot. 'My God, this is going to be heavenly.' The bath took a long time to fill but eventually she was soaking in the delicious warmth.

'Are you going to be wallowing in there all evening?'

'No, I'm nearly done. Are you going to use my water?'

'Ready already,' he said, entering the bathroom naked and cocking his leg over the side of the bath. He had a wolfish grin that made Catherine scramble to get out.

'Don't even think about it; my maid will be here soon.'

She wrapped a towel around her and knelt down in front of the fire in the bedroom, trying to dry her hair. As she did so she imagined herself back at home drying her hair with a dryer that was plumbed into the system. She could see the bedroom, the wardrobe holding all her trousers and tops, and she felt homesick. The big clock ticking on the mantlepiece told her it was nearly seven, so she left the fire reluctantly and put on some clean underwear. She dropped her used things in a heap on the floor and added Jason's to it, hoping the maid operated a laundry service.

There was a tap at the door. The maid entered and curtsied as she said, 'My mistress has asked me to assist you madam.' She moved to the bed where Catherine had thrown the dress she had been wearing. 'Is this the gown you wish to wear?'

'Yes, thank you.' Catherine moved towards her and was helped into her dress and all the tiny buttons at the back were soon fastened. It usually took Jason ages and she smiled thinking of the dexterity of youth.

'If madam would sit at the dressing table, I will arrange your hair. As it is damp, the pins I put in will give it some curl tomorrow.' Catherine obeyed and was delighted with the sophisticated style she managed to create.

'What's your name?'

'Sarah, madam.'

'Well, Sarah, that style is lovely, thank you.' Just at that moment Jason walked in, completely naked.

'Woah', he said, when he saw Sarah and rushed back into the bathroom. Catherine laughed and was pleased to see Sarah laughing too, behind her hand.

'Thank you, Sarah. I can manage now, and my husband needs to get dressed in time for drinks before dinner.' Sarah left and Catherine shouted, 'You can come out now and you'd better hurry. It's nearly seven thirty.'

When they arrived downstairs, they heard the clink of glasses and quiet voices coming from the drawing room. They entered and saw Jane sitting on a settle close to the fire and Cecil handing her what looked like a sherry. 'Good evening,' he said. 'I hope you've found your room comfortable. Please sit and I'll serve the drinks.' Jane patted the place next to her, looking at Catherine who obliged and Jason chose a seat opposite them but left the one by the fire for Cecil.

When Catherine was offered a drink, she said she would have whatever Jane was drinking. 'Right-oh, one Madeira coming up.' Catherine took it with a thank-you and turned to Jane. 'I have a problem and I do hope you can help me.'

'I will if I can.'

'I have only this dress and a day dress. Nothing to wear to dinner in the evenings and nothing to wear to the masked ball.'

Jane smiled. 'That's really easy to remedy. Cecil has always been very generous to me and I have many gowns for evening wear and special balls. I think we are a similar size so I can lend you what you need. We have twenty minutes before dinner. Bring your drink and we'll go up to my room.' They stood, making the men stand too. Jane explained their mission and the men were left alone.

'I think I should tell you, Jason, that earlier this year our son, Nathaniel, drowned in the lake. It has had a devastating effect on us, and Jane has only just been able to be sociable to anyone. I didn't want to tell you in front of her because she would probably have wept.'

'I'm deeply sorry for your loss and that you had to tell me. We knew something had happened to him before we came here. Catherine has been building her family tree for many years. It is not done on a piece of paper but on an amazing invention called a computer. After Nathaniel was born, she looked at the family tree and saw his name. Before we came back in time, she saw he had passed away.'

'Dinner is served,' announced the butler and Jane and Catherine joined them in the dining room. As the first course was being put in front of them, Catherine said, 'Jane has been wonderfully generous lending me gowns for all occasions. I feel so much happier now I have something to wear for the masked ball.'

'That's excellent, my dear, but it reminds me that I don't have an evening dress suit.' Jason looked hopefully towards Cecil.

'Hmm, I'll see what I can find but you are taller than me and a little broader. If not, my tailor may have something.'

'There's no time for something to be made, surely, and I must be honest and say I cannot afford to buy a suit.'

Cecil frowned his disapproval of penury being mentioned in front of the ladies. 'We will discuss this later when we have left the ladies.'

Jason was not sure what he had done wrong, but the atmosphere was now strained, and he was grateful to Jane who skilfully changed the subject.

'We must spend an hour or two decorating our masks tomorrow. We can do yours too if you gentlemen think it beneath you to glue and stitch.'

'It is most definitely lady's work,' said Cecil, 'and anyway we will be going to visit my tailor and if there's time, we could have a practice shoot to prepare us for Sunday. Does that suit you, Jason?'

'Definitely, I shall look forward to it.' The atmosphere seemed to have cleared, the food was delicious and at the end of the meal Cecil stood and announced they would have their drinks in the study and the ladies could return to the drawing room.

Once in the study Cecil explained to Jason that it was considered rude to talk about money, especially when women were present. 'I know you have travelled from a more modern era where such things are probably permissible.'

Jason nodded and accepted the brandy he had been offered. 'When we were having afternoon tea, we mentioned a sand timer from a ship called the *Daphne*.' He looked towards Cecil to see if he remembered.

'Yes, and then we were interrupted by the Haywards arrival. Is there more to tell?'

'A great deal, Cecil. The timer seems to have special powers to protect the women in Jane and Catherine's family. When you turn it over and watch the sand fall it seems to prime it to take you, usually when you are asleep, to a situation where a family member is in danger. We believe that Daniel's arrival in your time was engineered by the timer so he can stop Nathaniel drowning.'

Clive took a sharp intake of breath and stood up, pacing with agitation. 'So, in order to change what happened we must find the timer?'

'Yes.'

'We mustn't tell Jane this. It'll raise her hopes and if it doesn't work, she'll be deeply upset all over again.'

'Is it possible to find the timer without her?'

'I think so. We can begin tomorrow by quietly asking her father. He's coming to the ball.'

'Do you think he'll believe my time travel story?'

Cecil snorted with laughter. 'No. We must find a way to ask about the timer on the *Daphne* without giving the real reason. Leave that to me to think about. Now we must return to the ladies.'

Chapter 22

2048

Izzy had done everything she could to compensate for the loss of Daniel and her parents. She had gone back to work, a buyer in a seed and grain distribution company, and every weekend she spent at the sailing club, whatever the weather.

Ruby had been initially bribed to join her but after seeing all the young lads there, she had not needed to be bribed again. Not only did she enjoy the attention, but she also enjoyed learning to sail. Izzy told her she was a natural, seeming to understand where the wind was coming from and the angle the sails needed to be to catch it, without tuition.

'It just makes logical sense,' said Ruby. Izzy grimly remembered how she herself had struggled to understand the difference between a broad reach and a reach when she was learning.

Sailing was a physical exercise and Izzy knew she was fitter and healthier than she had been for years. She now ate with appetite and Andy was delighted with the change in her. He dutifully went to the sailing club with her and soon became invaluable at serving tea and cake in the club house. At first, he was invited to sail when people needed a crew or just thought he would enjoy it, but he refused each time. He failed to see the pleasure in getting cold and often wet every weekend and didn't mind saying so.

But, underneath the veneer of 'getting on' with her life, Izzy was busy researching and planning. The fate of the *Daphne* was uppermost in her mind. She was desperately trying to discover what happened to the ship and all its contents. If it sank, then the timer sank with it. She knew Xen had discovered the timer by a wreck when he had been diving but the wreck was not the *Daphne*. She also knew her dad had bought the timer at an auction at a manor house. She would have liked to able to ask him where that was then reasoned he would be investigating that himself.

121

As well as trying to find out where the timer might be, she was also working towards using the portal at Brimham Rocks herself. She loved Andy very much and really appreciated all he had done, and was still doing, to support her but ...

Hidden in an old cloth bag under the bed in Daniel's room was a Victorian outfit. She had bought old coins and they were in the bag too.

Her feelings of guilt led her to try extra hard to please Andy. She cooked his favourite dishes, baked cakes she knew he loved until one day he called a halt.

'You're working too hard, Izzy. You never rest. You don't have to do home-cooked meals every night when you've worked all day. Let's have a takeaway, a microwave meal or go out to a pub. Please let up on yourself.'

'I thought you liked what I cook.'

'I do. You know I do. I'm just saying you don't have to give me treats all the time.'

'Thank you, that's thoughtful. You've given up every weekend to support my sailing and I felt I had to try my best to please you.'

Andy laughed. 'I'll tell you what we'll do. I'll go to the sailing club every Sunday, when it's race day but not Saturdays, if you will stop all this excessive effort on food.'

'I do love you,' said Izzy going over to hug and kiss him. 'That's a deal.'

*

Andy, unwittingly, had opened an opportunity for Izzy to time travel on a Saturday. She would leave home as if she were going sailing but go to Brimham Rocks instead. It was a cruel thing to do, she knew. She would leave him a note under his pillow. He would be distraught when she failed to come back but, eventually, he would go to bed and find it.

Before that day came, she had to source another outfit and a Victorian night dress if possible. Sometimes she wondered what she hoped to achieve by going back to 1859. Was she just, selfishly, wanting to hug her son and parents again? She knew the answer was yes but also hoped she could do something to help them come back.

She decided to look at the census for 1851 to see if there was a maker of sand timers in the Harrogate area. She had to pay a small fee but couldn't find the occupation listed. She wondered if there was something else it could have been called. She had been reading quickly so she started again and found an Hourglass maker. It was a start and now she felt more optimistic.

But what was she thinking of? Mum and Dad were quite capable of asking about the sand timer. She should stay at home, go to work, go sailing on the weekends and forget about going back to the past. That was the sensible and logical thing to do. Something, though, was driving her to do it.

*

It was November and chilly but global warming meant it was bearable. Traditionally there was less sailing in the winter, so one day Izzy went shopping in Leeds. There were retro shops there where you could buy old clothes. She managed to buy a Victorian nightdress, long sleeves, buttoned to the neck, very frilly, and a smart skirt, blouse and jacket.

She also bought some modern clothes so she could show Andy what she had bought. After lunch she wandered around small, curiosity shops mainly looking in windows. Suddenly she stopped, her heart jolted with shock. There was a large sand timer in a window.

She pushed open the door and the smell of dust and aged furniture filled her nostrils. The doorbell clanged, disturbing an elderly shop assistant. His thick grey hair flicked back as he looked up and she saw a pair of shrewd blue eyes looking at her. He'd been sitting down but stood up slowly, wincing slightly. 'Are you wanting to browse? If so carry on but I'm willing to help if you're looking for something in particular.' He waved one hand airily and Izzy smiled.

'I would really like to look at the ship's sand timer you have in the window.'

'Ah,' he said and went to the window. He took a duster from his pocket and used it to pick up the object. He wrapped the duster partially around it and held it out to her. 'It takes a lot of cleaning so please touch it using the duster.'

With a shock she realised he knew the timer had power and was protecting them both. She took it from him carefully and upended it to see the inscription on the bottom. It was from the *Daphne*. This was all too much for her and she asked if she could sit down for a moment, she was feeling faint. He rushed towards her, rescued the timer and sat her down on a chaise longue then fetched a glass of water.

'If you lie down for a moment, it will allow the blood to flow back to your head.' Izzy did as she was told, and he placed a cushion under her feet.

'Thank you. I'm so sorry. I'm really not the fainting type.'

'No need to apologise. You are the most interesting thing that has happened in my shop all week.' He looked at her face. 'Some colour is returning to your cheeks. Do you feel any better?'

'Yes, I think I could drink some water now.' She sat up, carefully and took the glass from him. It was cold and very welcome. 'Now, where were we? I think I was about to ask how much the timer was.'

'Right, well I'm going to ask if you're sure you want it?'

'Oh yes, I really want it.'

He sat down opposite her on a dining chair that creaked ominously. 'It gives you strange dreams you know.'

'I don't see how it can; it's just a beautiful, nautical artefact and my father will love it. So how much is it?' She was holding her breath and let it out with a woosh when he said, 'It's free to ladies that are so thrilled they faint when they see it.' He was smiling at her, his eyes twinkling.

'Thank you. Will you wrap it for me, or put it in a bag?'

'Of course, madam.' She waited while he did so and then stood and held out her hand. He shook it and smiled back. She put the wrapped timer in one of her many bags and walked out into the fresh air, appreciating it after the fusty shop.

Now, she knew there was no choice. She must take the timer back into the past, find her parents and Daniel and hope the timer will bring them back.

On the way home in the taxi Izzy wondered if she should just use the timer to send her back to the past and not go to Brimham Rocks. Could she trust it?

Usually, it stayed in the present time and after you had completed your mission it brought you back. What was the mission? She needed to look at her mum's computer to see if there was anything obvious in 1859 in her family tree. This could be achieved easily because she had a key and had been going there once a week to check everything was alright and to water the plants.

She would go on Monday, after work.

*

It was raining when Izzy stepped out of the taxi and unlocked her parent's front door. She had grown up in this house. It had been her anchor when she was at college and discovering who she was, avoiding the temptations of drugs and booze. Her bedroom had little of her in it now because Daniel used it when he had a sleepover. But today she was only interested in her mother's family tree that she knew was still on an old memory stick in the desk drawer.

After her adventure in India, orchestrated by the sand timer, they had all looked to see if the baby born to Jane Carstairs was there. It showed him and he outlived his parents. They were all so pleased because Mum and Izzy had helped at the birth.

She put the lights on in the hall, the living room and finally the study. Dad's big leather armchair was still there and so was the old computer. She found the memory stick, slipped it into the USB slot and searched for the family tree. It was easy and soon she was scrolling to entries in the nineteenth century. There was Jane, married to Major Cecil Carstairs and two-year-old Nathaniel who died in 1859.

Izzy took a deep breath and feeling as if she'd been winded. On the screen in front of her was the reason for all of this mayhem. The timer wanted someone to go back and save Nathaniel from dying. It was almost certainly why Daniel found the portal at Brimham. He was being manipulated by the sand timer.

Izzy switched everything off, called a taxi and went home. She had just a few days to finalise her plans. She was going back in time on Saturday.

Chapter 23

It was snowing when the carriage arrived at the door to take Cecil, Jane and their visitors to Burton Hall. Once again Catherine felt as if she was taking part in a film as a footman held an umbrella over her while another helped her to climb in.

It was quite cramped inside the carriage, the men sitting opposite the women, their knees, covered in rugs, almost touching.

'I hope it stops snowing soon. I really don't want to have to stay the night,' said Jane.

'No, especially as we said we would go home, and they may not have beds for us. I may have been a soldier but now I like my comforts and sleeping on the floor is not my idea of fun,' said Cecil. Catherine and Jason nodded their agreement.

Catherine was feeling nervous even though she knew she looked elegant in a cream silk dress. The full skirt, just skimming her feet, came in tight at the waist and the top fitted her figure well. The neckline was scooped and the sleeves long but not restricting. It had a myriad of buttons down the back, and she wondered when zips had been invented. It had been fun getting dressed and having her hair done, then meeting Jane and Cecil for drinks before they went. But she must stop thinking about that because they were arriving at another beautiful house, brightly lit to welcome its guests.

There were more footmen with umbrellas and then they were in the entrance hall being helped off with their coats. Music was playing somewhere ahead of them.

Jane whispered, 'Masks everyone.' They dutifully lifted their masks in front of their faces and moved forward to the ballroom. They were welcomed by their hosts, Mrs Hayward, Mark and Amrita, and then moved into the room where guests were already dancing. They stood together, watching.

It was a dance in sets of four, the couples moving in a sequence. Catherine had enjoyed this kind of dancing but there had been a caller telling you what to do next. It seemed these were common dances, and everyone knew what to do. The music was lively, and Catherine wanted to dance but felt it would not be proper to suggest it.

'I dare say our dances may not be the same as yours. Perhaps if I danced with Catherine and you danced with Jane, we could help you.' Cecil suggested. They all agreed and formed a square. When the sequence began again, they joined in and soon they knew what to do and it was fun. When the music finished everyone bowed or curtsied. Couples wandered around and chatted to each other; masks held in front of their faces. Waiters were circulating with drinks, and they all accepted. Catherine sipped a medium-sweet white wine. Idly she thought it would be easy to drink too much and then worried they might do exactly that and make a faux pas.

Another dance was announced and people who did not want to dance moved towards the chairs around the edge. Cecil found somewhere for them to sit and there was a small table for their drinks. When they were comfortable, he excused himself and went to speak to an elderly man and his family.

'Oh, I know who he's talking to. No mask could disguise that portly figure. It's my father, Lord Marshall. I expect we'll talk to them later so please address him as, 'my lord, or your Lordship. He does enjoy his title,' said Jane smiling happily. It was obvious to Catherine that she loved him dearly.

'Cecil's bringing them here,' said Jane and she stood so Catherine and Jason followed suit. They curtsied, bowed and were introduced.

'It's a pleasure to meet you,' said Lord Marshall. His voice was deep and rich, as pleasurable to the ear as Christmas pudding to the palate. He continued. 'Cecil tells me you're interested in ships, my *Daphne* in particular.'

Jason was uncertain how to answer but was saved by Cecil who added, 'I said you were an enthusiast of all things nautical and had quite a collection of memorabilia and were looking for a ship's sand timer.'

'Yes,' said Jason. 'I currently have a sextant, a compass, a telescope and a ship's bell. I heard a rumour that your ship,

Daphne, had been damaged in a severe storm. That made me wonder if it was to be repaired or if its contents were to be sold.'

'The rumour was quite correct, Mr Brownlow, but I'm afraid the contents have already been auctioned. I did keep the sand timer for a while in a glass cabinet at home, but then it went into my next ship, the *Iris.*'

'My Lord, ladies and gentlemen. Supper is now being served in the dining room.'

'We must go in,' said Lord Marshall. 'No one will make a move until we do.' He held his hand out to his wife and the group followed them towards the dining room.

It was a buffet but there were small tables with chairs arranged around for those who preferred to sit and eat. Lord and Lady Marshall wanted them to sit together. The table was small for six people but when Lord Marshall looked around for a servant, he was there immediately bringing a second table and placing it beside the first.

'That's better,' boomed his Lordship and beamed at everyone. Jane was chatting quietly to her mother and Jason decided to ask a question. 'I wonder, Your Lordship, if you could tell me who manufactured the sand timer for the *Daphne.* Perhaps he would make one just like it for my collection.'

'I suppose he might but he's a rum one, that Silas. There are some who think him a wizard. He's a recluse who just prefers his own company. But he's a talented man and his work's exquisite. If you want to ask him, best send your wife. He's had some bad run-ins with men. Been beaten half to death by one who accused him of making bad magic and giving his pigs swine fever. He lives near Jane and Cecil. They'll be able to give you directions. Now I'm going back to try some of that delicious-looking pudding. Are you joining me my dear?'

His wife refused, enjoying being with Jane and not ready to stop talking. Jason turned to Cecil. 'We're coming back for the shoot tomorrow morning. That might be a good time for Catherine to pay Silas a visit.'

After the buffet there was more dancing. The floor was less crowded, some people being too full or too tipsy to be energetic. Catherine was neither and Cecil was happy to help her through every new dance. Cecil watched Jane dancing with Jason and felt

129

delighted to see her flushed and laughing. He wondered if he dared come to her bed that night. It would be worth a try.

When it was midnight carriages began to arrive for those not saying the night. When she got to the door and was handed her coat Catherine saw, with relief, that the snow had stopped but was glinting on the ground, suggesting it would crunch underfoot. She was grateful for the assistance into the carriage and shivered all the way back despite the blankets.

Cecil offered a hot drink, tea or mulled wine but Jason refused. 'I think Catherine's too tired to stay awake any longer and if the shoot is still on, we have an early start. We'll just thank you for a delightful evening and go to our room.' They bowed and were soon undressing in front of their fire.

Catherine yawned. 'That was much more enjoyable than I expected but I'm too tired even to talk.' She climbed into bed when there was a tap at the door. Sarah entered. 'I see you have managed without my help, so I will leave you. Goodnight, madam, Sir.'

'Thank you, goodnight,' called Catherine from under the covers and waited until the door clicked shut before saying, 'It's unreasonable to expect servants to stay up so late, just to undo a few buttons and brush your hair.' Jason nodded his agreement and climbed into the bed, snuggling up to steal her warmth. They went to sleep quickly.

Tea was brought to them in the morning and the maid re-kindled the embers of the fire. Catherine thought with longing of their house at home with its underfloor heating. She leant up with one arm out of bed to reach her cup of tea and shivered. She laid down again, pulling the eiderdown up to her chin. 'You must get up Jason or you'll miss breakfast, and you'll need the calories being outside shooting poor defenceless birds.'

'You'll be happy to eat those birds if they're dished up at some point.'

'Mmm,' came the muffled reply from under the covers. Jason grimaced and got out of bed. He had never killed a bird, or any animal, and he was not looking forward to doing so. He had also never shot a gun but that appealed to him. He just wished they were shooting at targets. He dressed quickly and went downstairs to the breakfast room.

130

About an hour later Sarah came to Catherine to help her get dressed. It felt strange, as if she were a child again. The clothes made her feel warmer and she thought of Jason already out in the cold and was glad she was staying behind with Jane.

Jane was eating her breakfast and greeted Catherine warmly. 'Good morning, Catherine. I hope you slept well. Help yourself from the dishes. It was cooked fresh for us and is still really hot.'

'Thank you, I did sleep very well.' She filled her plate with scrambled eggs, bacon and toast and brought it to the table. 'I really enjoyed the masked ball. Did you?'

They talked about the costumes, food, dances and then Jane said, 'I was thinking you may be missing Daniel and want to see him today. Would you like me to invite him to lunch with us?'

'That's a very kind thought. I was thinking of going to The New Inn to see him this morning but I'm sure he would enjoy coming here instead.'

'That's settled then. I'll send James with a note. Now what would you like to do now?'

'I would like to go to Silas's cottage to ask him to make my husband a sand timer. Your father was talking to Jason last night. He said Silas will only talk to women and asked me if I would go.'

'That's perfect. I usually go once a fortnight and take him a basket of food. We can go together. To be honest I find him a little repulsive and would be pleased to have a companion with me. I'll let Cook know what we're doing, and we can get our coats and hats on.'

Ten minutes later they set off, Jane carrying the basket.

Chapter 24

Catherine and Jane began to walk by the side of the wood. The path was clearly defined but narrow, so they had to walk one behind the other. Here and there they had to duck under gaunt branches and avoid brambles. The day was chill and misty.

Catherine felt as if she was walking in clouds with the soft snow underfoot. The bottom of her skirt was soon wet and clinging to her legs, threatening to trip her. She walked a little slower and lifted her skirt at the front. When they reached a stile, Jane put the basket down on it and rubbed her arm.

'What's in there?' asked Catherine.

'Some ham, cheese, bread, butter and a jar of raspberry jam.'

'It's my turn to carry it when we get over the stile,' said Catherine. 'Is it much further?'

'No. After about fifty yards we'll come to a five-bar gate. We go through it and walk diagonally across the field where there's another gate. We'll be able to see his cottage from there. I'll be glad to get there now because I'm beginning to feel cold.'

Catherine closed the second gate and saw the cottage, although she thought it a hovel. The roof had an ominous dip in the middle as if the house could no longer manage the weight of it. Trees were encroaching, saplings growing in front of the windows, unchecked. It was a one-storey building with a window either side of the door. Catherine shuddered. It was like a witches' house invoking the stories of 'Little Red Riding Hood' and 'Hansel and Gretel'. She slowed down and Jane strode in front and knocked on the door with her fist. As they waited, they heard shuffling footsteps coming to the door which was opened a crack.

'Who are you? What do you want?' The voice was rasping, and the words were followed by a fit of coughing.

'It's Jane Carstairs. I have a basket of food for you, and I've brought a relative, Catherine Brownlow.'

'Two young ladies this morning. Well then, enter and welcome.' Silas stepped back and opened the door wide. Catherine thought he looked like Gandalf from '*Lord of the*

Rings' but his eyes were dull, possibly with cataracts. By now she was used to Victorian odours, but he reeked of neglect.

When they were inside, and her eyes were accustomed to the gloom, Catherine noticed it was all one room. To the left of the door was a bed, the clothes tumbled and grey. To the right was a fire with a cooking pot hanging over it and there was a crude table with two stools tucked under. The only sign of comfort was an upholstered armchair, the fabric worn into holes, by the fire. Silas shuffled towards it and sat down with a groan. The women were left standing.

Jane took the basket from Catherine, moved to the table and began to unpack it, telling Silas what she had brought as she did so. When everything was on the table she said, 'May we sit down? Mrs Brownlow wants to ask you something.' Silas nodded and waved vaguely towards the table. The women pulled out a stool each and sat.

'I believe you made a very special sand timer for Lord Marshall's ship, the *Daphne,*' said Catherine.

'I did. Put a lot of work into that timer. It were a labour of love.'

'It's still in use but not on the *Daphne* anymore. It has special powers. If any woman in our family is in distress, it tries to help them.'

Silas looked at her sharply, frowning. 'Are you calling me a sorcerer?'

Catherine shifted on the hard stool and wondered how to proceed. 'I think you're an amazing craftsman and with the love you put into the work you did not realise how special it was. I was wondering if you could make another, just like it, for me.'

Silas stood up, his knees creaking, his face screwed up with pain. He put another log on the fire and came to the table. He looked at Catherine for a long time and then at Jane. 'I can see the likeness. You both have similar features to her. And that auburn hair, just like hers. She had just a few freckles over her nose and milk-white skin. I loved her with all my heart, but I was a humble craftsman, and she was proper gentry. Her name was Alice, your aunt Mrs Carstairs. I couldn't have her, but I vowed to protect her.'

He rubbed one hand over his face and turned away from them. Catherine thought he might be crying.

He sat down in his chair and said, 'I can't make another like that.' He spread out his hands in front of him. 'My fingers are too gnarled these days for delicate work. I'm sorry.'

The women looked at each other and both stood up.

'We must go now,' said Jane. 'I hope you enjoy the food and I'll come again with some more soon.'

'Thank you for telling me about the sand timer and I'm sorry if I brought you sad memories,' said Catherine. They let themselves out of the door, finding the fresh, chill air welcoming. They both breathed deeply and looked at each other, their smiles tinged with sadness. They walked back to Lime Bank Hall talking little, both deep in thought.

When they were nearly back Catherine remembered Daniel was joining them for lunch and her spirits rose.

Chapter 25

2048

During the rest of the week Izzy made sure her colleagues knew she was not feeling well. She feigned constant headaches and on Friday she excused herself, leaving early, saying she had an appointment to go to the doctors. They would not be surprised when she failed to arrive on Monday.

Before Andy came home, she packed the large sailing bag that usually held the sails, with all her Victorian things along with the timer still wrapped. She also squashed in two large cloth bags that had no logos. When she arrived in 1859, she was going to change her clothes, repack everything and hide her sail-bag containing her modern clothes.

She had finished by the time Andy arrived home and she told him she had booked a meal in an Italian restaurant. He loved pizza and she really wanted to please him.

They went out, had a lot of red wine and came home feeling tipsy and happy. As soon as they shut the front door and removed their coats, she took the rest of her clothes off.

'Oh ho,' said Andy and followed her example. They made love on the carpet in the living room, the slight decadence adding to their pleasure. Finally, they went to bed and Andy sank into a deep sleep immediately. Izzy had hoped the wine would have relaxed her, but she was frightened and felt guilty at not telling her lovely husband what she was about to do. Eventually she did sleep but she woke early and brought Andy breakfast in bed.

'You're beginning to make me feel suspicious; a meal out last night, now breakfast in bed.'

'I just woke early and there's no work today, so I thought I'd treat you. I'm going to the sailing club this morning so there's no rush for you to get out of bed.'

She called a taxi and when it arrived, she shouted out goodbye and was on her way to the past.

At Brimham Rocks Izzy let the taxi go and walked up the main path, then turned left and meandered between the rocks until she reached the top of the portal. There were few people around, mostly families or climbers, because it was a chill November day. The sun was shining, but it was giving out little heat. She looked down, searching for handholds and decided the descent would be easy. She left her bag on top, climbed down and then reached up and pulled her bag down. She threaded her arms through the handles, so it was across her back. The hand holds on each side of the rock were obvious. She put a hand in each one and pressed.

This was it. She just had to say the right words and she would go back in time. There were children's voices calling to each other that gave her the impetus she needed. It would be difficult to explain why she was climbing about on the rocks with a great big sail-bag on her back. 'Eighteen fifty-nine,' she shouted and the rock trembled.

*

1859

A snowy squall hit her almost threatening to push her off the rock. She pressed herself against it, waiting for it to pass, but it continued buffeting her with its icy breath. Going down was not an option so she threw her bag back up to the top and hauled herself up. She was out of breath when she was again on top of the rock and wished there was somewhere to shelter so she could change her clothes. No place came to mind so she would have to do it as quickly as she could.

Izzy unzipped the sail-bag and snowflakes drifted into it. No, she must remove her clothes first. It didn't matter how wet they were. It was almost like torture to take off her warm coat, her jumper, her boots and her trousers before opening the bag and dragging a long undergarment over her head. It was supposed to be laced but now was not the time to fiddle as she gasped with cold, her fingers numbing, trying to get the dress the right way

136

round and over her head. She slipped her arms into the sleeves and felt a little less exposed but again she was unable to do up the buttons. She managed the one at the top and left the rest while she pulled a cloak around her and put up the hood. Finally, she pulled on the boots and managed to tie the laces despite her deadening fingers.

The two bags of clothes, one containing the timer, were not really weatherproof and she thought miserably that if she got to the farm today, everything she owned was going to be soaked through. She stuffed her modern clothes into the sail bag and searched for somewhere to stow it. Walking back the way she had come she found a lip of rock with a gap underneath it. She shoved the bag under, and it was deep enough to hold it without being visible if you were standing. It would have to do. Now she picked up the other two bags and made for the road. When she was on the level, she turned towards Burnt Yates hoping the snow would stop, otherwise the road might disappear into drifts.

Izzy trudged miserably on for what seemed like hours, leaning against the driving snow, knowing she must be almost invisible, white from head to toe.

At first, she thought she was imagining a different sound, a creaking, then a snort from a horse brought her to a stop and she turned to look behind her. She could see a cart being pulled by one horse, its head down, plodding though the deepening snow. Izzy stepped off the road onto the edge where the tips of miserable grass peeped through and waited for it to go past.

It stopped. A man hunched up with a hat pulled low and a blanket over his knees shouted, 'Come on lassie, ride up wi' me. This weather's not fit for a dog.'

Izzy hesitated. How did she know he wouldn't rape her or steal her money?

'Come on. No need to be afeared.' She nodded and heaved her bags up to him one at a time and he twisted and placed them in the cart behind him. He held out a hand to help her up, but she managed it unaided.

'I'm delivering to Burton Hall. Where are you heading?'

'I was looking for Blackberry Farm, near Burnt Yates.'

'In that case you're out of luck because you've passed it. The best I can do is leave you at The New Inn. You'll find a good fire there to dry you off and the food's good.'

'Thank you. I really appreciate you giving me a ride. Is it far?'

He shook his head. 'We'm just comin' int' village now.'

They rounded a corner and she saw what looked like a picture on a Christmas card, silent, the snow muffling sound and covering roofs, softening every shape. Izzy could not admire it for long because her driver was bringing the cart to a halt, outside the inn. She climbed down awkwardly, her feet sinking into a drift, and then turned to receive her bags from him. He flicked the reins and the horse pulled away. He raised a hand, and she shouted her thanks to his back then entered the inn.

The warmth enveloped her, and the smell of food wafted making her realise she was frozen, wet, and hungry. The fire, hissing and popping as it devoured a huge log drew her. Izzy stood in front of it and watched her dress steaming. When it became too hot for her face, she turned to dry the other side and then looked around. There were a few people, all men, and they had empty plates in front of them. They were all looking at her. 'Good afternoon,' she said. There was a murmured response and a few heads nodded and then they went back to talking and drinking.

'Welcome to The New Inn. Can I get you something? You look like you've been out in this storm for some time. What would you say to some mulled wine and a plate of dinner?' Izzy moved to the bar, her damp skirt dragging against her legs and said, 'It sounds wonderful but I'm not sure I have enough money.' He told her the cost and she pulled out her purse, laboriously sorting through the coins.

'There's no need to pay now. Go back to the fire and I'll bring it to that table when it's ready.' Izzy followed his pointing finger and moved her bags beside it then returned to the fire. She had only stood for a few moments when he brought her the wine. 'This'll help to warm you. Dinner will be ready shortly.'

The wine was very hot, but she sipped it, feeling the liquid warming her as she swallowed. When her food arrived, Izzy moved to the table and sat down. It looked wonderful, succulent meat, some carrots, gravy and a chunk of bread. It was hard to eat daintily, like a lady when she was so hungry, but she tried, feeling the eyes of the men watching her. The men gradually left and eventually Izzy was alone with the barman who was clearing the tables. When he reached her, he asked if he could take her glass and empty plate.

'Yes, please do. The meal was absolutely delicious, thank you.' She waited until he had taken everything back to the bar and then stood and walked over to him. 'I wanted to go to Blackberry Farm but, in the blizzard, I missed it. I was wondering if you knew a boy called Daniel Mansfield who's staying there?'

She saw Sam's polite smile broaden into a wide one. 'Yes, I know 'im but 'e's not stayin' at Blackberry Farm. He was, but now 'e's 'ere.' He gestured up the stairs. 'I'm thinkin' you're related; very distinctive ginger hair, same as 'is.'

'I'm his mother. Which room? I really would like to see him.'

'Well, it's number six. He was in there with his grandparents, but they've gone to stay at Lime Bank Hall. Would you be wanting to share that room with him tonight?'

'Yes please, and I still owe you for the meal.'

'I'll put it on the tab.'

'Thank you.' Izzy picked up her bags and asked if there was another key to number six. Her heart was singing, anticipating seeing Daniel but then Sam said, 'Here you are, a key to number six but Master Daniel's not there. He went to have lunch at Lime Bank Hall. He'll be back in time for supper, I think.'

'Oh. Thank you for telling me. I'll go up now and unpack my clothes.'

Izzy's boots clattered on the bare wood stairs and the floorboards creaked as she walked along the corridor to her room. She unlocked the door and went in, closing it behind her. It was dingy, but she was pleased to see the dying embers of a fire in the grate. She dropped her bags, put a couple of split logs onto the fire and poked it, then knelt and blew to encourage them to catch light. When she was satisfied she had saved it from extinction, Izzy unpacked.

Her night dress was damp, so she draped it over a chair and stood it in front of the fire. There were hangers in a closet which she used to air the rest of her clothes in the relatively warm room. She looked at the beds, a double and a single and hoped Daniel was using the single. The double bed had a thick eiderdown on it and looked so inviting. She pulled off her dress and boots, snuggled under the covers and was asleep almost immediately.

Chapter 26

2048

Andy had spent Saturday morning working but decided, after a sandwich lunch, to go for a walk. The sun was shining weakly and after many days of dull grey skies and rain it was inviting. He liked to walk quickly and chose a cycle path that was still in the town but ran parallel to the railway line. It was flanked by trees and he felt as if he was in the country. Eventually he arrived in Knaresborough and decided to get a bus back to Harrogate.

When he got home, he made a cup of tea, found an open packet of biscuits and sat down to watch television. He dunked the crisp ginger biscuit into his tea and imagined Izzy saying, 'Oh that's disgusting.' He smiled, swallowed the soggy piece and dunked again.

After an hour or so, the programme he had been watching finished. He wondered why Izzy was late home. It was dark and there was no way she could still be at the sailing club. He sent her a text. There was no reply. He felt anxious now and rang her, but a message said her solafone was switched off. He rang all the people who usually went sailing and they all said she had not sailed that day and they had not seen her. He finally rang Xen. He sounded really concerned. He said Izzy had told Ruby last week she would not be sailing today.

'I'm scared, Xen. This is so unlike her. Yesterday she couldn't do enough for me and I said she must be up to something. I think she might have gone to Brimham Rocks.'

Xen offered to meet him there in the morning to see if she had left any evidence but also said Andy should report her missing to the police.

He phoned the police and spoke to the same sergeant who had conducted the search for Daniel. He suggested the two could be related and were possibly an abduction. He sent a constable to Andy's house to take a statement.

Andy's stomach was churning. He wondered if he was going to be sick. He sat on the bathroom floor, just in case, and then cried. He'd tried so hard to support Izzy and to quash his own grief to help her. Now it all flooded out with gasping sobs. He'd lost his son and now he'd lost Izzy.

The doorbell rang. He struggled up and washed his face, still drying it on the towel as he opened the door. He invited the policeman in and took him into the kitchen. They both sat at the table and the policeman produced a notepad. Andy offered to make a cup of tea and the young constable accepted. He asked questions as Andy moved around, filling the kettle and getting two mugs. When the mugs were full, he sat down again.

'You said you thought your wife had gone sailing. What would she have taken with her?'

'Her big bag of sails, and her phone so she could pay for lunch and teas. In the bag she would have put a change of clothes and a towel in case she capsized.'

'Right, I've made a note of that. Would you show me where this bag is usually kept?'

Andy nodded and stood up. He went into the garage through a connecting door. 'It should be here.' He pointed to a space on the floor and it was the constable's turn to nod. They returned to the kitchen and sat down again. Andy wished he would go away. He felt queasy again and exhausted.

'We've nearly finished,' said the constable as if he had read Andy's thoughts. 'I noticed the car in the garage. Does your wife have a car of her own?'

'No. When she goes sailing, she always uses a taxi.'

'What taxi company would that be sir?'

Andy told him and said what time she had left the house that morning. The constable said he would contact the taxi company and was hopeful the information they would give him would be useful. He stood up and Andy saw him to the door. As he went through it the constable said, 'Please let us know if she comes home tonight.'

'Yes, I will, thank you. Goodnight.'

Andy had not eaten since his ginger biscuits, but he was not hungry. He checked the doors were locked, lights were off and went upstairs to his bedroom. He felt under his pillow for his pyjamas and heard the rustle of paper. He opened the folded paper and read,

'Please, please forgive me!
I've gone back to 1859 to help them return to our time. When I went to Leeds shopping last week, I actually found the sand timer in a shop. I was so overcome when I saw it, I fainted! The shopkeeper gave it to me. He even said he knew it created strange dreams. I believe the timer's mission is to save Nathaniel. He's Major Carstairs and Jane's baby. The one Mum and I delivered in the hospital at Lucknow.
You see now, why I have to go.
I will do my best to be as quick as possible.
Please believe how much I love you.

Izzy
xxxxxxx

Andy phoned the police. He told them he had found a letter from her under his pillow. It said she had decided to leave him, so they could delete her from their missing person file. The sergeant thanked him for letting them know and was sympathetic.

Andy undressed for bed and then sent a text to Xen cancelling their meeting at Brimham with a brief explanation. When he put out the light and pulled the duvet around him, he wondered if he would be able to sleep. The realisation that there was nothing more he could do helped him relax and he did, eventually, fall asleep.

*

1859

Daniel sat on the edge of the armchair when he was invited by Jane to sit down. He was not feeling comfortable in her presence even though she was being pleasant. 'Your grandmama will be here shortly. I've sent a servant to tell her you've arrived. While we're waiting would you like a drink? I usually have something before lunch.' She waved a hand towards the sideboard where there was a decanter and glasses made ready.

143

'Thank you. Would you like me to get one for you?'

'That's a kind offer, yes please.'

Catherine came into the room to see him pouring Madeira into two glasses. 'I can see you have made yourself at home, Daniel.' She went up to him, gave him a hug and said she had missed him. 'Is that second one for me?' He nodded and she took it and went to sit down. He brought the other to Jane and then went back and poured himself a smaller one. He sat with them and smiled as Catherine raised her eyebrows. He was far too young to drink alcohol in his own time and here he was drinking Madeira.

Jane asked Daniel if he had been working that morning.

'Yes, I wrote three letters, two from people on your estate and one private one. The landlord, Sam, likes me doing it because all my customers buy a drink while they're waiting. It's much warmer writing there than outside on market days and, of course, I can be available every morning.'

'I can remember when you argued with your mother about the importance of neat handwriting. You hated having to practice it. I expect you're glad now that she kept insisting on a high standard.'

Daniel smiled but said nothing because lunch was announced, and they were to go into the dining room.

He was relieved to see it was a buffet so he would not embarrass himself by not knowing the etiquette. He was also not sure how much Jane knew about his family coming from the future and thought it best to keep quiet and copy what the others did.

'Catherine, please go first and help yourself. The platters will stay there throughout the meal so you may return for something different or to have more.' Catherine did as she was asked and soon filled her plate.

When she was seated, Daniel was invited to go next, but he said he would prefer it if Jane went. Jane nodded and when she had sat down Daniel went up to the buffet. He piled his plate high to the amusement of both the women.

'I see you have a good appetite, Daniel,' said Jane.

'To be honest that was why I wanted to go last. I would have been embarrassed to have taken so much salmon if you still had to serve yourself.'

'And there we were, thinking you a gentleman, letting the ladies go first,' said Catherine. They all laughed and the slight tension there had been eased.

As the meal went on Jane explained to Daniel that Catherine had told her about the portal at Brimham Rocks. 'I understand you come from the future and am curious to know what we are to expect. Cecil has fought at the Crimea and the Indian Mutiny. He has retired from active service now because his leg still pains him from time to time. But what I want to know is, will there be any more wars in our lifetime?'

Daniel shook his head and Catherine spoke. 'I'm pleased to be able to tell you there will not be any more while Queen Victoria is on the throne and she will still be there at the turn of the century.'

'My goodness that's forty years from now. Thank you for telling me that. Now, Daniel, tell me what is different for young people in your time.'

'The main difference is the use of what we call technology. Many amazing inventions mean that young people play and communicate without being with other people. It's really hard to explain. You know ships can signal to each other using flags,' he watched Jane nod, 'well the next invention was morse code. It meant people could send simple messages without being able to see them.'

'Cecil is very interested, like Prince Albert, in all new inventions and he told me about this morse idea. I think they use it on the railway. So, you can use something like that to talk to friends without them being with you.'

'Yes. I miss my friends and my Mum and Dad, but Grandma and Grandad have made me feel much better. Where is Granddad?'

They explained about the shoot and laughed when Daniel said he would hate to kill any animal.

'But you love meat and made short work of that salmon. Someone had to kill in order for you to eat,' said Catherine.

'I know, but someone else does it. If I had to pull a trigger or wring a chicken's neck, I'd become a vegetarian.'

The conversation then turned to the masked ball and Catherine described the dances, the musicians and people's costumes with great enthusiasm. She even went to her room and brought her and Granddad's masks to show him.

It was an enjoyable afternoon and Daniel wished he could stay longer but Jane said the men would be returning soon and he took the hint and left, not forgetting to thank Jane.

Chapter 27

Daniel walked as briskly as he could, but the snow had begun to freeze, and he slid along the path. He liked the crunch his feet made that seemed to echo, for everywhere was so quiet. He thought about Jane and how calm she seemed when faced with people from the future. Grandma seemed to be very relaxed in her company too. He decided he liked Jane now. She was no longer the odd woman who had made him feel uncomfortable.

The cold was seeping under his clothes and Daniel shivered. He thought of winters at home, in 2048. It never snowed, due to climate change, and he didn't think he was bothered about that. Snow might look beautiful as it glinted in the light but now, in the dark, it was just viciously cold. Christmas cards still had pictures of children building snowmen and riding on sledges. Perhaps that would be fun but now he was just looking forward to the big fire at the inn.

He stood in front of the fire holding his red hands closer to it when Sam said, 'Afternoon, Daniel. Did you have a tasty lunch?'

'Yes, thank you Sam, it was delicious. What's on the menu tonight?'

'Chicken. Got three turning on't spit right now. Oh, and you've got a visitor waitin' for you in yer room.'

'Oh, who?'

'She said she was yer Mam.' He grinned at the effect of his words. Daniel rushed to the stairs, took them two at a time and then ran down the corridor. At the door to his room, he tried to put his key in the lock but there was a key in the other side. He banged on it with his fist shouting, 'Mum, Mum, Let me in!'

The door opened and they rushed into each other's arms, Daniel whispering, 'I can't believe you're here.' His mother's muffled voice saying, 'I've missed you so, so much.' It seemed to Daniel the longest and best hug he'd ever had.

They parted and Daniel said, 'Where's Dad?' as he looked around the bedroom.

'He's not here. He had to go to work and keep things going at home until we get back.'

'Right, and that's not going to be soon, is it? You know the rock only works one way.'

'I know. I wanted to come but then I *had* to because I found the sand timer.'

'Grandma and Granddad have been talking about finding it here, but you found it in our time. Weird.'

'Yes, and it's definitely the same one I touched that took me to India where I met Jane and her husband Captain Carstairs.'

'He's Major Carstairs now. I had lunch today with his wife, Jane, and Grandma at Lime Bank Hall.'

'I thought you were staying at Blackberry Farm. This is almost too much to take in. I had no idea Jane lived near here. How's Grandma and Granddad? Are they well? How are they coping with being in Victorian times?' She put her hand to her head. 'I'm getting a headache.'

Daniel laughed. 'Slow down Mum. There's plenty of time to learn all about my adventures. Why don't you lay on the bed and shut your eyes? That might help the headache.'

'You won't go anywhere and leave me, will you?'

'No, I'll just sit here and write my diary while you rest.'

Daniel heard his mother's breathing slow and steady and enjoyed the peace. He got out his diary, wrote about having lunch and then coming home and meeting his mum. When he had finished, he glanced at her sleeping, hardly able to believe that she was here, with him.

He thought about the sand timer and looked in her bag to find it. Her clothes were hanging all around the room, so it was easy to find. He unwrapped it and looked at it. He turned and looked at the bottom where it had *Daphne* inscribed and he watched the sand fall. How could this be a portal to the past or future. It didn't vibrate or glow or anything. He wrapped it up again and put it back in her bag. It was too early to go down to dinner and after his huge lunch he was not hungry. He went to his own bed, laid down and fell asleep.

*

148

Daniel was walking along a riverbank. He marvelled at the warmth coming from the sun. Birds were singing in the trees that stood beside the river and ducks were doing what ducks do, dipping down for food. He came to a jetty where two rowing boats were moored, and a toddler was crouched trying to float his toy boat. He looked up and smiled at Daniel who crouched down beside him. 'I'm not sure you should be here. Where's your mama or papa?' The lad twisted and nearly fell as he tried to point behind him. Daniel picked him up, looked around and saw the bushes shaking and strange noises, grunts and oohs. He walked towards the sounds and suddenly a woman stood up, her naked breasts swinging as she bent down to pull up her skirt. It was Emily. Daniel knew he should turn around so she didn't realise he'd seen her, but he couldn't stop looking.

Major Carstairs, a satisfied smile on his face stood and pulled up his breeches. Then they both saw Daniel. Emily screamed and he shouted, 'Who the hell are you, spying on us. Put down my son at once.'

His shouting upset Nathaniel who began to cry. Emily, now properly dressed, moved to Daniel and took the boy from him. As she did so he said, 'The boy was playing right beside the water trying to float his toy boat. He could have fallen in and you wouldn't have known.'

Major Carstairs blanched. 'I'm sorry,' he said. 'You've probably saved his life.' He felt in his pockets for a coin, found a florin and held it out.

Daniel shook his head and put his hands deliberately behind his back. 'I don't want your money. I'm just glad the boy's safe.'

The Major blustered at first but then he bowed and said, 'That's hard for me, knowing I'm indebted to you but thank you again.' He took Nathaniel away from Emily and they began to walk back towards the large house in the distance.

*

Daniel woke up. That was a strange dream he thought. I should have taken the money. Granddad needs it. He opened his eyes. There was no fire, and it was very dark. He felt the covers.

He was on a duvet. This was his own bed in 2048. He sat up, swung his legs out of bed, calling, 'Mum, Dad, I'm back.'

*

Izzy yawned and stretched, noticed the fire was dead and got up. She wondered where the light switch was. Then she realised there was probably no electricity and stumbled in the dark looking for an oil lamp or candle. 'Daniel, wake up, I think we've missed dinner.' There was no reply, so she felt her way to his bed. He was not there. She felt disorientated and cross. He'd promised to stay with her.

Izzy's eyes were becoming accustomed to the gloom. She could now make out shapes and went to the window and pulled back the curtains. It was not dark but dusk; the sun was very low in a beautiful red sky. There was no snow left and she was amazed. It must have warmed up considerably.

She wasn't sure what to do, so she opened the door. The corridor looked dingy and uninviting. She closed the door again and looked around the room. On top of the fireplace was a candle and a taper but there was no fire laid so she couldn't light it. She only had her underwear on so she put on her dress, doing up as many buttons as she could, then threw a shawl around her shoulders. She went back to the door, opened it and walked slowly along the corridor and down the stairs to talk to the landlord. There was plenty of light now.

Sam looked at her with surprise, his bushy eyebrows raised. 'Can I help you madam?'

'I'm looking for Daniel, my son. I thought he would be down here but he's not. Have you seen him?'

'I'm afraid I don't know any Daniel and, I don't recognise you.'

Izzy looked at him in disbelief. 'I came in earlier today and you said I could share Daniel's room.'

'I find that 'ard to believe seein', as I said, I don't know no Daniel.'

Izzy wondered if she was going mad but managed to say, calmly. 'Shall we start again? My name is Mrs Mansfield, and I would like to rent room number six.'

Sam nodded and said, 'I'll get the key.' He took a key off the hook and held it out to her.

'Thank you,' she said. She had just reached the stairs when Sam added 'Will you be wanting a meal? I finish serving at nine.'

'Yes, please,' she said and went back upstairs to her room. It felt lonely without Daniel and she had no idea where he'd gone. She hoped he would come back when he was hungry. Her son had changed so much she scarcely recognised the young man she had met a few hours ago. He seemed so tall, mature, so grown up. Having to cope, being thrust into a different time zone, seemed to have made him an adult and he was not quite fourteen. His birthday was December 4th, just a few weeks away.

The snow had gone; it wasn't dark so it couldn't be November. She wasn't sure what month they were in but knew she dare not ask the landlord. He would certainly think her mad then. When she had time travelled before, the dates roughly matched. She had left 2048 in winter and arrived in winter, but it seemed so much warmer now. When she went to sleep there was a fire in her room. Now it was neatly laid and seemed not to have been lit recently.

Suddenly Izzy knew what had happened. Nathaniel had died in June 1859. Daniel had touched the timer while she was asleep and sent everyone back nearly six months. That was why he was not here. That was why the landlord had not seen her before. That thought threw up more questions.

> Had Daniel saved the boy's life and gone back to 2048?
> Had her parents returned to 2048 too?
> If so, why hadn't she gone back to 2048?
> Was the timer still in her bag?
> If it was, did it have another task?

Izzy felt the migraine returning and tried to stop her teeming brain. She stood up and went to her bag. The timer was still there but not wrapped in the same way. Daniel must have touched it. What should she do now? She was exhausted and realised she felt hungry. She went back along the dark corridor, down the stairs and saw the bar was now quite busy. It was nearly all men and she felt conspicuous and embarrassed when she saw them all looking at her. She knew it was because this was a small village

151

and strangers, especially women alone, were rare. She held her head high and went to the bar.

'What can I get you, Mrs Mansfield?'

'I would like a drink of erm …'

'Ale?' he suggested,

'Yes, please and a meal, whatever you have.'

'I have roast chicken tonight. Will that do yer? Or I could do yer some cold meats, cheese and bread?'

'The chicken smells wonderful, I'll have that. Do I sit anywhere?'

'Wait while I pour your ale and then I'll take it to a table that's nice and quiet.' She waited and followed him to a table in a niche where she could eat without prying eyes.

'Thank you, that's perfect.' She sat down and sipped her ale, wondering what she should do next.

The dinner was huge and delicious. Izzy ate it all feeling over-full but more relaxed than at any time since she had left home. She sipped her ale and thought. She needed a plan and the only one she could think of was to go to Lime Bank Hall and see if her parents were there. But even though she had slept in the late afternoon, she now felt extremely tired. It was probably the soporific effect of eating a large meal and drinking ale. She wondered how alcoholic a pint of ale was. She went up to the bar to pay for her meal, but Sam said he would put it on a tab, seeing as she was a resident.

Izzy put her purse back in her pocket and went upstairs. If her parents were staying at Lime Bank Hall, they would still be there tomorrow. She would cope better with meeting Jane and Major Carstairs if she had had a good night's sleep.

She undressed and snuggled down under the blanket, appreciating the weather and the bedroom, being warmer than when she'd arrived.

Chapter 28

Catherine and Jason enjoyed their evening with Cecil and Jane. The shoot had been a great success, despite the snow, and the men arrived home red-faced with the cold and elated with the day's sport. They chatted about the other men at the shoot and their prowess with a gun, or not. Cecil praised Jason's efforts, as a complete beginner and Jason said how good a shot Cecil was.

'I should be good when you consider I was a soldier. I've had plenty of practice.'

When the men had finished their stories, Catherine and Jane related their meeting with Silas and Jason's face lost its hopeful smile when they said Silas had arthritic hands and could no longer do delicate work.

They told them Daniel had come to lunch and made them smile exaggerating the heap of salmon he'd consumed. Jane also said that Daniel had assured her there were to be no more wars during Queen Victoria's reign and the Queen was going to live well into the next century. Cecil was impressed with that knowledge and looked to Jason for confirmation that it was all true. Jason said Daniel was correct in all he'd said.

The evening ended with a night cap and Catherine felt the effects, hoping it would help her sleep.

When they went to bed, Jason and Catherine snuggled under the covers that seemed inadequate. Catherine wished she was at home under her duvet, but the thought didn't last long because sleep came quickly.

Catherine woke up feeling unbearably hot. She threw off her covers and went into the bathroom mumbling under her breath about hot flushes. Some light was gleaming through the curtains and she pulled one back a little. The snow had gone, the sun was up, and she could feel the warmth through the glass. She looked at the clock on the mantlepiece and it said it was five o'clock. She frowned, closed the curtains and went back to bed. How could it be so bright so early on a November day? She closed her eyes, turned over and went back to sleep.

Jason woke her saying, 'It's nine o'clock and no maid. What's happened to our morning tea? If we don't hurry, we'll miss breakfast.' He rushed into the bathroom, had a quick wash and dressed. Catherine got her clothes ready and as soon as Jason came out of the bathroom, she went in.

They descended the stairs, side by side, debating the possible menu. Catherine preferred scrambled eggs; Jason fried.

'To be honest I'd settle for bread and marmalade, I'm that hungry,' said Jason. They entered the dining room expecting to see the sideboard covered in platters, but it was empty. There was nothing to eat and no people.

'Curiouser and curiouser,' said Catherine. 'Did you look out of the window this morning?'

'No, I was in too much of a hurry. Why?'

'Well, there's no sign of the snow and when I got up at five o'clock the sun was up and shining.' Jason moved to the dining room window and looked out. 'The garden's full of roses, Catherine. Something's happened since last night. I think we've gone back in time.'

Just then they heard a child laughing coming from somewhere upstairs. They looked at each other and said, simultaneously, 'Nathaniel'.

'Jason, if they find us here, we'll have a lot of explaining to do. Let's go back upstairs, pack our things and go to The New Inn.' Jason nodded and they returned to their bedroom creeping as quietly as they could.

Catherine packed only the things she had brought with her. All the dresses, nightdresses and underwear Jane had given her she left lying on the bed. Jason added his extra shirts and his dress suit. They both used the flush toilet once more and Catherine wished she had started the day with a bath. After a final glance around to check they had left nothing they went downstairs. They saw no one, let themselves quietly out of the front door and set off at a brisk pace enjoying the sunshine.

Some hours later Emily was hanging a dress in Jane's wardrobe that she had pressed when she noticed there were a lot of clothes missing. 'Excuse me Ma'am. Some of your evening gowns and day dresses are missing. Have you given them to the poor?'

'No, let me see.' She stood up from her position at her dressing table and came to the wardrobe. 'Yes, I see. Mostly things I've not worn for a while. How strange.'

It was several days before anyone entered the guest bedroom that Catherine and Jason had been using and discovered the clothes on the bed. Jane looked at it all and suddenly in her mind she saw Catherine and Jason. The momentary flash of memory frightened her, and she sat down on the bed.

'This is, indeed, a mystery but as all the missing garments appear to be here, I think we should leave it at that. Emily, will you launder everything and return them to my wardrobe?'

Emily bobbed a curtsey, as she said, 'Yes Ma'am.' She gathered all the clothes and went downstairs to hand them over to the washer woman.

Jane sat still for a few moments feeling unsettled. Why did she suddenly think of Catherine and Jason? She had last seen them in the field hospital at Lucknow and yet she felt she'd seen them recently. Eventually she rose to her feet and went to the dining room for lunch. Cecil was already there, and she wondered if he had felt anything similar.

'For no apparent reason I found myself thinking of Lucknow and Catherine, the nurse who helped me and her husband, Jason, who saved your life.'

'How odd. I've also been thinking of them. It will soon be Nathaniel's second birthday so perhaps that's why.'

Emily went into the kitchen. She had taken the load of clothes to the laundry to be washed and stood for a moment in the doorway.

'Can I help you, Emily?' asked Cook who was beating something in a large earthenware bowl.

'I don't think so, but …'

Now she had Cook's interest. She stopped beating, put down the bowl and waited for Emily to speak.

'You will think me mad, but I wondered … when the mistress didn't need me if I could sometimes help you? I would like to learn English cookery. I feel I would be good at making food look decorative.'

'Well, that's a surprise but a pleasant one. I could certainly do with extra help when we entertain, and I'd be happy to teach you some of the basics. At the moment I'm creaming butter and sugar to begin making a cake. If you're free now, I'll show you how to do it. It's going to be chocolate, one of the master's favourites. He likes it decorated with whipped cream and walnuts. Here, put this apron on.'

It was market day. Joe and Mary were selling cheese, and vegetables. When the rush was over Mary said, 'It's strange, Joe, but I've been dreaming about a young man helping us out. In my dream he was living with us, sleeping in Ruth's bedroom. It started fine but then turned into a nightmare. You got smallpox and died! It was so vivid, Joe, like it really happened.'

Joe laughed. 'Look at me, my dear, fat, hale and hearty. Whatever put that idea into your dream? I don't know. Ah, here comes Mr Hancock. He might buy cheese; he often does.'

George Hancock stopped and, as predicted, he bought some cheeses and some marmalade. When he had completed his purchase he said, 'Tell me, how is your Ruth getting on at Burton Hall. She's such a comely lass. I've been thinking of calling on her. When will she next have a day off?'

Mary bobbed a curtsey, almost speechless to hear him talking of calling on Ruth. It was Joe who managed to say, 'Thank you for your interest, Sir. She'll be home next Saturday, and we would be honoured if you wished to call. I'm sure Mary will bake for the occasion.' Mary nodded, bobbed again, unable to speak until George moved away.

'Joe, I can't believe it. He wants to call on our Ruth an' he's a gentleman.' They had a quick hug of delight. If he wanted to marry Ruth, their daughter would be set up for life. Mary had already forgotten her dream in her excitement.

*

George walked on through the market and arrived at The New Inn. He fancied a drink and as it was nearly lunch time he would linger and have that too. A couple of older people he did not know were just going in, so he paused and raised his hat, allowing them to go ahead of him. They approached Sam and asked for a room. He gave them number three, apologising for the fact it was at the front and could be noisy when people sat outside in the evening. 'It's the only room I have left. Some people stay over on market days.'

When they had set off up the stairs Sam turned to George. He served him a tankard of ale and noted his order for a cold lunch. 'Lunch will be ready in ten minutes, Sir. Where are you going to sit?'

'It's noisy outside, Sam. I think I'd prefer indoors. I want peace and quiet.' Sam handed him the ale and George sat where Izzy had sat the previous evening. He sipped his drink, cool and refreshing and thought about Ruth. He couldn't say why she was in his thoughts so much but knew he could hardly wait until Saturday to see her. He hoped she would have some feeling for him too. He dreamt on, his thoughts only halting when Sam brought him his lunch.

*

Amrita was walking in the sunshine through the woods surrounding the estate. She had a cloak on because her sari was made of thin, diaphanous fabric. The cloak warded off the slight chill of early morning and she was enjoying her walk. She decided an English summer was delightful. It was warm, rarely too hot and everywhere was green and beautiful. Where she came from in India the summer weather was very hot. The ground became parched, cracked and everywhere was dusty brown.

As she walked Amrita thought about her wedding. She was not a Christian but knew Mark and his family were and she didn't want to upset anyone. There had to be compromises when you lived in a foreign country, and she really loved Mark. She had already chosen the fabric for her wedding sari, although Mrs Hayward had been annoyed that she would not wear the white, enormous creations brides in England usually wore.

157

Ruth was also musing, as she dusted the dining room, moving ornaments and placing them carefully back in their correct place. When she had finished, she was to start on the study, completing it before Mr Hayward was ready to begin his day. She liked the study with its bookcases, heavy oak desk and leather armchairs. Suddenly a picture of George Hancock came into her mind. He was a kind man, a gentleman too. She'd been dreaming about him in the night and she blushed at her forwardness. Mr Hancock had been courting her and she had allowed him to kiss her and touch her breasts and then …

'Good morning Ruth. Have you finished in here or should I leave and come back?'

Ruth blushed and curtsied. 'I'm sorry, Sir, you startled me. I have just finished.' She collected her cleaning things and scuttled out of the room.

Chapter 29

2048

Daniel found Dad sitting at the kitchen table, cradling a cup of tea. When he saw Daniel, he stood abruptly bumping the table and spilling his tea. They hugged for a long time, both of them crying.

'Mum didn't come back with you, did she?'

'I don't know. If you haven't seen her, I suppose she didn't. What day is it? Do I have to go to school?'

They released each other and Dad shook his head. 'It's Sunday so you've got a day to get ready to pick up your life.' He moved to the hot tap to make Daniel a cup of tea and then microwaved two cooked breakfasts. Daniel collected the toast and they sat down opposite each other. They both began to eat and Daniel said, 'Microwaved breakfast is not as good as fresh cooked, but it's quick and easy, I suppose. Mary and Sam both cooked lovely bacon and eggs.'

'Who were Mary and Sam? A couple you met on your travels?'

Daniel laughed. 'No, sorry, I shouldn't have said it quite like that. Mary was the woman, married to Joe, who took me in when I arrived at Blackberry Farm. Sam was the landlord of The New Inn.'

Dad had finished his breakfast and sat back, looking at Daniel. 'You remember the picnic at Brimham Rocks?'

'The scariest day of my life. Of course, I remember. Can you imagine climbing back up the rock and Ben not there. Then the car park was not there anymore, nor were you and even the road was a dirt track.'

Dad held up his hands. 'Before you tell me all about it, I must tell you that the picnic should be today. I need to phone Xen and tell him we can't make it. I'll have to make up some excuse, although I suppose I could tell him the truth. He knows Mum went to find you.'

159

Andy sighed and wiped his hands over his face. 'It's been a terrible six months. The police went frantic looking for you and when it was no good you were filed as a missing person. Then when Mum left, I had to tell lies to her company. I said she'd had to go and look after a sick relative and would be away a month or so. Now I'll have to lie all over again. I'm missing her so much.'

He stood up and went around the table. He put his arms around Daniel and kissed his head. 'It's wonderful you're back safe and you seem to have grown. Not sure if your school uniform will fit you. Anyway, while I'm phoning Xen, go and have a shower and turn yourself from a Victorian gentleman to my precious, two thousand and forty-eight, teenager.' He took his arms away from around Daniel and the boy went upstairs.

'I'll tell you all my adventures when I come back down,' he called.

Before Andy had picked up his solafone, Xen rang.

'Something's happened. We've gone back in time. We were in November and now we're in June. Today we're supposed to have a picnic at Brimham Rocks. Have Daniel and Izzy come back?'

'Daniel yes, Izzy no.'

'Oh no, perhaps they were not close together when he touched the timer. What about Izzy's parents?'

'Well, they don't live here so I don't know. I think if they were back, they would have rung by now.'

'Yes, I'm sure you're right. I just hope Izzy still has the timer and then they might all be able to get back.'

'I've yet to hear all of Daniel's story and he might know more. I'll let you know and make my apologies to Joanna about the picnic. Bye.'

Andy cleared up the kitchen, recycling all the packaging and putting cutlery and cups in the dishwasher and then turned as Daniel arrived, clean and looking much more himself, apart from his hair.

'You'll have a hard job explaining the length of your hair when you go to school tomorrow. As far as school's concerned you've only been away the weekend. I'll get some scissors and see you in the garden.'

Daniel picked up a tea towel and went and sat in a garden chair. It was warm, birds were singing and everything looked neat and tidy; the trimmed lawn and weedless flower beds so different from Victorian times. He realised he could smell the roses and there were no pungent smells like horse dung, cow dung or unwashed bodies. He lifted his face to the sun and began to relax.

Andy arrived wielding scissors and he succumbed to a haircut. When he'd finished Andy said, 'Now sir, would you look in the mirror and see how you like it.' He was holding up Izzy's hand mirror and Daniel grimaced at his reflection.

'That's terrible! I think it might be better if you use your hair clippers and make it extra short all over. I can start a new trend at school.'

'OK.' Dad went indoors and returned with the clippers. He went all over Daniel's head and had to admit himself it looked much better. Daniel said he was happy and they went back indoors.

'Let's sit in the living room, in comfortable chairs and you can tell me all your adventures.'

'OK, but I don't want to tell Uncle Xen or anyone else. Once I've told you I want to try and get my head around going to school tomorrow.'

When they were sat, feet raised, Andy said, 'So, fire away.'

Daniel did his best to describe the long walk to Blackberry Farm and Joe's appearance at the cottage door with a shotgun. Then the kindness he and Mary showed him and so on. Dad listened and reacted with laughter, gasps of surprise and sadness when Daniel cried when telling him about Joe's death.

Finally, Daniel talked of his delight at meeting Mum and how he had looked in her bag and found the sand timer. He went on to talk about his strange dream of walking by the river and finding Nathaniel dangerously close to falling in the river.

'That was not a dream, Daniel. You really did save that lad from drowning. That was what the timer wanted you to do.'

'How do you know that? Have you travelled in time?'

'No but I know a lot of people who have, Granddad and Grandma, your Mum, Xen and Ruby.'

'Ruby? I know about the others but not her.'

'No, Ruby touched the timer when she was seven, and warned us not to go anywhere that day. In doing so she saved Mum's life. Xen, some time later, used the portal at Brimham and took us all back five years so Ruby has no knowledge of what she did.'

'That's so weird.'

'Yes, and all that talking must have given you a thirst. I'll order some coffee?' They heard the coffee machine burbling and hissing. When the noises stopped, Daniel filled two cups and sat down again. He took a sip of the hot frothy liquid and sighed with contentment. 'I really missed frothy coffee. But I suppose after drinking so much of it I'll probably miss mulled ale.'

'You drank ale, alcohol?'

Daniel grinned. 'Yes, loads. At first it made me feel funny, but I got used to it and could easily drink two tankards without feeling any effect.'

'That's not legal now so you'll have to miss it.'

'I know but it was often a choice between ale or milk. Which would you prefer?' He knew his dad didn't like milk and they both laughed.

Dad then suggested they went to Grandma and Granddad's house to look at her family tree stored on a very old computer. 'We could see then if Nathaniel lived a long life.'

They stepped outside and walked towards the car, but Daniel asked if they could walk. 'I'm really used to walking, but I can drive a horse and cart too. Did I tell you that?'

They chatted as they walked. Dad told him about Mum taking up sailing and introducing Ruby to it. He talked about how his absorbing job at the research laboratory had helped him cope when everyone he loved was away.

When they reached the house, Dad used the key to let them in and they went straight to the study. He put the computer on and was soon scrolling back on the family tree. There was Major Carstairs married to Jane and their son Nathaniel lived until he was sixty-five. He married but had no children.

'Last time we looked at this,' said Dad. 'Nathaniel died in 1859. You really did save his life.'

Chapter 30

1859

Catherine and Jason unpacked their few belongings and went straight back downstairs. They had had no breakfast and nothing to drink at all that day and now it was lunchtime. The smells were intoxicating. Jason ordered four tankards of ale and a meal each. Sam brought them to a table near George, carrying all four with practised skill. 'It seems you have a thirst on you. Have you come far this morning?'

'Just from Lime Bank Hall and it was a lovely day for a walk.'

'If you've been to Lime Bank, then perhaps you know Mr Hancock sitting behind you, steward of the estate.' They both turned to look at George who nodded and they nodded back. 'No, we've not met him,' said Jason.

'Right, well, lunch will be ready soon, enjoy the ale.'

They drank thirstily and when one tankard was finished, they began to talk quietly, in case George could hear them. 'What are we going to do now? Daniel's not here because we're back in June. He was the whole reason we came. I wonder if he found the sand timer. If he did, why didn't we return too?'

Catherine shrugged before answering. 'It's possible we may be stuck here, in the past, until we die. In which case we are desperately poor. We cannot afford to stay here more than a night or two.'

Jason sighed, 'Perhaps there's a cottage we could rent. If we self-catered it would be cheaper than eating out all the time.' Catherine said nothing because their lunch arrived, a large plate of rich stew with a small loaf of bread between them. Jason broke off a piece of bread and then George stood and came to their table. He bowed and they stayed sat but bowed back.

'Please forgive my impertinence but I heard you say you might be looking for a cottage. If you decide then please contact me. Here's my card. Enjoy your lunch. Good day.'

'Well, if it comes to that, we know where to go but we still need an income,' said Jason.

'I've just had an idea. Daniel was a scribe and he worked for Mr Hancock. He wrote letters for the illiterate tenants who farmed Jane and Cecil's land. You could do that.'

Jason mopped up his gravy with the last of the bread before replying. He burped, apologised, and then said he thought that would be a good idea. They drank the rest of the ale and then decided to go for a walk. When they had arrived in 1859, the market had been closed due to smallpox, but now it was open.

They strolled arm in arm looking at the varied goods on each stall. Many of the fresh food stalls were nearly empty, most of the customers having come in the morning. Some traders were even loading what little remained on to their carts.

Catherine paused at one selling candles and candle holders, but Jason said their finances couldn't run to it. She made a face, remembering just how dingy their bedroom at the inn was. The smell of horse dung mingled with unwashed bodies, newly baked bread and salty bacon. There was a fresh meat stall crawling with flies being ineffectually wafted away by the owner. The stench of blood there eclipsed all other odours. Catherine hoped Sam had his delivered direct from the farm. She wondered how people stayed healthy when general hygiene was so poor. She thought about her great-grandmother saying, 'You have to eat a peck of dirt before you die.' How much weight was a peck?

Towards the end of the market was Mary and Joe's stall. They were smiling and chatting to customers and other stallholders. When Joe saw Catherine and Jason had stopped at his stall, he greeted them with the same cheery smile. 'Good afternoon, can I serve you with anything?'

'I'd like that loaf and a slice off that cheese,' said Catherine pointing to each. Jason looked at her in surprise but said nothing. Joe positioned the cheese wire and looked enquiringly at Catherine. She motioned with her hand to make it less and he moved the wire a tiny amount. She smiled and nodded. Jason paid and Mary wrapped the cheese in cheese cloth and gave it to Catherine. 'Thank you,' they said in unison and laughed.

As they walked away Jason said, 'I thought we agreed to be frugal and not spend any money.'

'This is being frugal. It's our picnic tea and will surely cost less than a meal at the inn.'

164

'Well before I can eat anything, I need a long walk. Coming?' Catherine grinned and they walked along the road towards Harrogate.

'I know it's too far to walk all the way to Harrogate before tea, but I'd really like to see it now, in Victorian times. There would be many buildings we'd recognise all looking new and clean, not grey and polluted with a hundred and sixty years of traffic filth.'

'Yes, but I don't suppose we'll have a reason or the money to go there. I think I will have to call on Mr Hancock tomorrow and assume this is how our lives will stay. If we had the timer, we might find a way back, but I assume that disappeared after Daniel had saved Nathaniel.'

'Another thing we could do is call on Jane and Cecil and introduce ourselves all over again. I'd like it if they let us stay again. I'm not looking forward to having no baths and using a chamber pot in the night.'

'Yes, we could. Meanwhile I'm now peckish and looking forward to home-baked bread and proper farmhouse cheese.' They looked around for a suitable place to picnic and saw an oak tree offering shade just a few yards from the road. There seemed to be no occupants of the field, no sheep, goats or cows, nor did it have any crops. It was a meadow with wildflowers nodding in the gentle breeze.

'Perfect,' said Catherine, 'Will you go over the fence first and then help me?'

The fence was not high, and Jason could almost step right over it. When he was on the other side he waited while Catherine looked up and down the road then hitched up her skirt and petticoat and climbed up and over. They walked to the oak tree and sat in the shade then shared the cheese and bread which was delicious.

'It's a pity we didn't think of buying a drink too,' said Jason lying down, his arms bent up supporting his head. 'But drink or not this is such a beautiful place. Just listen, nothing but bees humming and birds - look isn't that a skylark?'

Catherine looked up and then joined him lying back, her head resting on one of his arms. 'It is. It's climbing higher and higher, almost out of sight but we can still hear it. I think they've become extinct in our time, such a shame; it's a really joyous sound.' She shut her eyes, listening and fell asleep. Jason could hear her gentle breathing and lay still. He shut his eyes too but could not relax enough to sleep. He was thirsty and worried about money. If he agreed to rent a cottage, he was not sure if they could afford their bill at the inn. More than anything he longed for the ease and comfort of their old life.

Jason allowed Catherine to sleep until she woke naturally but then he moved his cramped arm from under her, despite her protests and stood up. 'Come on sleepy head, you must be as thirsty as me and we still have to walk back.'

Catherine grinned, rubbed her eyes and got up stiffly. They scaled the fence again and set off back towards the village. Carts going home from the market passed them, the drivers waving cheerily.

As they neared the village, they saw a lone woman walking towards them. When they got nearer Jason nodded to her and said, 'Good afternoon,' then he stopped abruptly.

*

Izzy stepped out of the inn door and breathed in deeply. The sun shone, the market was busy and despite the uncertainty of her future her heart lifted. If she had sacrificed herself to a life in Victorian times so Daniel could go back, it was worth it. She imagined him with Andy hugging so hard they couldn't stop, just as she had when she met Daniel here. Her dreaming ceased when a cart rumbled past, the horse snorting and its hooves clattering on the cobbles.

Izzy had made up her mind before leaving the inn. She was going to visit Jane and Major Carstairs at Lime Bank Hall. Now she had to ask directions. Looking around she ignored men, surely a lady in this era would not approach a man. It had to be a woman and there was one just turning away from a stall. She was placing a punnet of strawberries carefully in her basket. 'Excuse me. Could you direct me to Lime Bank Hall?'

'Going for a position, are you? Well, if you walk that way then take the first lane on the left, you'll come to the back of the house. Good luck.' She turned away. Izzy thanked her, not allowing her irritation to sound in her voice. How could she possibly mistake her for a servant? She had believed she was dressed as a lady. What would Jane think of her if she arrived looking like a servant girl. Should she knock on the back door or boldly knock on the front? It was a less confident Izzy that set off towards Lime Bank Hall.

A cart rumbled up behind her and Izzy stepped onto the verge until it had gone. She was feeling warm now and wished she had less clothes on. As she stepped back onto the road, she saw a couple walking towards her arm in arm. She envied them their happiness, obviously comfortable together and she thought again of Andy. If she got home, would he forgive her for leaving him without explanation?

The couple were getting closer and the man wished her good afternoon. She had passed them but then stopped. They had stopped too and turned round. Suddenly she became a little girl again, who had lost her mummy and daddy, and she rushed to cuddle them both.

Tears ran down Catherine's cheeks as she said, 'Izzy, Izzy what are you doing here?'

Izzy wiped her eyes with her sleeve. 'I wanted to come, I was missing you and Daniel so much. I tried so hard to get on with my life, but then I started buying old money, hired some outfits. Then I found the sand timer, so I didn't hesitate. I only got here yesterday; no, it was November. Oh, you know what I mean. I met Daniel and then, when I was asleep, he must have used the timer. I felt so bleak when I realised he'd gone. I didn't know what to do so I decided to visit Jane and Major Carstairs. Then, before I got there, I met you.' Tears ran down her face again.

Jason offered her a handkerchief. It had a monogrammed *C* in one corner, and he felt guilty knowing it was one of Cecil's. 'Come on back to the inn. We're both desperate for a drink and we can talk there. I think Mum would prefer to be sitting rather than talking in the street.'

Izzy nodded, sniffed and they walked the short distance back to the inn. It was very noisy and crowded as men drank away their earnings at the market that day. Jason told Sam they would drink their ale in their room as it was so busy, so he placed the tankards on a tray and Jason carried them upstairs. At the top he hesitated. 'What room are you in Izzy?'

'Six.'

'Good, let's go to yours; it's a lot bigger than ours.' Izzy squeezed past him to open the door. Catherine went straight to the chair and sighed as she sat. The others perched on the beds.

'Have you still got the timer, Izzy?' said Jason after nearly downing his drink in one go.

'Yes. It's in that bag by the window.'

'Good. We need to formulate some kind of plan to get back home. Before we do that, I need another drink. Can I get you another?' Both women nodded and he went back to the bar.

While he was away Catherine told Izzy about their stay with Jane and Cecil and their calm acceptance when told they came from the future.

'It was much more comfortable than here. We had our own bathroom with flush toilet and bath. Oh, before Dad gets back, I must tell you he's very worried about money. He's almost none left and everything we're ordering here is on tick. Have you got much?'

'I'll have a look.' As she was tipping her coins onto the bed Dad arrived with another tray of drinks. 'I've ordered dinner and Sam said it'll be ready in about half an hour. Izzy that looks a healthy heap of coins. At least if we stick by you, we can still eat for a few days. Have you ladies made a plan?'

'No, said Izzy. 'We were waiting for you.'

Chapter 31

2048

Daniel dressed in his school uniform and looked ruefully at the length of the trousers. They were also uncomfortably tight. He'd enjoyed the food and ale in 1859 but he ate far more bread than in his own time.

At breakfast, healthy cereal and fruit, he asked Dad if he would order some larger trousers. This was normally Izzy's department, so Dad frowned. 'How do I order it and what size should I get?' Daniel showed him the label on his trousers, and they agreed one size and length higher should be enough and Daniel knew the website.

'I could do it myself but then I'd have to pay for it,' he said grinning.

'I'll do it now and then I must go to work. Mum's usually the last to leave and locks up. You'll have to do that.' He stood up, picked up his briefcase, then came round to Daniel and gave him a hug before leaving. 'Good luck with your first day back at school.'

Daniel looked at the messages on his phone. He'd been having chats with friends who were complaining he'd ignored them all weekend. He apologised but avoided making up lies to explain it, although Dad said they'd have to say Mum was ill to explain why she was not at work.

Daniel approached the school gates with some anxiety but when he met friends none of them remarked on his short trousers or his height. In lessons he found he'd forgotten some things and the maths teacher was cross. 'What's wrong with you today? We only did this last Thursday and you've forgotten already.' He then explained it all again and Daniel listened, feeling upset because he couldn't say it was six months ago and a lot had happened to him in that time.

The lesson he enjoyed most, apart from gym, was history. They were learning about the first world war and the lesson was

169

on screen. There was no teacher present for these types of lessons, but cameras ensured they concentrated and did not play about.

The type of money used in that time was explained and Daniel felt excited. He understood pounds, shillings and pence while the other students were finding it difficult. They had to add up some sums of money as a written task and Daniel found it easy.

'I don't get it,' said Sadi. 'Whoever thought it made sense to use base twelve and then base twenty and then there's farthings and halfpennies? It's stupid.' Daniel felt smug. He finished the task in record time and thought there had been one good outcome of Victorian experiences.

When he got home, he felt bleak entering the house. Dad would not be home for over an hour and it was very quiet. Then the games console bleeped. He changed out of his uniform and started to play. He was still there when Dad came home.

'Have you done your homework?' Daniel's eyes didn't leave the screen, as he shook his head.

'In that case you'd better stop playing and make an effort.' Daniel pulled a face but did as he was told.

'Sorry, it's just so good to be back, feeling normal and doing all the things I used to do.'

'I understand that. You've had some R and R, so now get on with your homework while I cook dinner.'

Daniel stood and stretched then went into the kitchen and hugged Dad. 'I'm so glad to be home. What's for dinner?'

*

1859

'I think the first thing we should do is keep together. To this end I told Sam we were not going to use our room but would sleep in here with you. What do you think?' asked Jason.

'It seems you have made that decision anyway, so the question is pointless,' said Catherine.

'That means I have to have the single bed,' said Izzy. She made a rueful face and took her nightdress from under one of the pillows and threw it on the other bed.

'Sorry, I should have asked you both before I spoke to Sam. Shall I go back and say I've changed my mind?'

'No,' they said in chorus and giggled.

'Just talk to us first before making any more decisions. You're behaving like a Victorian gentleman; as if the opinion of women is worthless,' said Catherine.

'I've got the point, sorry again. Shall we collect our things from number 3?' Catherine nodded and got up stiffly.

Izzy had been sitting on the double bed. When they'd gone, she moved to the single one, laid down, sighed and closed her eyes. She felt safe now Mum and Dad were here. She knew she should be thinking of a plan, but she was so tired.

When Jason and Catherine returned with their clothes, she was deeply asleep. They unpacked quietly but Catherine knew it was close to their booked dinner so she would have to wake Izzy now. She squeezed between the beds and stood for a moment looking down at her. She was still her little girl and she loved her so much. She had tears in her eyes and her voice cracked as she said, 'Izzy you have to wake up now. It's time for dinner.'

Izzy's eyes flicked open and then shut. She sighed, opened her eyes again and said, 'In my dream I was at home hugging Andy and Daniel. It's so hard waking up and finding us still here. Did you say it was dinner time?' She sat up. 'I can smell it, roast lamb, I think. Hope there's mint sauce.' She stood and ran her fingers through her hair. She looked at Mum, 'Do I need to brush it?'

'No pet, it looks fine. Let's go down.'

The bar was shockingly loud, raucous laughter, back-slapping with many men drunk. When Sam saw the family coming down the stairs he pointed to a table in a corner. The ladies sat down while Jason went to the bar.

'Good evening, Sir. What can I get you?'

'Three tankards of ale and three dinners please.'

'Right you are. Food'll take about ten minutes, an' I'll bring it over.' Sam poured the drinks and Jason carefully carried them to the table. He sat down, took a deep drink and said, 'That's a good brew.'

Catherine frowned and said, loudly, 'Can't hear you above the din.' They all drank in silence watching the scene, and heard voices raised now in anger. A man stood up his chair scraping on the flagstone. He'd balled a fist and was threatening to use it.

'Now, Jack, we'll have none of that,' shouted Sam from behind the bar. Jack didn't seem to hear but everyone else did. The room quietened and the air was tense with anticipation. Jack looked around at all the eyes upon him and sheepishly lowered his fist. He pulled his cap onto his head and made an unsteady exit. There was a collective sigh, some feeling relieved, and others disappointed there'd been no fight.

Sam plated their dinners and carried two to their table, placing them in front of the ladies. 'You did well, Sam; there could've been a fight,' said Jason.

Sam grinned, 'Well I knew there were ladies present. Anyhow I didn't want my chairs broke. Would you like more drinks?' Jason nodded and the women shook their heads, murmuring, 'No thank you.'

Sam returned with another drink and a dinner for Jason then went back to the bar. When he had moved away Jason tucked into his dinner and there was no conversation until they were all replete.

'That was filling and delicious. I've been thinking. Shall we turn the timer tonight, go to bed and see what happens?'

Catherine and Izzy both nodded and then Izzy said, 'It might take us home but if it doesn't, I hope we don't go into winter again.'

The evening was still warm, so they had a short stroll around the village then back to their room. When the women were in bed Jason turned the timer over. They all watched the sand run through then settled down to sleep.

In the morning Catherine opened her eyes and was miserable to find them all still in the past. Light was filtering around the edges of the curtains, so it seemed likely they were still in the summer. It was very quiet, but she thought the smell of bacon was wafting from the kitchen below.

Jason stirred next and she heard him sigh. 'We're still here then.'

'Yes, Izzy's going to be upset when she wakes. I had a really vivid dream. We were all at Brimham Rocks. You turned the timer over. There was an explosion, and I woke up.'

Jason sat up. 'My dream was similar, but it was not so much an explosion as an earthquake. How odd we both had the same dream. Do you think it's significant?' In his excitement Jason had forgotten to keep his voice quiet and woke Izzy.

'I hoped so much last night I'd wake up at home. What are we going to do?'

'Can you remember dreaming?' asked Catherine.

'Mmm, we were all at Brimham Rocks and there was a big bang.'

Jason looked at Catherine and raised his eyebrows. Simultaneously they got up, had the briefest of washes and got dressed.

Izzy flounced over in bed. 'What's all the hurry? I'm going back to sleep.'

'We're going downstairs to order breakfast and we want you down with us in ten minutes,' said Jason.

'Why. I'm not moving until you explain.'

'We all had the same dream, Izzy, so we think we should go to Brimham Rocks this morning. The timer is telling us what to do.'

Izzy sat up, alert now. 'OK, I'll be down in ten.'

During breakfast they talked about what they should take with them to Brimham. Izzy said it was a long walk, looked like being another warm day so she voted to carry nothing. Then if the plan didn't work, they could return to the inn. Catherine agreed but Jason wasn't so sure.

'I agree in the main, but I think we need to keep the sand timer with us. Was the timer in either of your dreams?'

'No, I don't remember it,' said Izzy.

'It was in mine,' said Catherine.

'It was in mine. I turned it upside down just before the earthquake.' The women looked at him and Catherine said, 'This

173

is beginning to feel exciting. The sand timer must, obviously, come with us. Let's get our bonnets on and get going.'

Chapter 32

Long before the family had left the inn, George and Cecil were deep in the woods moving stealthily looking for poachers. The day before, George had found the remains of a small deer, namely its head with tiny antlers just sprouting. Any predatory animal would never be so precise. It had to be poachers and George was determined to find them. He never worried about the locals snaring rabbits. Rabbits caused no end of damage to vegetable plots and he didn't begrudge poachers having a free meal of stewed rabbit. Venison was different.

They had reached the area where the remains had been found and paused. They stood still, listening intently for anything other than the buzz of insects. Everything was quiet, there were no birds singing or flying with flapping wings. The wood had an atmosphere as if, like them, it was holding its breath.

The gunshot was shockingly loud. Birds took to the air in alarm and Cecil and George ran between the trees, jumping fallen branches making no effort now to keep quiet.

There were three poachers, and they were kneeling around the still twitching body of a stag. One was trying to hack off the antlers while the others were tying the legs to a sturdy pole.

'Hurry, Pete we must get going. Someone might've heard the shot.' As he said that Pete held up one antler, the bloody end dripping. He threw it behind him and began on the other. They were all so intent on what they were doing they jumped in fright when Cecil shouted at them.

'Bloody thieves, scurvy poachers. This is my land and that's my stag.'

He might have said more but these men were not going to be prosecuted if they could help it. They stood up, slowly looking at George and Cecil and then began to run. Pete turned, fired a shot in their direction and then ran after the others.

'After them,' said George, firing his shotgun in response. He turned to see if Cecil was going to give chase, but he was face down in the leaf mould. 'Oh my God, Cecil. Cecil, speak to me.' As he said that he pulled Cecil over onto his back and wiped the debris from his face. There was no response. The shot had punched a hole in his chest. Blood was pumping out. George kept saying Cecil's name but knew there was never going to be a response. His master, his friend, was dead.

George gathered Cecil into his arms and cried, rocking him as he might a child. As his sobs abated the shock lessened and he began to feel angry. He would recognise those poachers and see they were brought to justice. He even knew one of their names, Pete. Pete had taken Cecil's life and he was going to hang for it.

George shifted and placed Cecil's head gently on the ground. He stood stiffly, then picked up his gun and walked to the Elliots' cottage. It was the closest and he knew Mr Elliot had a brawny son and owned a cart.

An hour later Cecil's body and that of the stag were side by side on the cart.

'We'll take the stag back to your place and you can have the meat and share it with others as you wish. I'll take Major Carstairs' body to the Hall.' George spoke with the weariness and depression he felt.

When they reached the cottage, Mrs Elliot came out to pay her respects and help with the unloading of the carcass. She also placed a sheet over the body. They were all silent for a moment with heads bowed and then George got up on the cart and set off on the worst mission of his life, to break the news to Jane.

*

Unaware of the drama that had happened, Jason, Catherine and Izzy had stopped walking. They estimated they were quite close to Brimham Rocks, but it was uphill, the sun was overhead and very hot.

'I've just got to have a sit down and a moment to regain some energy. It must be about lunchtime and I'm flagging, blood sugar down. I'd give anything for a chocolate bar and a cold drink,' said Catherine.

'I can't produce a chocolate bar but can offer a drink. I'm surprised you hadn't heard it sloshing about in my holdall. Mind you I stuffed a shirt around it because I was worried about damaging the timer.' Jason undid the straps of the bag and produced a pottery flagon. 'I asked Sam after breakfast what I could carry on a walk to quench our thirst and he gave me this. When I say gave, he did note it down on our tab. I've no idea whether it's water, ale or even wine.' He pulled the cork and sniffed the contents. 'Some kind of beer but it doesn't smell the same as the ale we normally drink.'

He handed the bottle to Catherine who drank thirstily then handed it on to Izzy. Izzy drank a gulp and made a face but had another before passing it back to Jason. He glugged a lot before putting the stopper back on, wiping his mouth on his sleeve and grinning at them. 'Not bad, but I prefer Sam's ale on tap. Are you ready to move on?'

'Yes,' said Catherine, 'but I could do with a helping hand.' Izzy pulled her up and Jason stood, after carefully packing the flagon back into his bag.

'When we get to Brimham what, exactly, do you think we should do?' asked Izzy.

'I'm open to suggestions,' said Jason, careful not to impose his idea, 'But, what about standing on top of the portal and then turning the timer upside down. After that wait and see what happens.'

'Doesn't the timer work mostly when you're asleep? I know we'll all be tired after the walk but I'm not sure I can sleep on a rock in the daytime,' said Izzy.

'I could sleep right now,' said Catherine. 'But the experiences we've had with the timer means anything can happen. The timer is in charge. I haven't got a better idea, so let's try that.'

About half an hour later they arrived at Brimham to find it busy with tourists. A man was acting as guide and talking about the rock formations, encouraging people to see recognisable shapes in them.

Jason, Catherine and Izzy stood well away from the small crowd. 'I didn't expect this,' said Catherine. 'When we arrived here there were no tourists.'

'There were none when I came but it was in the middle of a snowstorm,' said Izzy. 'Shall we move from these people and see if we can find another route to the portal?'

They walked quietly away until the strident voice of the guide became just a distant murmur then looked for possible tracks between the rocks and began to climb amongst them going uphill. When they thought they were at the right height they turned to go to the cliff edge, and there it was. The flat-topped rock, with the beautiful view across the valley, looked so innocuous. It was hard to believe it had any power at all.

'We seem to be well away from the tourists so shall we make a start?'

'Just a minute, Dad, I must find my sail bag. I hid it under a rock. It's got my clothes in it and my solafone. Izzy bent down peering under fissures and then said, 'I can't find it. I was sure I'd squashed it under this rock.'

'I know why you can't find it,' said Jason. 'You arrived in 1859 in a snowstorm in November. Daniel used the timer and put the whole world back to June. That sail bag is probably still in Phil's garage. He hasn't yet offered you the chance to use his Enterprise.'

'Oh, I never thought of that. So, I won't have been sailing with Ruby, or be known at the club when I get home. This time travelling really messes with your head, doesn't it?' Izzy settled on to the rock with Mum and looked expectantly at Dad.

Jason opened his bag and brought out the sand timer. He knelt, turned it upside down and then sat. They all watched the sand fall. Nothing happened. There was no sound at all apart from a skylark's singing as it flew high, and insects buzzing among the wildflowers. They were all waiting for the loud bang or explosion that happened in the dream.

'Perhaps nothing happens until the sand has run completely through and that'll be several hours,' said Jason looking at Catherine and Izzy. They looked odd, shimmering. Then he could see through them at the rock behind. His heart pounded with fear as the two women he loved most in the whole world completely disappeared. He jumped to his feet shouting their names and then looked at his hands to see if they were shimmering, but they were solid, normal.

He was still in 1859 and alone.

Chapter 33

2048

Catherine felt nauseous. Her eyes were tight shut. Every muscle was tensed and to relax in anyway would cause pain. She was sitting hunched and was aware that whatever she was sitting on was hard. They'd been sitting on the rock. She listened. There were no bees buzzing, no skylark singing. It was very quiet. Taking a deep breath, she unscrewed her face and opened one eye. Coming into focus was her dishwasher. The realisation that she was at home, sitting on the kitchen floor, helped her relax. She opened both eyes wide and breathed, 'Oh, thank you, thank you God.'

It took Catherine a couple of attempts to stand up. It was eventually achieved by rolling onto her knees and levering herself using a chair. 'I'm getting too old to be hurtling through time.' She'd spoken out loud but knew neither Jason nor Izzy were with her. She went into all the rooms downstairs calling both their names but there was no response.

Upstairs was equally silent. The urge to pee was suddenly very strong and after that she ran a deep, hot bath. It was sheer heaven, she thought, soaking away the stress and cleaning off the filth of Victorian Britain. Before the water cooled too much Catherine washed her hair and found herself singing,

'I'm gonna wash that *time* right outa my hair,
I'm gonna wash that *time* right outa my hair
and send it on its way.'

When Catherine was dry and dressed in a comfortable track suit, she ordered a cup of tea and sat in her favourite armchair. She sipped it but it was still too hot for comfort. Her phone was at hand to ring Andy, but her eyes wanted to shut. She would do it in a minute. The warm bath, the long walk and stress of time travelling made her so sleepy.

Her tea was cold when she woke.

*

179

Izzy struggled up from her bathroom floor and reached the toilet in time to be sick. It was a noisy retching and she wondered why Andy or Daniel hadn't come to investigate. She stood up, washed her face and went downstairs. Where were they? Then it occurred to her they were probably at work and school respectively. In the kitchen the clock on just about every appliance showed it was 2.30 in the afternoon. 'Coffee please,' she said

'Good afternoon Izzy, coffee will be ready in 2.5 minutes.' Izzy smiled with delight to hear the familiar electronic voice. This was how one should live, no lighting fires and hanging kettles over them, or stoking a range. Just ask and things switch on and happen automatically. She would have to get up and remove the cup from the machine, but it was all so easy. While she was waiting, she looked through the window at the grey drizzly weather.

It's odd, she thought, I've travelled through all those years, arrived more or less at the same time of day, in the same month. Just the weather is different.

The coffee was ready. She sipped it and sent a text to Andy at work and Daniel at school. Solafones were not allowed at school but everyone took them and were eagerly using them as soon as they left the premises. Izzy felt hungry, opened the fridge and smiled to see cream cheese and smoked salmon. She made them into a sandwich and relished every mouthful, realising how basic the Victorian food had been. It was now 3pm and she wanted to shower and change into modern clothes before Daniel came home.

Her body felt light and free dressed in simple T-shirt and cotton trousers. She looked down at the clothes she'd been wearing piled in a heap on the floor; so cumbersome and hot. No wonder Victorian women were prone to swooning. She had not attempted to wear a corset but thought if one was pulled tight in a heat wave, a woman might die.

Izzy brought the clothes downstairs and put them in the washing machine. At some point she must take them back to the hire shop. It was June now and she hired it in the autumn to come.

As far as the hire shop was concerned Izzy had never been there. Perhaps it would be better to offer them to the local amateur dramatic group. Her reverie was broken by Daniel entering the front door, shouting, 'Mum?'

She went into the entrance hall where he was dumping his school bag and they hugged happily. There were no tears this time, just delight to be back together and everything normal again.

In the kitchen she called for tea and Daniel added, 'and a cold coke.'

'Tea in five minutes. Coke is poured,' intoned Shakespeare, the name they had given to their electronic slave.

'So how was going back to school?'

'Good. Great to see all my friends and no one mentioned my trousers had suddenly become too small.'

Izzy looked at his trousers, inches shorter than they should be. 'Has Dad ordered you some more?'

'Yes, they should be here any minute.' The front doorbell rang. 'That'll be it now.' Daniel collected the parcel and opened it on the table while Izzy drank her tea.

There were two pairs of long trousers, track suit bottoms and three T-shirts. When Izzy queried the shirts, he held out his arms to show her the one he was wearing, fitting too snugly.

'It seems I've not only grown taller but fat.' He grimaced and Izzy laughed.

'You're not at all fat. You've just lost that skinny kid look.'

'Are Grandma and Granddad back too?'

'I assume so, but I'll ring to make sure.' She took the phone into the living room so Daniel could have his drink in peace and returned five minutes later looking serious.

'What's up?' asked Daniel.

'Grandma's back but Granddad isn't.' She began to cry, and Daniel hugged her. 'I thought it was all over, everything back to normal and it's not.'

'Has Granddad still got the timer?'

'I don't know. He was the one who turned it over.' She pulled away from him and wiped her face and blew her nose on a tissue. It's so civilised to use tissues, she thought.

'Grandma will be feeling a bit lonely. Should we invite her over for dinner?'

'I did invite her, but she said she wanted to be at home in case Granddad came back.'

'You could suggest she leaves him a note and then entice her with something for dinner she will have really missed.'

Izzy went to the freezer and looked in the fish department. 'I really missed fish. We could have fish pie or fish and chips or a salad with cold salmon.'

'You decide, Mum, Grandma likes all of those.' She stood in thought and Daniel went to his bedroom with all his new clothes. He had changed when he came down and Izzy resisted the temptation to ask him if he had hung up his new uniform trousers. There was no point in treating him like the teenager he was, when he had behaved like an adult for six months.

'I sent Grandma a text,' he said. 'She couldn't resist a fish dinner and will be here at six thirty. She wants to give you time to see Dad before she arrives.'

Andy came home an hour later and rushed to Izzy, putting his arms around her and telling her how much he'd missed her. Then he pulled Daniel into a group cuddle and when they moved apart, they all had tears of joy streaking their cheeks.

Chapter 34

1859

Jason sat on the rock hardly able to believe Catherine and Izzy had gone back to their own time. He felt he should wait until they came back but knew that was illogical. There was no choice. He had to walk back to the inn. With a deep sigh he got wearily to his feet, picked up the bag with the flagon and sand timer and set off.

He felt he'd trudged for days. He had always tried to keep healthy and up until recently had continued to run every day. Then his knees had begun to complain, and he'd stopped. That's what happens when you get old, he supposed. The sun was still shining but getting low in the sky by the time he got back and entered the inn. He went straight to the bar and ordered two ales. He then dragged the flagon out of his bag and asked if it was usual to have it refilled.

'I buy them filled up but there's no reason why I can't give it a rinse and put the ordinary ale in it. Do you want me to do that now?'

'No, but if I go for another long walk it would be useful.'

'No ladies with you?'

'We met some friends and they've gone to stay with them. There wasn't room for me but I'm happier staying here.' It went against the grain to lie but Jason couldn't see any other way. He could hardly say, 'My wife and daughter used a portal and went back to two thousand and forty-eight.'

Sitting down felt glorious after the long walk and several deep draughts of ale made the situation less depressing. He still had the timer. He had enough money because Izzy had given him all her coins. The problem was what to do next?

He could go and visit Clive and Jane, explain all over again about travelling through time. If they invited him to stay with them it would be much more comfortable than here. Jason was feeling really hungry having eaten nothing since breakfast. He went to Sam and asked if he could make him something.

'Bread, cheese and a chunk of ham with some pickles?'

'That sounds perfect. Thanks.'

Sam said he would bring it to his table when it was ready, and Jason went back to his second tankard of ale. When the food arrived, he wanted to stuff it in as quickly as he could, but he was supposed to be a gentleman, so he tried to eat steadily, not greedily.

Jason had just finished his meal when George Hancock entered, went straight to the bar without acknowledging anybody and ordered a brandy. Sam's bushy eyebrows raised a little when George drained his glass in one go and asked for another, and an ale.

'Something wrong, George?' he asked and stopped filling the tankard when George said, 'Poachers!' They've shot Major Carstairs. He's dead.'

There was silence in the room. George had spoken loudly, and everyone knew of Major Carstairs. Most of the people in the room worked for him. They were all waiting to hear the whole story and they were not disappointed. When he'd finished George turned to all the people in the room and said, 'If any of you know these poachers, I want you to tell me. They should hang for this.'

'Probably not local, out o' towners if you ask me.' There was a murmur of agreement to Jack's words. 'They'll not dare come back.'

'I want all of you to spread the word about this. Someone must know who they are.' The voices were angrier now as they shouted, 'Aye,' and 'They should pay for what they done.'

George looked around at all the faces, caught Jason's eye and took his ale to sit with him.

'I'm truly sorry about Major Carstairs.'

George nodded, his expression grim. 'I should've shot first. They were running away, I never thought one would turn and shoot at us. I've never been a soldier, never killed a man.'

'Nor have I, Mr Hancock and I don't think you should blame yourself. How is Mrs Carstairs?'

'Devastated, as you would expect. I left her sobbing, holding poor little Nathaniel who didn't understand. Emily was trying to comfort her mistress, but she seemed just as affected. I went to see the rector and he said he would go to comfort Mrs Carstairs. That was a great relief. Then I went to the undertaker. I couldn't organise a date or any details but at least he could begin making the coffin. I'm sorry, Mr ...?'

'Brownlow.'

'Yes, Mr Brownlow, it must be the brandy making me talk so much.'

'I think you're still shocked by what's happened, so please, don't apologise. Can I get you another brandy or ale?'

'Yes, please. One of each. I'm not a great drinker but tonight I'd like to get drunk.'

'Did you have lunch?'

'No.'

'Then I think I'll get you a plate of bread and cheese too.'

Several hours later, when everyone else had gone home to bed, George had become a maudlin wreck, crying and blaming himself for Clive's death. Jason felt quite drunk himself but managed to get up and go to speak to Sam.

'I don't think George's fit to walk home. Can he have a bed here tonight?'

'Yes, but I wonder, Sir, if you'd give me a hand wiv' 'im? He's a big'un.'

Jason left Sam pulling off George's boots and went unsteadily to his own room. He shut the door after lighting a candle and looked bleakly around. There were dresses and bonnets, and nightdresses under the pillows. He missed them so much. He sat down on the edge of the bed and pulled off a boot. Tears began to flow unchecked down his face. He knew it was because he was drunk and because he'd spent the evening with a totally depressed man, but he couldn't stop. By the time he'd yanked off the second boot he was sobbing. He undressed and pulled on his nightshirt.

Jason pulled back the covers and got into bed. He should go to sleep easily. He'd walked miles, after all. But every time he turned over the room swam. He sat up, fighting nausea, waiting for the room to be still and began to think.

Cecil must have died before they got to Brimham Rocks. That was why the timer hadn't let him go. If he used the timer, it would take him back in time to prevent Cecil's death. Then he'd wake up at home.

Flinging the covers back he stood up carefully and went to his bag thrown onto the single bed. He fumbled with the straps then took out the timer and turned it upside down. He stood it on the mantlepiece then blew out the candle and went back to bed.

Chapter 35

The ground was soft and damp beneath Jason's bare feet, but he trod warily fearing twigs, stones or worse, brambles. Shafts of early sunlight gave the leaves on the trees a brilliance, glossy with dew. Birds were busy flitting, grabbing the early worm or unsuspecting grubs. Had this been an ordinary walk he would have rejoiced, his heart full of the glory around him. But he could hear rough voices.

'The quicker we get 'im tied ont' pole the quicker we can git. Hurry with them antlers Pete.'

The poachers were directly in front of him. Jason froze, uncertain what to do. The odds were not good. If they looked in his direction, they'd see him. He moved stealthily behind a large tree, his heart thumping. He knew what was going to happen but had no idea how to prevent it. Perhaps he could trip the man who turned and fired. Not a good idea in bare feet. Tackle him then with all his weight so any shot went askew. Hit him with a stick. He looked around for anything stout enough to be a weapon. There was nothing.

Cecil was shouting. The men were moving, running, but not in his direction. He wasn't close enough to achieve anything and then the shot. Birds rose into the air squawking. Then all he could hear was George's lament.

Jason woke. He was on top of the bed and feeling chilly, so he went under the blanket and tucked it around him. He'd failed to help Cecil and he needed to think what to do. Perhaps he could ask George to take him into the woods and show him exactly where the poachers had been. How would that help? Perhaps he could spend the night at that spot, use the timer, knowing he was in the correct place.

The whole idea was daft. The timer took him from his bed to the woods. The timer knew exactly the place. If Jason was to go back the next night, he had to be prepared. He would go to bed fully clothed, with his boots on and take a weapon.

At that thought he fell asleep waking only when there was a knock at his door.

'Come in,' he called, and a maid peeped around the door.

'I'm sorry to disturb you, Sir. Hope I didn't wake you. Mr Hancock is asking for you. He's having breakfast, Sir.'

'Give me five minutes and I'll be ready.' Jason sat up feeling a headache behind his eyes and went to the washstand. The cold water refreshed him and when he'd washed his body, he put the basin on the floor and put both feet in it. He sucked in the air with the cold and saw, with disgust, floating bits of leaf and twig rise up. When his feet were clean and dry, he pulled back the covers revealing a very grimy sheet. Some of the leafy bits he swept onto the floor but left the sheet exposed, hoping the maid would change it.

Whenever he left home to go out Catherine always reminded him to check he had his keys, a tissue and phone. He could hear her in his mind and put his purse in his pocket. How he longed to have a phone and be able to ring her.

When Jason went downstairs George was wiping his plate with the last of his bread. His hangover had not seemed to diminish his appetite. He gestured to Jason to sit with him.

'I want to thank you for drinking with me last night and organising my stay here. How are you feeling this morning?'

'Just a bit of a headache. Some breakfast and fresh air later will help.'

'I'll treat you to your breakfast if you'll help me today.'

'You don't have to bribe me to help. I'm happy to do whatever I can.'

'It was not a bribe. A thank you for being a friend when I needed it.' He signalled to Sam and in a few minutes a large, cooked breakfast arrived for Jason. While he was eating George outlined his plan.

'I would like you to walk with me to the site of Major Carstairs' murder. The poachers ran off and I wondered if, in their haste they'd dropped anything. Another pair of eyes searching the area would help.'

'I'm happy to be another pair of eyes.' Jason hesitated, unsure how to say what was on his mind. He decided to just say it. 'One of the poachers is called Pete.'

George sat back in his chair, looking at Jason with an incredulous expression. 'How can you possibly know that? You weren't there.'

Jason smiled, 'I went there last night in a dream. One of the men asked Pete to hurry cutting off the antlers.'

George wiped his hands over his face and spoke slowly. 'I don't think I told everyone about cutting off the antlers, when I related the story. I don't understand, but if it's true, that could be really useful.'

Jason had finished his meal and stood up. 'Are you ready to go to the woods now?'

'Yes. I'll just go and pay what I owe to Sam.'

'I'll fetch my hat and meet you outside.' Jason went back to his room and saw the maid had cleaned his filthy bowl and made the bed. He picked up his hat and went back downstairs an idea formulating in his mind.

*

2048

Catherine stretched and then relaxed, turning over to look at the clock. Too early to get up but she had no sleep left in her. If she got up early, normally, Jason would moan at her to come back to bed because he didn't want to get up. But there was no Jason, so she threw back the covers, pulled on her dressing gown and went downstairs. She ordered tea, ready in five minutes, and stood thinking about the night before. It had been such a warm, happy evening with Andy, Izzy and Daniel. They were delighted to be reunited and included her in their euphoria. The meal was one of her favourite dishes and she felt a glow as she remembered it all.

The tea was ready. She took it into the living room to sit in her favourite chair. While sipping it gingerly she remembered something. Izzy said when she'd come to water the plants, she'd looked at the family tree and saw Nathaniel had died in 1859. She'd asked if Catherine had looked at it since she came home. She hadn't but decided to do it now.

She carried the hot tea into the study and started up the old computer. She scrolled back on the family tree and saw Nathaniel had lived a long life. Daniel would be pleased, she thought. She idly looked above Nathaniel to Jane and Cecil and saw another change. Major Carstairs had died in 1859.

'That's why Jason hasn't come home. The timer wants him to save Cecil's life, again. I must tell Izzy.' Catherine sent a text, then sat back, finished her tea and remembered the last time Jason had been a hero.

The timer had transported Jason to a field hospital in Lucknow during the Indian Mutiny. Jason had found Cecil in a bed, wounded in the leg. His injuries were not life threatening but then a sepoy was serving breakfast and Jason noticed as he went from bed to bed the men all had fresh blood on the bandages or clothes. He was not just bringing breakfast. The man was the grim reaper, bringing death. Jason tackled him, bringing him down just as he was about to kill Cecil. The stiletto knife skittered across the floor and before the fight progressed the alarm had been raised and soldiers pulled the men apart.

Whatever Jason had to do, Catherine felt sure he was going to put himself in danger. She felt anxious and helpless. She would have liked to speak to Izzy but by now she and Andy would be at work and Daniel would be at school.

Catherine got dressed and went out into the garden. Her first task was dead heading the roses and then she began weeding. It felt odd to know she had been away for weeks, but the garden showed no sign of neglect. As far as the garden and the rest of the world knew she had not been away at all.

After an hour her back was aching, and she decided to stop. It was satisfying to have made a difference and her mood was lighter. There was nothing she could do about Jason except trust the timer.

Chapter 36

1859

'I've been talking to Sam about the name you gave me. He says there's a Pete who goes around the farms in the summer helping with the harvest. It seems he doesn't have a regular job and turns his hand to anything that makes money,' said George. 'I've no proof and think it unlikely we'll find anything to point to him in the woods.'

Jason didn't answer. He just followed George into the woods and along a broad path. The sun was filtering through the leaves dappling here and there where the trees were not so dense. Insects were humming, birds singing but the death of Cecil made it impossible to enjoy the walk.

George paused for a moment. 'It's this way and you'll need to walk behind me. No room for two.' He walked steadily and then stopped, allowing Jason to stand beside him in a small clearing. 'This is where we saw them, tying up the stag and Cecil was standing where you are when he shouted at them. See the antlers?' George watched as Jason moved towards the antlers and crouched down.

'There are a lot of footprints here, more than three men.'

'Of course. I had to have help to remove the body and the stag.'

Jason had a vision of a modern crime scene, tape all around the area, no one allowed in or near the body until forensic scientists had done their job. He stood up and walked to the tree that had hid him last night. From there he turned to George. 'Can you show me the direction they ran in and where the man was when he fired the shot?'

George moved towards him, pointing. 'They went that way.' Both men walked in that direction. 'See, there are recently snapped twigs,' said George. 'There is nothing to help us here.'

'Just one more thing before we leave,' said Jason. 'Would you go back to where you stood with Cecil?' When George had returned to the spot Jason added. 'Now am I in the right place to be the killer?'

'You need to take one step back. Yes, that's perfect.' There was a thick thorny bush nearby and Jason thought he could hide there, ready to spring out and stop the murder.

'Would you like to come to my cottage, now? My housekeeper, Alice, will have baked today. She makes excellent cake. I feel we've done all we can here.'

'I'd like that very much.' They returned to the broad path and turned away from the village.

'We're walking in Cecil's woodland and my home is in a clearing just at the end of this path. It's ideal for me to walk to the village or to Lime Bank Hall.'

Jason smiled in appreciation when he saw the cottage. 'George, it looks delightful and much bigger than my idea of a cottage. It seems more like a manor house.' They both stood as Jason admired the porch sheltering the front door, the windows either side of it with three windows above.

'It's a spacious house; more than one gentleman needs but I hope to marry and have a family one day. Please, come in.' He opened the door and stood back allowing Jason to enter. The air was filled with the delicious smell of bread and cake. In the hall to the right of the front door was the parlour, and Jason was shown in and asked to sit.

The room felt almost claustrophobic to Jason, for almost every inch of floor space was covered with furniture. The atmosphere felt heavy with thick brocade curtains at the window and solid oak chairs. There were so many chairs he hardly knew which one to sit on. Eventually he chose an armchair beside the fireplace but then worried it might be George's favourite.

The walls were covered in pictures and Jason stood up to study them. Most were paintings of animals, set in woodland. They all had heavy, dark wood frames. The signature on several seemed the same and he wondered if the artist was local.

George entered and said, 'I've ordered tea and cake. Which should be here soon. Do you like my pictures?'

'Yes, the workmanship is excellent. I was wondering if the artist was local.'

George smiled, obviously pleased as he admitted he was the artist. The arrival of refreshments meant they moved to sit, and George poured tea and offered the cakes himself.

Jason bit into a moist cake and savoured the flavour of lemon. 'Delicious cake. Your cook is a treasure.'

The conversation meandered from quality staff to the trials of being an estate manager until Jason felt it was time he left and wondered how to broach his need for a weapon.

'Before I go, George, I have a strange request.'

'I'll help if I can. What is it?'

'I need to borrow a weapon; not a gun, a stout stick or even a spade would do.'

George stood up and fetched a stout walking stick. 'What about this?'

Jason stood, hefted it but shook his head. 'I need something heavier.'

George nodded. 'Let's go to the outhouse and see what's there.' The outhouse was attached to the house at the back and contained gardening tools. Jason picked up a spade and said, 'This is perfect. I'll not keep it for long.'

'May I ask why you need a weapon? If you think you're in danger from someone I'd be happy to help.'

'It's difficult for me to explain; a secret that I cannot reveal at present.'

'In that case I'll not press you. Perhaps we can meet again for a drink or a meal together in a day or two when all the funeral details are complete.'

'Yes, I'd like that. Thank you for your hospitality, and the loan of this.' He brandished the spade and it sufficed as a wave goodbye, then set off to walk back to The New Inn.

*

It was lunch time at the inn and Sam was busy. Jason nodded to him and went up to his room. He stood the spade against the wall and then sat down on the bed. He lay back on the pillow and began to think about the evening. Should he turn the timer once and arrive as he did before with a short time before the murder or should he turn it twice? When he'd been in this position

193

before, turning the timer twice had meant he arrived earlier by a few minutes. He decided to do that. It would give him time to find the thorn bush and prepare himself. The bed was comfortable and soon Jason was sleeping.

When he woke, he thought he'd just had a short doze but in fact the evening meal was nearly ready. He worried he'd be unable to sleep when he went to bed. The timer seemed to prefer the person asleep before transportation. Perhaps a quick walk would help. He got up, stretched, and picked up his hat.

Down at the bar he paused and ordered dinner to be ready in an hour and then set off to walk in the direction of Brimham Rocks. He passed Blackberry Farm and looked to see if Joe was outside, but all was quiet. They had been so kind to Daniel, he thought and then his mind moved to Izzy and Catherine. He missed them very much, but it had only been a few days. Perhaps, if all went well tonight, he'd be transported back home. He found himself smiling at the thought.

A few hours later, replete with dinner and ale, Jason went back to his room and turned the timer upside down. As the sand ran through, he looked at the spade wondering how he could attach it to himself so when he was transported it came with him.

Izzy had left a deep bag with a flap and two leather straps. He tried the spade in it and pulled the flap around the handle, doing up the straps as tight as they would go. It seemed quite secure. Now he needed to tie the bag onto himself.

Catherine's bag had a detachable, long, leather strap designed to hold the bag over the shoulder. He pulled it out, threaded it through the handle of Izzy's bag and tried it over his head so the bag rested against his side. It was going to work. He went back downstairs, ordered a brandy and brought it back to his room. He hoped the brandy, plus the walk, would take away the tension he was feeling and allow him to sleep.

Before settling onto the bed Jason turned the timer again. He pulled the strap over his head, so it rested on one shoulder and drank the brandy. He lay down with his hand over the bag and closed his eyes.

Chapter 37

1859

Jason heard the sharp report of a rifle followed by a thud and muted woops of excitement. He opened his eyes to find himself looking at the recent kill and the poachers just beginning their task of trussing the stag for transport. They would see him if they looked up. Jason looked for the thorn bush. He crouched low and stealthily made his way there. He was glad he'd kept his boots on this time, so no worrying about stones or brambles.

The three men were talking quietly as they worked. This helped to cover any noise Jason made undoing the straps of the bag and pulling out the spade. It was heavy, much heavier than the one he used in his own garden. He felt nervous, wanting to time his attack to prevent anyone being hurt. He peered around the bush, his knees beginning to ache with crouching, hoping George and Cecil would arrive soon. I'm really getting too old for all this, he thought. He heard Pete being told to hurry. They'd be here any minute.

Jason saw them arrive, heard Cecil's shout and steeled himself. Suddenly the men were running. He stood up wielding his spade just as Pete raised his rifle. There was a loud bang and everything for Jason went black.

Cecil and George ran after the men but caught only one, Pete. When Jason hit him with the spade the gun fired into the ground, but Pete needed to get away and he'd swung the rifle round and brought it down upon Jason's head. Cecil guarded Pete with the rifle while George took the rope off the stag's legs and used it to tie Pete's hands behind his back and then tied his feet together so he couldn't run.

When Pete was secure both men turned to look at Jason.

'Is he dead?' asked Cecil.

George put his ear to Jason's face. 'No, I can hear him breathing but he's taken quite a blow to the head. Will you stay with him while I run to the Elliot's? They'll lend us a cart and a board to carry Jason. With their help we can get the stag into the cart too.'

'Yes, go on. I'll see if I can stem his bleeding.' George ran back to the main path and Cecil knelt beside Jason. He pressed his handkerchief onto the wound and then wondered how he could keep it there. He looked at Pete, who had stopped struggling, trying to get free. Cecil stood and moved quickly towards him, stretching out his hand. Pete shut his eyes and whimpered, expecting a blow. Cecil smiled grimly and pulled off the man's neckerchief. It was not very clean, but it was long enough to make a bandage. 'I'm not going to hit you, though it's tempting. There'll be punishment enough when you meet the magistrate. Attempted murder, as well as poaching. Could mean a hanging.'

By the time George came back with two strong men and a cart waiting on the main path. Jason's head was bandaged but he was still unconscious.

'I've asked my young son to fetch the doctor to my house, Sir, because I wasn't sure where you wanted this gentleman taken.'

'I think he should be taken to my house,' said George. 'His name is Jason Brownlow, a recent acquaintance of mine.'

There was then a lot of action as two men hefted Jason and took him along the narrow path to the cart. They covered him with a blanket. George drove the cart to his own house and Jason was carried into a room at the back. He left Jason in Alice's kind and capable hands then drove the cart back for the stag.

By the time George arrived the stag and prisoner were waiting at the side of the path. They were quickly loaded, and the stag went to the Elliot's cottage, with instructions to butcher and share the meat with the other tenants. The prisoner was placed in the village lock-up until transport to a magistrate could be organised.

This had all taken a long time and George invited Cecil back to his house for something to eat. Cecil shook his head but before they parted, he said, 'I know the name Jason Brownlow. I think he's the man who saved my life in Lucknow. If so, he must be handsomely rewarded for saving me a second time. He looks different, older by more than two years. I'll call tomorrow morning and hope to find him conscious. If you're worried about him, call the doctor and I'll, naturally, pay the bill. This has been a successful day, eh George? See you tomorrow.'

Jason woke with a pounding headache. He opened his eyes and recognised nothing. Where was he? He almost cried with disappointment. Wherever this was it was still in Victorian times. He put a hand up to his head and discovered a bandage. Then he remembered what had happened in the wood. Had he saved Cecil? Probably not or the timer would have taken him home. He felt depressed at the thought.

'You're awake, Sir. I'm right glad to see that. I'll fetch Mr Hancock and then I'll get you some brandy and water.'

'Thank you.' Jason recognised George's excellent housekeeper and cook and relaxed a little. At least he knew now where he was. He tried to sit up, but pain seared through his head and he sank back on the pillow. The bed was very hard. He felt with a hand and realised he was on a table or board. This must be George's dining room, he thought.

George came into the room. He was smiling and holding a glass of brandy. 'How are you feeling? You had a severe blow to the head.'

'I tried to sit up but failed. Would you help me?'

'Of course.' As George helped him Jason groaned and put his hand to his bandaged head.

'This will help,' said George offering the brandy.

Jason sipped it and felt the warm glow of the spirit moving down to his stomach. He finished the drink and grinned. 'It has helped, thank you. I think, if you would steady me, I could get off the table and sit in a chair.' George helped and Jason was glad of it because he felt weak. Sitting in the armchair was much more comfortable and Jason, feeling more alert asked. 'What's the time? Have I been unconscious for a long while? George, please tell me Cecil's alive. Did you get the poacher?'

George laughed and held up his hands. 'I can see the brandy has revived you. Cecil is fine. We caught one of the poachers, Pete Makepeace and, no doubt with a bit of persuasion, he'll reveal the names of the others. Do you remember hitting Pete with a spade?'

'No. I remember he was about to fire his gun, but nothing more.'

'You rose out from behind a bush like a spectre and walloped the arm holding the gun. It fired harmlessly into the ground. Pete swung round and hit you with the butt. You were felled but we managed to wrestle him to the ground. He's now in the village lock-up. I believe you saved our lives and we're in your debt. Cecil is coming tomorrow morning to see how you are.' He paused and then added, 'I do have some questions for you, but they can wait. You look exhausted. Rest now and you may feel like eating something when you wake.'

Jason closed his eyes and slept for an hour. When he woke the pain was less. He tentatively shuffled to the edge of the chair and levered himself to his feet. The room swam a little but soon steadied. He walked the two steps to the table and stood still, assessing how he felt but everything remained stationary. He was nearly at the door when George entered. Alice followed, her round face smiling, carrying a tray heavy with tea and cakes.

'You're on your feet. That's good. Are you hungry? Let's sit at the table.' George removed the blanket and wooden board, and Alice placed the tray on the table. She then folded the blanket and took it out with her.

George poured the tea and told Jason to help himself to cake. There was a comfortable silence as they ate and drank. When they were both on their second cup of tea and the plate of cake almost empty George spoke. 'Do you feel well enough to answer some questions?'

Jason nodded but the pain waved in again and he winced. 'Yes, I can answer some questions but must remember not to move my head too much.'

'Cecil thought he recognised you as the man that saved his life in the field hospital at Lucknow. Was that you?'

'Yes. It was the day Nathaniel was born, about two years ago.'

'Aye, well that's the mystery. You see he remembers you as younger, having a slimmer figure and dark hair. Just two years later you are stouter, have age lines and grey hair. Could such a change really have come about in just two years? Perhaps you've been ill?'

198

This was the perfect way out, to say he'd been ill, but Jason liked and respected George. He wanted to tell him the truth. 'It's very difficult to explain,' he said, without looking at him.

'I would greatly appreciate it if you would try. You see I found my garden spade. You'd felled Pete with it. How did you come by my spade, locked inside my outhouse? We're barely acquainted yet I feel I know you well.' Jason squirmed in his chair, but after a considerable silence he looked at George and began.

'I come from the future, the year 2048.' He saw George frown with disbelief and pressed on, anxious now to convince him. 'In my room at the inn is a ship's sand timer. It came from one of Jane's father's ships called the *Daphne*. It has the power, when turned over, to take a person back or forwards in time. But it is only motivated to work when one of Jane's relatives is in difficulty. My grandson, Daniel, came back in time to save Nathaniel from drowning. The timer then took him back to his own time.'

George raised his eyebrows and said, 'Clive told me about a lad he'd found holding Nathaniel in his arms. The baby had been too close to the river and Clive had not been watching him. He didn't tell Jane about it so I'd rather you didn't mention it. This is a strange tale you're telling but please go on.'

'I was at the inn when you came in distraught because Clive had been killed by a poacher. We spent the evening together and you were so drunk I arranged with Sam for you to spend the night. That's why you feel you know me. I knew I had to go back in time one night to save Cecil, but I had no weapon. You invited me here, we had tea and lemon cake and then I asked you to lend me the spade.

'That night, back at the inn, I turned the sand timer twice and arrived in the woods just in time to whack that poacher with your spade.' He paused for a moment, but George waited, sensing he was just gathering his thoughts.

'I think I'm still here because I was injured. Travelling through time makes you feel queasy and disorientated. I expect, now I'm feeling better, the timer will return me to my family. I have no more to say except I have told you the truth. Please do

199

me the courtesy of believing me.' He felt exhausted with the effort and closed his eyes, wishing he could lie down and sleep.

Chapter 38

1859

It was the following day when Jason woke to find himself in a strange bedroom, wearing a very long nightshirt. Daylight was glowing around the edges of the curtains. George must have carried me upstairs and put me to bed, he thought. He propped himself up on one elbow, waiting for a wave of pain but it was just a distant throb. When he sat up fully, he saw some clothes had been placed on a chair. They were not his so were probably George's. He got out of bed slowly, expecting the room to revolve, but everything was still.

At the washstand he found soap, towel, even a shaving brush and razor. It was the cutthroat type and Jason decided to ignore it. After a wash and getting dressed in clothes too long for him, Jason was pleased to feel well.

He went downstairs and followed the aroma of cooking to the kitchen. Alice was stoking the range. She turned giving a little shriek and covering her mouth with her hand when she saw him.

'Oh, Sir, you did give me a fright.'

'I'm sorry but I'm feeling so much better I wanted to come and thank you for seeing to my wound.'

She flushed with pleasure and pulled out a chair at the table. 'If you would sit, Sir, I'll make you some tea and breakfast. Mr Hancock has a fine dining room but usually takes his breakfast here. He's not risen yet.'

Jason smiled and sat down, at ease with this pleasant woman. She placed a cup of tea in front of him and said, 'The bread's fresh baked this morning. Would you like some bacon and egg with it?'

'That sounds wonderful. I'm very hungry.'

'In that case I'll do two eggs.'

The smell of bacon frying must have wafted up to George who arrived just as Jason's meal was placed in front of him. Jason tried to stand but George placed his hand firmly on his shoulder. 'No, don't stand on ceremony. Enjoy your food and I'll

201

join you.' His breakfast was ready in a few minutes and the two men ate almost in silence.

'That was delicious, Alice, thank you,' said Jason when he'd wiped his last piece of bread around his plate and eaten it.

'Thank you, Sir. I'm glad you enjoyed it.'

'Do you remember, Jason, my telling you that Cecil is coming this morning?'

Jason moved his hands apart a little and grinned. 'I'm afraid I wasn't at my best yesterday and remember nothing after talking at the dining table. You've been very kind, bringing me to your home and looking after me, but I would like to go back to the inn after Cecil's visit.'

'I took the liberty of cleaning the clothes you were wearing, Sir, and they will be dry and pressed in a couple of hours,' said the housekeeper.

'Thank you,' said Jason.

'In that case let's take a walk around the estate. Cecil will arrive at eleven, so we have time.'

Cecil arrived promptly at eleven. George and Jason were waiting in the parlour, refreshed from their walk. Alice was ready in the kitchen, kettle boiling on the range with a plate of fresh baked cakes, still warm from the oven.

'I'm delighted to see you much recovered,' said Cecil as he pumped Jason's hand, holding it with both of his before letting go. 'I had my doubts you would return to us, yesterday and here you are so very much alive.'

'Thank you. I've been well looked after by George and Alice.'

'Shall we sit down?' said George and Cecil strode straight to the armchair beside the unlit fire, saying, 'Mr Brownlow, sit here next to me.'

'I'll happily do that if you will address me by my first name, Jason.' He sat down and George sat opposite them both.

'Jason it is then, so you must call me Cecil. No doubt you're already on first name terms with George.' Jason nodded and was pleased to feel only a small twinge in his head. Alice came in carrying the refreshments and Cecil greeted her. 'Ah, Alice, the best cook in the estate. I keep trying to steal her from George, but he'll have none of it.'

Alice blushed as she placed the tray on a low table in front of George.

'Thank you, Alice, that all looks lovely. You don't have to stay. We can manage.' She curtsied and George began pouring coffee and handing out the drinks and plates. While George was busy Cecil bent to open his leather satchel. He pulled out a bottle of French brandy, stood and gave it to George. 'A little gift for all the help you gave me yesterday. If you care to open it now, I'll not complain.'

George was surprised and smiled. 'Thank you, Cecil. I'll fetch some glasses. He went to a sideboard and said, 'Will you join us in a brandy, Jason?'

'I will, thank you. The brandy you gave me yesterday really revived me. I'm becoming quite partial to it.'

The brandy was sipped along with the coffee. All the men enjoyed the cake, and the conversation was about their adventure the day before.

When Cecil had finished eating, he returned to his satchel and brought out another bottle of brandy and handed it to Jason. 'I know you saved my life yesterday. That thug was pointing his gun directly at me. I don't know how to show my gratitude, but I would be pleased if you would accept this.'

Jason took it and placed it on the small table beside him. 'Thank you, Cecil.'

'I also brought you this. You may have read it already, *David Copperfield* by Charles Dickens.'

'I have read it,' said Jason, thinking he had also seen it as a film and serialised on television. 'It's an excellent story.'

'I'd like to give you this copy because it's been signed by Mr Dickens himself. I was fortunate, while spending a few days in London, to be able to hear him reading. He was so eloquent and read with such enthusiasm. I could almost see his characters, so alive did he make them seem. A remarkable and talented man.'

Jason took the offered book, reverently, and opened it to see the signature inside. 'You shouldn't part with this, Cecil. One day it will be very valuable.' George shared a conspiratorial look with him and smiled.

'That's exactly why you must have it, Jason. Please accept it.'

'It's a wonderful gift, thank you.'

George topped up their brandy glasses and said, 'A toast to Jason Brownlow with thanks for his prowess with a spade.' They raised their glasses and were all smiling, the brandy influencing all of them.

'Well, I must go home. I promised Jane I'd be back in time for luncheon though I have little appetite after consuming so much cake. You must come and see us soon, Jason. What about tomorrow? Come and meet my wife, about twelve and then you can take luncheon with us.'

'I would like that, very much. Thank you,' said Jason. They stood and watched Cecil stride away down the path. Jason felt anxious and guilty. He liked Cecil, George, Jane, Sam and all the people he'd met in 1859 but he really wanted to go home and fervently hoped he would not be able to meet Cecil and Jane for luncheon.

When they went back inside Alice was hovering in the entrance hall. 'I just wanted to tell you that your clothes are all ready for you. I put them on the bed, Sir.' She gave a little curtsey and was already at the kitchen door when Jason said thank you.

'In that case, George, I'll go up and change.' George nodded.

In his room Jason stood, clad in his own underwear, looking in the small shaving mirror. The bandage made him look like a wounded soldier. He began to unwind it. The process was painful because his congealed blood had stuck to it, so he filled the basin with cold water and put his head in. He gave a little gasp; the water was fresh and cold. After soaking for a short while the bandage came away. He dried himself and looked back in the mirror. The wound was not bleeding and the area around it was a dark purple. He looked much better without the bandage. A few minutes later he was dressed and carried his brandy and precious book downstairs to take his leave of George.

The farewells were brief, George saying they would meet again soon. He wished Jason an enjoyable visit to Cecil and Jane's house and warned him he may have to explain his time travel again. Jason was about to set off when he turned back to George.

'If I should go back to my own time and miss the luncheon appointment, would you explain my absence to them? I wouldn't want them to think ill of me.'

'Don't worry. I'll do that for you should it be necessary.' George waved and Jason went back towards the village. He felt strangely ambivalent. He wanted to go home but did not want to leave these new friends.

When Jason arrived at the inn it was crowded. They cheered when they saw him. People he didn't know clapped him on the back and commiserated with him at the sight of his wound. Sam poured him a brandy, 'On t' house for the hero what saved the Major's life.' Everyone pressed him to relate the scene with the three poachers and how he'd prevented one of the poachers shooting Major Carstairs. The noise in the bar was deafening, the ale and the occasion making everyone speak louder than usual. Jason had never been such a centre of attention and found it exhausting.

Sam helped by producing a huge plateful of meat pie and thick gravy, muttering, 'On t' house', again.' He renewed his energy by clearing the plate.

It was nearly four o'clock when he was finally able to leave the few well-wishers who were left and take refuge in his room. His mouth ached with smiling and he wanted to lie down on the bed and sleep.

He kept seeing in his mind Catherine and Izzy disappearing at Brimham Rocks. He'd felt the rock shake and they'd all dreamt about it beforehand. He felt very strongly that he too had to go there in order to return home.

Instead of resting on the bed and allowing himself to sleep, Jason put his book and brandy in the bag holding the sand timer that he was very careful not to touch. He left all his spare clothes and night-clothes in the room and his purse of money, hoping the maid would be honest enough to give it to Sam. If this didn't work, he could always come back.

When he got downstairs, he was relieved to see that Sam was not behind the bar and there were no customers. He let himself quietly out into the afternoon sunshine and began to walk.

Chapter 39

Jason had not brought a drink and the walk was longer than he remembered when he was with Catherine and Izzy. He knew that was illogical. It had just seemed like that because they were chatting as they walked. There had been tourists at Brimham Rocks last time. Jason thought it would be unlikely now because it was later. The sun was low in the sky and had lost its warmth.

He predicted correctly. There were no other people there and Jason walked up the path and turned left. He felt exhausted and thirsty when he got to the flat rock. He sat down on it and looked at the view. Dry-stone walls separated fields of grazing sheep, trees with bright green leaves threw long shadows. It was peaceful. He sighed, almost reluctant to get out the timer. It would be unbearably disappointing if it failed to work. A chilly wind blew at him. He shivered and dragged his bag towards him. He stood the timer on the rock after he'd turned it over and quickly shrugged his bag back on. He didn't want to leave the brandy or his copy of *David Copperfield* for someone else to find.

Nothing happened. Jason stared at the timer and then spoke to it. 'Please take me home. I've tried hard to do your bidding. Please … He felt a vibration that grew in intensity. The rock was shaking, violently. Jason rolled off it. Just as he did so there was an explosion so close, so deafening he found himself shaking and burying his head under his arms.

When everything was still and quiet, Jason sat up still quaking with shock. The big, flat rock had split across leaving a jagged edge. The section he'd been sitting on had tumbled down into the valley. The timer had gone too. He rubbed his hands over his face and stood up. He looked down at the rock realising the portal to the past had gone for ever. He had no idea if he was in his own time but even if it was Victorian time, it was late and would soon be dark.

Jason stood stiffly and began to walk slowly along the little path that weaved amongst giant rocks. He arrived at the broad one that went up to the Visitor Centre or down to the car park. Looking towards the car park he felt excited. He could see a barrier and surely the car park was tarmacked. He quickened his pace. It was tarmac. He wanted to kiss the ground like the pope. He was back in his own time of automatic cars, wondrous electronic gadgets and his family.

There was one car in the car park. Jason looked around, wondering if he'd be able to ask for a lift. Two men carrying climbing ropes were coming towards the car, jingling with carabiners on their belts.

'Excuse me,' said Jason. 'I really need a lift towards Harrogate. Can you help me?'

He saw the men looking at him with amused expressions and was suddenly embarrassed. How could he explain his eccentric clothes?

'We're going to Harrogate so hop in.' Jason got into the car and when the two men had put their gear into the boot they set off. The driver asked Jason where he wanted to be dropped and Jason gave his address. 'I have to pass that street so we can drop you at your door. Hey, did you hear that explosion? I nearly fell. It seemed to shake the whole area. Did you see anything?'

'I heard it and I was near a flat rock. When the explosion was over it had split in two. Perhaps it was an earthquake.' Both men in front of him nodded.

The journey was only half an hour. The men talked to each other making plans for another climb the following week. This suited Jason who sat, tired but grateful to be back in his own time. He was also grateful they didn't ask him about his odd choice of clothing.

The car stopped right outside his house and Jason thanked them for the lift. The car pulled away and he pressed the keypad on his front door.

Catherine heard the door and was walking towards him as Jason came in. She ran the last few steps and he held her in his arms for a long, long time.

The End

About the Author

I was born in London in 1946, the middle child of three. The family moved to Harlow in Essex when it was a very small, new town with an enthusiastic community spirit.

I went to S. Martin's College of education and became a primary school teacher, returning to Harlow for my first job. The following year I married John, we moved to Biggleswade in Bedfordshire, and during the next seven years, our two children were born. During this time, I studied with the Open University and gained a BA.

John was offered a promotion if he would move to North Yorkshire. He accepted with pleasure, having had many camping holidays in the area. The gentler pace of life was good for growing children and for a writer.

Writing has always been something I enjoyed, poems, stories and holiday diaries but, when I took early retirement, I went to a creative writing class. Out of that a self-help group was formed called The Next Chapter. We wrote stories and poems but were all excited when a local author suggested a course called, 'Write a book in a Year'. I wrote my first novel, 'Forced to Flee' about the ethnic cleansing of Albanians in Kosovo, during the collapse of Yugoslavia.

There was still a need to write and, as I have enjoyed many fantasy stories, 'The Pathway Back' became my next project. The idea for the sequel, 'The Pathway Forward', was forming as

I wrote it. At the end of The Pathway Forward the reader will have realised there was to be one more. The Rocky Pathway is the third and the last in The Pathway Series.

While writing all four novels I have been creating a memoir, so keep an eye open for, 'When Life throws you a Lemon.'

Printed in Great Britain
by Amazon

65777616R00129